What others are saying about *Climatized*...

"In *Climatized*, Sally Fernandez has deftly created a novel out of perhaps the biggest deception in the history of the modern world. She has made herself a credible expert on the real causes of our mostly natural global warming, and on the members of the cabal that has misled us. She also presents a plausible scenario that a very cold 60-year solar minimum will descend on the planet soon, with or without any change in human CO_2 emissions. The plot to create a world government of unelected bureaucrats will thus be brought down by the very natural cycles the deceivers have tried so hard to deny. Then the Western world will have to turn around the deadly and ultimately ruinous 'environmental' policies which have held us in thrall for the last 30 years."

—Dennis T. Avery, *New York Times* Bestselling Co-Author
of *Unstoppable Global Warming: Every 1,500 Years*

"Sally Fernandez' novel *Climatized* is a tour de force of exciting fictional characters engaged in non-stop action juxtaposed within a context of real people, current politics, and factually accurate information. She has found a stunningly innovative way to draw attention to one of the great issues we're dealing with today!!!"

—Tom Wysmuller, NASA, The Right Climate Stuff
research team

"Sally Fernandez has written an exciting novel that interweaves politics and science. Although it is a work of fiction, *Climatized* demonstrates that its author—having done her own investigating—has not been taken in by the hype of so-called 'climate change/ global warming' that continues to be prominently propagated by a host of politicians, media, scientists, and administrators of major scientific societies. Readers of *Climatized* can expect adventure plus enlightenment."

—Laurence I. ("Larry") Gould, Professor of Physics
(University of Hartford), Former Chair New England
Section of the American Physical Society, Member of The
Right Climate Stuff research team

"Riveting, powerful, intriguing—I could not put *Climatized* down! Fernandez once again brings the ignorance of man to the forefront. Will we remain sheep or will we break away from the fold? If we do not, we will be penned in and led to the slaughterhouse. It is time to start questioning our governments' true motives and who they actually benefit—US or THEM!!"

—Ann E. Howells, Wine Consultant, Florida

CLIMATIZED

CLIMATIZED

A Max Ford Thriller

A N o v e l

Sally Fernandez

DUNHAM
books

In loving memory of Dr. Patricia Ames,
a selfless aunt and eternal role model,
who contributed in large part
to the person I have become.

FOREWORD

I was completely astounded when Sally Fernandez, a novelist previously unknown to me, contacted me about 10 days ago and asked me to read and comment on a pre-publication draft of her new novel, *Climatized*. At first, I was surprised to find characters in her novel using my real name in the dialogue of this fictional mystery thriller that is full of political intrigue and obscure international locations. But as I progressed further into the riveting plot, I was completely blown away when she revealed an unusual clue scribbled on the back of a family photo in a fictional US Senator's office. This clue was in the form of an equation that I recognized from presentations I had made at international climate conferences and that our climate research team of retired NASA Apollo Program scientists and engineers had derived and documented in research reports published on our website. Most readers won't learn the meaning and actual significance of this clue until much later in the story, as Fernandez deftly weaves her fictional plot in and around the actual history and more recent events of the anthropogenic (human-caused) global-warming (AGW) movement. Her heroine, Maxine Ford, not only uses the old adage "follow the money" to solve this mystery; she also has to "follow the bodies" and survive attempts on her own life to bring this political thriller to its final conclusion.

Besides the suspense and reading enjoyment from following the characters in the unfolding plot of the sinister but plausible premise of this novel, readers will be educated regarding many important scientific facts. Many of these facts are totally at odds with the constant barrage of global-warming doomsday propaganda continually distributed by some politicians and hyped-up mass media news stories using selected alarming, but highly unlikely possibilities, from peer-reviewed scientific research publications by climate scientists' dependent on government grants doled out by political appointees.

Fernandez leads her readers to understand her fictional explanation for the current climate alarmism, and it lines up uncomfortably close to the conclusions our research team of NASA Apollo, Skylab, Space Shuttle, and International Space Station Program veterans from our own independent and objective scientific assessment of the current global-warming controversy.

—Dr. Harold Doiron, Chairman
The Right Climate Stuff research team
July 25, 2016

INTRODUCTION

E verything had changed. The country had stabilized and support for the president's plan had gained momentum. America was once again sailing on course.

But for this cast of characters unexpected winds lay ahead, starting with Major Stanley Stanton. His love for Maxine Ford was beyond reason, given her unwillingness to commit to him. Then he discovered who was holding her back. It hit him hard. But as with any hardy soldier, he was resilient and accepted that an abiding friendship was all he could expect. Of one thing he was certain: he would always protect her with his life. The real shock came when Max and Noble Bishop discovered their adoration for each other, forcing Max's role as his deputy director to come to a bittersweet end.

Their true feelings had erupted three months earlier, on that ominous night in July when the former First Lady and senator, Maryann Townsend, held Max at gunpoint. For Townsend it was a final vendetta against those who had caused the death of her one-time lover, the world-renowned terrorist Simon Hall, and her husband, the former US president Abner Baari. For Stanton it was a split-second decision forcing him to fire the fatal shot that killed the former First Lady. For Noble it was a hidden emotion when he witnessed Max's life in peril. Although a tragic ending to the legacy of the Baari Administration, it a new and interesting chapter for those who survived.

Life was about to get more complicated. This is their story... somewhat.

Chapter 1

———o——O——o———

UP IN THE AIR

C laus was pleased to see Ernst standing outside the hotel at
eight a.m. sharp. Now they could beat the weekend traffic
and arrive in Saint Léger within the hour. It was an easy drive
from Claus' home in Avignon, but the weather forecast for the
weekend called for conditions that were unseasonably sunny
with cloudless skies, abnormal conditions for an April day
without rain. He suspected the roads would be cluttered with
families opting to enjoy the various outdoor activities available in
the mountainous region. Most important, the weather was ideal
for rock climbing, one of Claus' obsessions. He often remarked
that the desire to climb coursed through his veins since receiving
his first Whiz Kid harness and carabiners at the age of five.
What choice did he have? Both his grandfather and father were
avid climbers. Oh yes, with the warm sun and the crisp air, it
promised to be a strenuous but invigorating climb, exactly what
Claus preferred.

Up ahead was the sign for Saint Léger du Ventoux. They
were about to pass through the quaint village in the Toulourenc
Valley at the base of the Mont Ventoux. The immense mountain,
towering six thousand feet into the air, was well known for

casting a permanent shadow on the tiny hamlet. In another half-mile east and a quarter-mile north they would reach their destination. Finally, Claus steered into the sparsely filled parking lot, pleased to see only a few visitors had arrived.

"How magnificent," Ernst said, as he viewed the majestic Saint Léger hovering above.

"She's got some of the finest crags and some the hardest routes," Claus said. Eager to get going, he hopped out of the car and headed for the trunk. "Help me with the gear?"

As Ernst followed behind he spotted myriad overhangs off in the distance. "It looks challenging."

"The route we're going to take is a single pitch and only a hundred and thirty feet high up the cliff. But don't let her fool you; she's a tough old crag."

"So what do we need—just ropes and belay devices?"

"That will do it." Claus looked at Ernst's feet and noticed that they were two shoe sizes larger than his. "Good thing you brought your own climbing shoes," he joked.

"I never leave home without them. But thanks for letting me borrow your other gear."

"No problem. Let's get going. It's a twenty-minute walk from here to the base."

As they walked along the narrow path lined with Austrian pines, Claus explained that the route was one of the most difficult, as well as one of the least ventured. "There are permanent bolts strategically placed up the rock face. They're positioned anywhere from fifteen to thirty feet apart, so we'll be able to descend without rappelling."

They both understood that with or without the bolts that provided protection, the descent was the most dangerous part of rock climbing—the part they both enjoyed.

"Hey, Ernst, you never told me what you do for a living or why you were even at the conference?" Claus was a little curious, but he was primarily killing time.

"I guess our climbing tales did dominate our discussions. No big secret. I'm a freelance consultant for biotech companies."

"So why the interest in a climate-change seminar?"

"I was bored." Ernst grinned. "You gonna let me start the ascent?"

"I know the route. You don't, so I'll take the first pitch."

Ernst didn't push. He knew there would be plenty of opportunities to switch roles back and forth between the lead climber and the belayer.

"Here we are!" Claus announced as they came around the last bend. Standing before them was a massive rock towering up in the air.

Ernst inspected the crag. He noted that the first bolt was secured approximately twenty feet up the rock face.

Claus noted his expression. "I assume you approve?"

"Absolutely!"

Claus expertly tied off one end of the rope to his carabiner with a figure-eight knot and then attached the carabiner to his harness. "I mentioned that this is one of my preferred routes. It's a rugged day's climb that calls for endurance and physical strength, but it's not *Dangerville*."

"I'm ready to rock and roll!" Ernst said. His eagerness was apparent.

Claus also deemed it time to get the show on the road or, rather, up the rock. After double-checking his equipment, he took the lead and began the ascent. Taking special care, he inched his way up the rock face as Ernst ran the rope through the belay device and then clipped the device to his harness. It provided the necessary protection in case the leader was to slip and fall before attaching himself to a pre-placed bolt with a carabiner. The belay device created friction, placing bends in the rope the belayer to tighten and secure the rope quickly, preventing the leader from falling beyond the last piece of protection.

Having maneuvered the rock face without incident and satisfied with the pace, Claus attached himself to the next bolt. Then, he took over the belay device and functioned as the belayer. He watched attentively as Ernst climbed to join him. At that point they had been ascending for well over an hour, covering half the distance, with Claus always in the lead.

"Now can I take the lead?" Ernst asked, satisfied he had proven his athletic prowess.

Claus gave the go-ahead.

Ernst moved upward toward the next bolt as Claus adjusted the belay. Thus far, the ascent had moved along with a rhythmic cadence. Then after passing a few more bolts, Claus was once again in the lead.

"I'm ready!" he shouted down to Ernst but there was no response. "C'mon, let's move it!"

"Give me a sec! I'm adjusting my gear!" Ernst shouted back. Moments later, he resumed the climb.

Finally, they had reached the top of the cliff. They each detached the rope, removing the tether from their harnesses, and then stood back to admire the three-hundred-and-sixty-degree view.

"Breathtaking!" Ernst remarked. "Well worth the climb."

"Ready for lunch? I'm starved." From Ernst's expression, Claus needed no verbal response. Immediately he opened his backpack and pulled out an assortment of sausages and cheeses, along with a crusty baguette.

Ernst grabbed two energy drinks and two protein bars from his backpack.

They noshed leisurely on their snacks and carried on with simple conversation while enjoying the refreshing cool air. But as the hour passed by they agreed to pack up and get off the mountain before losing the benefit of daylight. Within the next two hours, the sun's glow would cast itself on the back side of the mountain, leaving them hanging off a dimly lit crag. After a few more moments to stretch their legs, they gathered their belongings and organized for the descent. As agreed, they would not rappel, but would climb down together, sharing the roles of leader and belayer as they had before.

Ernst walked over to the permanent bolt fastened to the rock face at the edge of the cliff and clipped on a carabiner. He ensured the knotting on the rope was secure. Simultaneously, Claus tied the other end of the rope to his harness and descended to the first bolt twenty feet below. Ernst released the rope at a slow, even pace through the belay, using the device as a descender this time. As Claus increased his distance, Ernst kept the rope taut.

"Watch your footing down here!" Claus shouted, paying particular attention to the patch of scree they encountered on the way up. He continued to edge his way along the rock face using great caution, until he arrived at the next bolt. "I'm clipped on!" He attached his carabiner and waited for Ernst to climb down and take the lead.

"Whoa!" Ernst landed his left foot smack in the center of the scree, but soon regained his balance as the loose gravel scarcely missed Claus' head.

Either Ernst did not hear him or he was not paying attention, but for whatever reason it gave Claus pause. "Let's take it slow! We have plenty of time. Remember—you don't know this crag—I do!"

"Got it!" After a few deep breaths, Ernst continued.

They regained their cadence, taking special care as they maneuvered past each other and descended the mountain.

All of a sudden, Claus heard a foreboding snap. "*ERNST!*" he screamed as he slid down the rock face, scraping his head along the way.

With no time to spare, Ernst tied off his rope to stop Claus' acceleration. Had he not, they both would have plunged over seventy-five feet to the ground.

Dangling helplessly on the rope thirty feet below, Claus took a lungful and then exhaled. His ears rang with the sound of his body scraping against the rocks. It reminded him of a train coming to a screeching halt on unoiled tracks. *A horrible sound,* he thought as he shuddered.

"Find a foothold—and don't move!" Seconds later Ernst had him tied off, and the rope was secure. "I need to rappel down and take your weight."

For Claus, it seemed like hours, but it only took minutes for Ernst to reach him.

"What the hell happened?"

Claus tried to regain his breath, but all he managed to utter was, "The bolt let go."

"How could the bolt simply pull out of the rock?"

"I don't know!"

"It was fine on the way up. We both clipped on to it!"

"Let's just get off this mountain." Claus was clearly ill at ease.

Given the circumstance, Ernst took charge. "Take a deep breath; we've got only about thirty feet more to go."

Back on solid ground, Ernst inspected Claus' head. Fortunately, he had only a few superficial scrapes on his forehead, not worth a bandage. Then, after a bit of haggling, Claus insisted he was perfectly capable of driving Ernst back to his hotel. They wasted no time in gathering their gear and headed for the car. Once underway, Claus gradually returned to his former self, and their conversation took on a lighter tone. They chatted about their good fortune until Ernst proceeded to recount horror stories from his earlier climbs.

All Claus heard was his grandfather's voice echoing in his ear. "You'll never be able to read the mind of Mother Nature, so you'd better be able to read the minds of those helping you to challenge her." They were words he did not heed on that day. Claus was rarely rattled, but he had never climbed with a stranger before, only with close friends. But he had to admit that it was Ernst's quick action that saved them both.

Ernst was still rattling on about a fall he took until Claus interrupted. "I'd prefer you to keep those stories to yourself, at least until after our climb tomorrow."

"Point taken. So we're still on?"

Claus nodded but continued to keep his eyes on the road. The rest of the drive was relatively silent as they sped along the winding alpine highway. Finally, Claus spotted a neon sign on top of a building that flashed the name "Novotel," and he breathed a sigh of relief.

Antoinette checked her watch and then checked the wall clock; they both read 9:38 p.m. "*Il a promis.*" She soon decided moaning was useless and thought the Beaujolais wine might produce a better effect. After pouring herself a glass, she sauntered into the living room and waited for her husband. Unfortunately, her favorite Gamay grape from Burgundy was not doing its magic. She prayed that her worrying would prove unnecessary.

Antoinette recognized that Claus was an excellent climber. He had tackled the Matterhorn frequently with his hiking buddies. But the day hikes by himself or with only one other person concerned her, especially if she was not acquainted with that person. All she knew was that Claus had befriended another attendee during a weeklong conference. His name was Ernst from Lucerne, also an avid climber. They had made plans to climb Saint Léger on Saturday. She had approved on one condition — They would be off the mountain by sunset. That was two hours ago. Once again she checked her watch with growing concern. The time was 10:15. Suddenly, she heard a car pull into the driveway and she let out a huge sigh of relief.

"*Je sais que je suis en retard!*" Claus called out from the kitchen, apologizing for being late. When he walked into the living room, he found his wife standing in the center of the room with her arms folded across her chest. *Not a good sign*, he thought, and he moved in to embrace her with a hug, whispering *"Je t'aime"* in an effort to stifle any anger.

Antoinette surrendered to his ploy, but when she pulled away, she saw the bruise on his forehead.

Claus assured his lovely wife that it was nothing and then rotated his cupped hand as though he were holding an empty wine glass.

"Tu veux un verre de vin?" she asked without a trace of anger, thankful that he had arrived home safely.

"Absolument!" he replied, amazed by her easy acquiescence and more than ready for the glass of wine she was in the midst of pouring. Then, he prepared for the inevitable question.

As expected, the moment they sat down next to each other on the sofa, Antoinette asked, "So how was the climb?"

Claus filled her in on the day's events, careful to leave out a few details. *It all ended well; what's the point?* he mused. Then, switching the topic slightly, he began to wax on about how Ernst was such a great climber, hoping to butter her up for his next request. "Ernst leaves on Monday and asked if I'd climb the Lou Passo with him tomorrow. I agreed."

Antoinette knew that Lou Passo was located in the same region they had just climbed, but it was a rarely visited crag and considerably easier than Saint Léger. "Clau—"

"Arrêtez," he said as he held up his hand, stopping her response. *"Je l'ai déjà dit oui."*

"So, you've already said yes. Then what's left for me to say?" she asked with mild annoyance, annoyance that was rooted in her doubts about Ernst. He was not one of Claus' close friends.

Chapter 2

SPARKS FLYING

In 2017, at the behest of the Republican senators, a bipartisan committee to study climate-change initiative bills was established to monitor appropriation recommendations to the House. Prior to the formation of the committee, bills addressing climate change were scattered among various subcommittees established under the House Committee on Appropriations. It became extremely difficult to identify the overlapping appropriations and to determine the total dollar amounts allocated in the name of climate change. At first, the Republicans received a lot of pushback, but finally the Democratic senate base acquiesced, clearly a concession. The Democrats still needed the support of the Republicans to assign hordes of unallocated stimulus money they sought. It was also agreed that the committee would be co-chaired by a representative from each party.

Senator Winston Erog, a controversial Democrat from California, was appointed as one of the committee co-chairs. It was no secret that he was a staunch environmentalist. But he played the role of a fair debater and worked tirelessly to push legislation through for his constituents. He appeared to have won the respect of both parties. But his strongest asset was his deceptive physical appearance. His obviously corpulent body and his disproportionately small mouth, amazingly commanded attention when he spoke. Still, there were those who distrusted him.

The other co-chair was Senator Sherman Spark, a Republican from the state of Florida. But it was Erog's turn to call the committee to order.

As Erog watched the shuffling of chairs, he waited a while longer for the members to settle down. Then, at ten past one, he raised his gavel. "I call this session to order. Secretary Collins, please read the first item on the docket."

"Chairman Erog, Senator Richly from California will introduce H.R. 20500 for consideration."

"Senator Richly, you have the floor."

"Chairman Erog and respected Senators, I'd like to introduce the following bill, H.R. 20500, which was submitted by the Committee on Education and the Workforce. This act is cited as the 'Climate Education Act.' They are requesting ten million dollars for each of the fiscal years 2018 through 2022. The primary purpose of the bill is to support programs for teacher training in K through 12 and to develop models for climate-change curricula for both primary and secondary educational institutions."

Spark turned and eyed Erog. "Chairman, I respectfully remind this committee that this bill was already addressed in the last Congress. And now, as it did then, it smacks of brainwashing."

Erog lowered his gavel. "Senator Spark! Senator Richly has the floor."

Richly smiled. He had tangled with Spark in the past and enjoyed the challenge. Without hesitation, he addressed him directly. "Climate change is undeniable and there is overwhelming science that proves global warming is human-induced. However, a recent survey of elementary and high-school teachers, conducted by Professor Plutzer, the academic director of Pennsylvania State's Survey Research Center, showed that thirty percent of teachers polled emphasized in their teachings that global warming was most likely due to natural causes. Clearly, it flies in the face of the fact that ninety-seven percent of climate scientists agree that global warming is caused by human activity."

"Senator, you know that claim is poppycock."

Erog winced. "Out of order, Senator Spark. Senator Richly, please continue."

"Chairman Erog, I'd be interested in hearing what the Senator has to say."

"Senator Spark, please make your point—and quickly." Erog was clearly exasperated.

"This claim of ninety-seven percent is a deliberate attempt to coerce public opinion. The number sprouted out of a paper published by John Cook, a global-warming alarmist and founder of a blog site misleadingly named *Skeptical Science*. Cook, along with his cohorts, reviewed exactly eleven-thousand-nine-hundred-and-forty-four studies published in peer-reviewed climate literature. They found that roughly thirty-four percent endorsed the concept that man-made carbon dioxide is being emitted into the atmosphere. Out of that number came the infamous ninety-seven percent of those who emphatically endorse the position that humans are causing global warming. In fact, numerous scientists whose papers were cited by Cook took exception to his unsupported conclusion. This research is anything but scientific and does not represent the scientific community as a whole. However, careful evaluation of various surveys has taken place and support the idea that the number of qualified scientists believing global warming is primarily man-made is less than three percent—rather than ninety-seven percent."

"Interesting, Senator Spark," Erog droned, "but I fail to see any connection to the introduction of Bill H.R. 20500."

"With all due respect, the bill presents only one side of the debate, one that is still questionable. It's too murky for the taxpayers to support. And I don't think you'll get an executive order this time around," Spark argued.

"Senator Richly."

"Chairman, to the Senator's original point, he's accurate. The bill was presented in the last Congress, but in light of the Paris Agreement I ask this committee to review it once again. It's no secret that the UN Climate Change Conference held in Paris in 2015 was a valiant effort to obtain agreement to reduce carbon-dioxide emissions and adopt green energy as a renewable energy source, as evidenced by the attendance of one hundred and ninety-seven countries' diplomats. The goal, of course, is to reduce the global average temperature by three-point-six degrees Fahrenheit, with an ideal target of two-point-seven degrees, which is quite achievable."

Spark could not hold back. He loved to spar as much as Richly. "And to accomplish such a feat would require one-hundred-billion dollars a year over the next five years, with the financing coming primarily from developed countries to help the less developed countries. The mere fact that our former president, along with the leaders from Canada and Mexico, had to forge a North-America-wide climate partnership shortly after the Paris Agreement was a clear indication that it was dead in its tracks."

Erog glared in Spark's direction.

"Chairman Erog, I'd be happy to yield my remaining time to the Senator. Although we are very familiar with his feelings on the subject." Senator Richly purposely cited the Paris Agreement to further bait Spark. It worked. "I thank the committee for your time." He took his seat.

Spark ignored Richly's jab and kept his anger in check. He was next on the docket and wanted the committee's full attention, but he felt that the point bore repeating. "May I remind the committee that the Paris Agreement is a non-binding commitment and provides limited impact for the money spent? It's another blatant attempt to erode the United States' sovereignty."

Erog cut off the sparring. He was eager to move forward. "Secretary Collins, please read the next item for discussion."

"Senator Spark has requested that the chamber hear the testimony of Mr. Claus Veunet from the Climate Research Unit at the University of East Anglia."

"We always welcome scientists from the CRU. They've been an invaluable resource for the IPCC, the esteemed United Nations Intergovernmental Panel on Climate Change," Erog remarked, reverting to a pleasant manner. "But how is his testimony relevant to this committee, Senator Spark?"

"Chairman Erog, forgive me but you are aware that Mr. Veunet will not be speaking directly to any one initiative, but to the initiatives as a whole. This has been on the docket for months." *Damn him, he's trying to renege on his promise.*

"Okay, Senator Spark, Mr. Veunet has the floor."

Spark glanced toward the row of chairs in the back of the room. When he went to motion Veunet to take a seat at the table—he wasn't there. Agitated, he checked his watch; it was 1:45. *He's supposed to be here at one o'clock.*

"The committee is waiting, Senator," Erog urged. This time with impatience.

"Excuse me, Mr. Chairman, but evidently Mr. Veunet has been delayed." Awkwardly, Spark said, "With your permission, I will excuse myself from these proceedings and turn my chair over to Senator Ryan. It's imperative I locate Mr. Veunet."

Erog raised the gavel but without setting it down, he said, "Granted! Secretary Collins, please read the next item on the docket." His tone was boorish, but it was clear from the expression on his face that he was pleased to move on.

Spark left the committee room.

⌐⊶⊷¬

Out in the hallway, Spark frantically called the hotel only to discover that Claus Veunet had never checked in. Then he called Claus' home in France and spoke with his wife. Minutes later he hung up the phone. "Jesus Christ," he muttered as he rushed back to his office, foregoing any further committee business for the day.

"Hold all my calls," he barked to his secretary.

Secure in his office with the door closed and no chance of being interrupted, he placed a call to Switzerland.

"Luca, I need you in Washington."

"No, Sherman. We agreed that only Claus would go public and testify. The rest of us were not to be involved."

"Claus is dead!"

"*Oh mein Gott!* What happened?"

"It was a stupid climbing accident. I knew about his obsession and warned him that his testimony was of grave importance. I told him explicitly to lay off his daredevil antics."

"Sherman, please! He was a dear friend."

"No time for mourning. I need you in Washington." It took Spark twenty minutes more to lay out a viable argument as to why Luca needed to testify in Claus' absence.

Finally, Luca agreed.

"I'll get back to you when I reschedule the date." Spark ended the call abruptly.

Still distressed at the death of Claus, Spark sat back and recalled all the months that had gone into the planning for that testimony. A testimony that would rattle the world, a testimony with trillions of dollars at stake. He hated the cloak-and-dagger game, working behind the scene, carrying secrets he could not share even with his wife. *Thank God Luca is willing to step up to the plate.* He let out a deep breath. Then, he remembered that there was one more obstacle—Erog. He glanced at the wall clock and presumed the committee had adjourned for the day and Erog had most likely returned to his office. But before he fought that battle, Spark had to make one more phone call. He had to convince one other scientist to prepare to testify as well.

"Senator Spark, he's not available," the secretary said, as he rushed past her desk.

"What the hell was that all about?" Spark blurted as he barged into Erog's office.

"It's good to see you too, Sherman."

Senator Sherman Spark was a tall, slender man with salt-and-pepper hair, along with other classic statesman-like qualities. And when the two senators were in proximity, it accentuated Erog's grotesque features. But Erog was no less dangerous and Spark thought he was up to his neck in trumpery.

"You tried to weasel out of your promise to allow Claus Veunet to testify!"

"How can you say that? The entire committee sat back, waiting for him to speak."

"Well, he won't be arriving anytime soon. He's dead!"

"I'm terribly sorry to hear that. Seriously, Sherman. I know this meant a great deal to you."

"You don't seem sorry. And If I didn't know better, I'd think you pushed him off some goddamn mountain in France."

"I'll forget you said that. But now it's over. It's time to move on. We have business to conduct for our constituents."

"His testimony was vital, you son of a bitch!" Spark yelled and then reeled in his ire. "I worked hard to get him on today's docket. But it's not over. I want to reschedule the testimony."

"I don't understand."

"I have another scientist who can impart the same information."

"Sherman, let me be frank. While you've been willing to give me only a general idea as to the testimony, which I suspect has nothing to do with appropriations, I've agreed to this arrangement out of my respect for you. But I hope for your own sake you're not using these scientific minds—and this committee—to make a grandiose statement for your own personal agenda."

"Damn you! I'm trying to save this country from falling into a trap. Using this committee is the best way to get the truth out to the public. Be careful, Erog; people might start to question the appropriations you've pushed through bypassing the committee. I want a new date!" Spark demanded, slamming his fist on Erog's desk.

Erog knew Spark would hold true on his threat. His reputation for being a judicial-watch bloodhound, with a bark that included a bite, was not to be ignored. Spark, on the other hand, did not divulge on all he knew, holding some leverage in abeyance.

"You'll get your date." Erog's lips curled down into his customary smirk, making his mouth seem even smaller.

Spark stormed out of Erog's office, leaving the door open behind him.

Chapter 3

—⚬———⚬———⚬—

OPEN FOR BUSINESS

I t was a brutal weekend in Washington, DC, but not because of politics as usual. It was the massive Indian-summer heat wave, with its record-high temperatures, that caused the discomfort. The weather became the hot topic of discussion. It dominated the pub scene with the happy-hour crowd heatedly debating whether it was caused by greenhouse gases or a very strong El Niño stirring up the air and ocean currents. Either way, Max just wanted some relief.

She bounded up the front steps, balancing packages in both hands, and glared into the peephole. Once she heard the click, she freed up one hand and opened the door. She was elated to feel the rush of cool air coming from inside. Quickly, she dropped the shopping bags in the foyer and closed the door behind her. At once, the smell of fresh paint stung her nostrils, but it was of no consequence. Her newly renovated Victorian townhouse was finally ready to occupy.

The once elegant forty-foot long living room, with its high ceiling and tall windows, had been stylishly transformed into two office spaces and a reception area. Situated in front of the canted bay windows were two overstuffed sofas facing each other, with a glass coffee table in between them. The table was strewn with magazines, but not the usual outdated "doctor's office" variety. Max's clients would most likely find themselves flipping through the pages of *Forbes* or *The Economist*. The dining room functioned as a conference room, replete with an oversized Tuscan-style table she had uncovered at a local flea market. The carpet placed under the table had more of a Zen-like quality, with maroon and sage-green colors—not that Max had a Zen bone in her body. But it created the mood she was trying to achieve. The original kitchen remained intact, but multi-functioned as a copy room and storage space for office supplies. Her proudest achievement was converting the upper two stories into a spacious apartment that provided her with ample living space. It had been a long, agonizing decision that brought her to this place, but she could not have been more pleased with the outcome.

Her plan began to culminate shortly after that deadly night in July when it became clear it was impossible for Max and Noble, her boss, to continue working side by side at the agency. Coupled with their newly minted relationship and the trauma of a gun's metal barrel pressed against her temple, Max willingly offered to resign. What to do next, she did not know. She had been an analyst, she had been a spy, she had been an investigator, and as deputy director of the SIA she had functioned in all three capacities. But once the fog had lifted from repeated visions of that fatal shooting, she began to think more clearly and to weigh her options. One thing was clear—her inherent penchant for sleuthing needed an outlet.

For weeks, she and Noble discussed her various options, but in the end he encouraged her to continue to do what she did best—investigate, analyze, and solve. Excited by the newfound possibilities, she began the process to earn her license as a private investigator in the District of Columbia. She assumed that being the former deputy director for the SIA and a field agent for the CIA would pave the way for an easy FBI clearance and registration for a concealed handgun. All her plans were in place. But unfortunately for Noble, his plans to pursue other interests were stymied by Max's departure. At the behest of the president, Noble agreed to stay on as the director for another year.

Max walked over and sat down on her new sofa, partially to take a load off her feet and partially to admire her new workplace, until she saw the stack of boxes filled with contents that could no longer be ignored. "Well, they're not going to unpack themselves!" she sighed. She fastened her hair on top of her head haphazardly, stood up, and dove in. For the next several hours, she placed the massive collection of books on the shelves in their appropriate order, organized her file drawers, and set up other paraphernalia on her desk.

Thanks to Noble's skills, the computers and printers had been connected to the Internet with a virtual private network. Stanton handled the security system for the premises, which included using a retinal scanner to open the front door— something he insisted upon. He also loaded double-encryption software that secured both calls and texts into two smartphones: one for Max and one for her new partner. This protocol was all new to Max. For most of her career at both the CIA and SIA she had full built-in protection. But the day she left the agency, she not only had to surrender her top-security clearance; she also had to return her government issued xPhad, a high-tech gadget that was like an appendage to her, to replace it with an ordinary civilian smartphone. Now as a private citizen and considering her new undercover profession, she needed to take all precautions.

Max was growing weary and was ready to call it a day. She figured her associate could tackle the other office and help her finish up with the supply room in the morning as his first assignment. But before heading upstairs she had one last official act for the evening. She needed to hang out her new bronze shingle with her name etched in prominent letters, another gift from Stanton. First, she needed a screwdriver. Max walked into the kitchen and spotted her girly-looking toolbox sitting on the counter. When she opened the lid, she saw that the gift card was still inside. It brought a smile to her face as she reread the note: *It's time to fix things, other than the world. Love, Noble.* "How imaginative," she said aloud, thinking that Noble and Stanton had co-conspired on their gifts. Then she thought about how they had become quite the threesome over the past few months. Peculiar, considering how it started and the emotions involved.

Stanton was her ex-lover whom she still admired immensely; she especially admired his coping mechanism after their breakup. Whether he learned it as part of his military training or it was inherent, he never showed remorse and always treated her with tenderness. Strangely, it was Noble who had arranged for Stanton to transfer to Washington and head up the president's Secret Service detail. Max was still standing in the kitchen, holding the bronze sign in one hand and the screwdriver in the other, when a weird thought entered her mind. *Did Noble purposely try to bring Stanton and me together? Was Noble trying to rule out any possibility of a future with me?* She tapped her head with the bronze plate, hoping to bring her back to her senses. "Get a grip, Max!" Now armed with the pink-handled tool and the shingle, she headed outside into the stifling air. Fortunately, the blazing heat had cooled a bit as the evening hours set in. In no time flat, she expertly fastened the last screw to the shingle and Ford Investigations was officially open for business. *Now all I need are clients* was the first thought that popped into her head. When she stepped back to admire her handiwork, she blurted out, "What the hell am I getting myself into?"

"You're going to be great!" Noble sounded off, having arrived unexpectedly at her doorstep.

Startled by the interruption, she turned and waved her new screwdriver in his direction, faking a menacing stare.

"Whoa!" he cried, as he took a step back.

"It's not wise to sneak up on people!" She quickly softened her expression, and admitted, "But it's a pleasant surprise."

"You look like you could use a bite to eat?"

"You have a real knack for knowing what I need—I'm famished." She redirected her pink-handled weapon out of harm's way and moved in to give him a warm hug. At that moment, she noticed the flashing lights in the park. "What's going on over there?" she asked, even though she assumed he had no way of knowing. Hurriedly, she placed the screwdriver inside the hallway. "Let's go see."

"Max, hang on."

"C'mon, it will just take a minute."

"You want the reputation of being an ambulance chaser?" He knew it was a lost cause, but he gave it a shot.

Clasping each other's hands, they walked across the street and into Lincoln Park. But then Max loosened her grip and headed straight for the police car.

"Hey, Ray, what's up?" she asked.

"Just some poor stiff offed himself."

"It must be an important stiff to bring out the Capitol Police Chief. Any I.D.?" Max started to move in closer to where the body lay.

Noble stayed back and watched her take on the chief.

"Sorry, Max," the chief warned, "not until we inform the next of kin." He then moved in front of her, blocking her view. But not before Max saw the corpse sprawled out on the park bench. The inflexible arm in rigor angled downward. The gun lay only inches away from his fingertips on the ground.

As Max studied the scene, Noble became concerned by the strange expression on her face. He made a mental note to ask her about it later. But evidently his worry was unwarranted.

Max spun around with her usual gumshoe look and refocused on the chief. "Why all the mystery if it's just some poor stiff?" The moment the words left her mouth, her antennae started to telescope.

That expression was familiar. One Noble had seen many times before. He moved in to pull her back.

"Sorry, Director, but Max no longer has clearance." The chief was clearly asking Noble to play interference.

Max refused to be ignored. "Why do I need clearance?"

"Max, enough," Noble pressed.

Grudgingly, she let it go, but only for the moment, and agreed to leave the scene with Noble, foregoing any further interrogation.

———— ✦ ————

Noble waited until they were safely back inside her townhouse and then cautioned, "Remember, Max, you no longer have the same access to information you once had. You're going to have to learn to play by a different set of rules. And besides, this isn't your case." Giving her no time to respond, he tossed out the question that concerned him most. "Incidentally, what was that look all about?"

"What look?"

"When you saw the corpse?"

"So to what do I owe this impromptu visit?" she asked, hastily changing the subject.

Noble knew when it was time to back down and obliged for the time being. "I thought it would be nice to have dinner together."

"I assumed you'd be having dinner with Paolo tonight?" She knew that Noble often joined his brother-in-law for dinner on Sunday nights and rarely diverted from the boys' night out.

"You think only women have the prerogative to change their minds." He moved in for a seductive kiss and then asked, "How's steak sound?"

"Perfect! Give me a minute to change."

Max went upstairs while Noble waited in the foyer, gazing back at the siren lights through the window. He could see them turning off one-by-one as the cars and the ambulance were leaving the park. When he heard the sound of Max's heels clomping down the stairs, he pulled his eyes away from the scene.

"What?" She could not help but notice him eyeing her.

"You continue to take my breath away, my dear."

Max had replaced her shorts and tank top with a miniskirt and camisole. Her hairstyle of choice was a tousled mess of blond hair upon her head, but now it flowed elegantly on her shoulders, erasing all traces of her.

"Thanks! Give me one more minute to check my emails."

Noble followed Max into her office and watched while she spun through her emails on the touch-screen desktop. "By the way, I stopped by to see Amanda."

"Oh," Max said, trying not to seem too curious as to why.

"She's decided to go ahead on the cruise that I'd already paid for. She said it would make her feel better spending my money."

"How's she doing otherwise?" Max appeared mildly interested, but continued to focus on her computer screen.

"Her nerves are still a little raw since I broke off our engagement, but she said she was thankful that I discovered my feelings for you in time."

This time Max could not help but look up.

"She said it was best that I said 'I can't' before I said 'I do.'" Noble walked over and gave Max a kiss on the forehead. "I'm glad I discovered it in time as well."

Max stopped perusing the screen and stood up, prepared to leave.

"So what's going on with Stanton?" Noble thought it was only fair play.

"He's fine. He'll be fine. We'll be fine. We've always been friends and I suspect we always will be. Sweetie, he knew that I was never in love with him." Max cocked her head and eyed Noble suspiciously. "Why did you go see Amanda, anyway?"

"No biggie. I simply wanted to wish her a safe trip. And speaking of trips—"

She cut him off. "Noble! Why now?"

He quickly flashed her the "stand down" stare. She knew it well and backed off.

"I'm only planning to be away for a few weeks," he continued. "My plane leaves in the morning."

"You're really going away?" she asked calmly, refraining from further nagging for the moment.

"Honey, the president asked me to follow up on something for him. I can't tell you any more than that, which is probably more than I should have told you in the first place."

"You know you can trust me." On a dime, Max could turn her deep, commanding voice into a seductive tone. But that time her face betrayed her. It equated to a hound dog on a scent.

"Max!"

"I liked it better when we worked together. Remember when we were cleared to discuss everything, except of course, your last little escapade?" She smirked.

Max still did not know what Noble's disappearing act was about, but she believed it had something to do with the president. It started months before the death of Senator Townsend, when Noble left her at the helm to solve the mysterious attacks on the families of *La Fratellanza*. Although he checked in periodically, he never acknowledged his whereabouts. Then magically, the day the former First Lady kidnapped her, Noble came out of hiding. It was also the same day the president gave his most compelling speech to the nation, a speech that further economic downturn and stabilized the country.

"Why now?" she persisted. "I'm just getting established and it would be nice to have you around."

"You'll be fine. Jax starts tomorrow. Rely on him as you have me."

Max curled her lip. "Really?"

"You know what I mean. Jax will be a solid asset. Remember, he still has the means to get information that you're no longer privy to. And I'm sure by the time I get back you'll already have your stilettos dug into ominous places."

Lightening her mood, she asked, "I thought you were supposed to be spending time looking for your replacement?"

"I serve at the of the president." Noble smiled and then asked again, "Dinner? C'mon, let's go."

Max stood back with her arms crossed, eyeing him up and down. "I have a better idea—pizza. But first," she added with a coquettish grin, "an appetizer."

Noble chuckled as she turned around and headed for the staircase leading to her apartment.

◆───◆◆◆◆◆◆◆───◆

Max felt the gentle movement from under the covers and rolled over as Noble was about to slip out of bed.

"What time is it?" she asked, stifling a yawn.

"Four thirty." He rolled back over and held her in his arms for a moment, but could no longer prolong the inevitable. "Go back to sleep and I'll call you later."

"Why do you have to leave now?"

"You know I hate goodbyes. Besides, I have to go home to pack and make a few calls. Honey, remember that I love you."

"Noble," she cooed in her sexiest voice as she pulled him back to her side.

He surrendered, instantly melting in her arms. But when Max felt Noble release his embrace, she knew he was about to leave her.

Noble moved in for one last kiss. "Go back to sleep," he whispered, and then left her bed.

It was five fifteen. He quietly dressed as he gazed at her profile against the pillow. He could see the shape of her slim body under the sheets, producing an insatiable urge to want to climb back in bed with her, but he had no choice. Falling in love with Max was also an irresistible choice he did not have. They had worked closely together for over eight years on sometimes-vexing, oftentimes-dangerous cases. However, when he finally decided to settle down, he looked elsewhere, all the while unconsciously denying his feelings. That was, until he thought he could lose her.

They mutually agreed to allow their relationship to unfold. Their friendship was rock-solid, but the idea of becoming lovers frightened both of them.

"What if we screw it up?" Max often asked.

"We won't," Noble always replied. But after several dinners, increasingly passionate kisses, and a deepening relationship, Max invited him to stay the night. The next morning, they pledged their love forever—at least, they hoped it would be forever.

Chapter 4

A SHOT IN THE PARK

The seven o'clock alarm bellowed raucously, but Max remained curled up under the covers, waiting for Noble to silence the intrusion. "Dammit," she uttered, realizing that he had slipped away hours earlier. She rolled over and slammed down the snooze button with her hand, giving her a few more minutes to wake up. The unwelcome alarm sounded again.

Resisting further temptation, Max hopped out of bed and threw on a T-shirt that barely reached the top of her thighs and then sauntered into the kitchen. While she waited for her coffeemaker to dole out the last of the caffeine, she decided to walk downstairs to pick up the morning newspaper. As expected, when she opened the front door the paper was lying outside on the top step. She picked it up and flipped it open to view the headlines. "Oh my God!" Max turned and bounded back up the stairs to her apartment. Immediately, she grabbed her smartphone and hit a speed-dial button.

"Noble, have you seen the morning headline?" Before she gave him a moment to answer she broadcasted, "Senator Spark committed suicide! He was the dead guy in the park!"

"Explains why the chief was so tight-lipped."

"You don't seem surprised." Max was taken aback by his tepid response.

"You yourself assumed it was somebody important because Ray was on the case."

"I'm going down to the station to see if I can pry anything out of him today. In any case, what time are you heading out?"

"Max, it's not your case," he reminded her.

"I repeat what time are you heading out?"

Noble gave up. There was no point in trying to dissuade her from her insatiable curiosity. "My flight leaves in a few hours. I'll call you this evening when my plane lands."

"I miss you already."

"I miss you. I'll come back as soon as I can. In the meantime, we both have our work cut out for us. And congratulations, Madame P.I."

"I love you, Noble."

"I love you, too. Gotta go."

<hr />

Max grabbed the cup of strong brew that sat waiting and began to read the entire article. Somewhat surprised, she learned nothing more than what she already knew. Senator Sherman Spark, a Republican from the state of Florida, was found dead in Lincoln Park, apparently from a self-inflicted gunshot wound to the head. The rest of the article focused on his various accomplishments, including his latest appointment to a committee established to review climate-change initiatives. The article continued with the usual list of survivors: his wife Isabelle, two sons, a daughter, and five grandchildren. *Hmm,* she thought, *nothing nefarious enough for someone to want to kill himself.* Then, out of the blue, a scene flashed in front of her eyes. Almost like a reflex, the self-generated virtual reality caused her to shudder. She shook her head. *Stop it! Focus on the case.*

Max tossed the paper down on the table and gulped the rest of her coffee, providing the final oomph she needed. Hurriedly, she showered and dressed. Then she trotted back downstairs, grabbed her oversized handbag from her office, and headed out the door.

✦────•⟨✣⟩•────✦

Max knew her way around the US Capitol Police building on D Street, having made a slew of official visits over the years. The building itself was rather innocuous and a bit worn at the heels, but within no time she meandered down the narrow corridor, walked past the secretary, and barged directly into the chief's office in her usual brazen manner. "Okay, Ray, what gives?"

"Good morning to you too, Max. I see I have to remind my secretary that you no longer work for the SIA."

"How could you release to the press that the Senator shot himself before you even investigate?"

"It was pretty open-and-shut. Anyway, what's your interest?"

"A prominent senator commits suicide for no reason. It doesn't seem open-and-shut to me, at least until you're sure of the reason. Was there a suicide note?"

"Max, you're chasing rainbows. I'm not releasing any more information, so quit while you're ahead."

"How come there were only Capitol police and no DC cops at the scene last night?"

"Because we got the call and were told to handle the case."

"Call from whom?"

"Max, that's it! I wish you the best of luck with your new agency, but I think you have the sequence all wrong. First, you get the client, and then you get the case—not the other way around."

"You used to be one of my best sources, Ray."

"Look, I'd help you if I could, but this case is closed."

Max could not explain why, but she had just another one of those overwhelming feelings that would envelop her at a moment's notice. The one that told her that this was only the tip of the iceberg.

"Thanks, Chief. I'll back off."

The Capitol police chief and Max had worked on many cases in the past. And he was well aware that she was not one to back off. He knew he would have to keep his ears to the ground, paying extra attention to her snooping. "Thanks, Max. And I really wish you luck with your new venture. Stay safe out there."

"You, too." Max turned and left.

Chapter 5

—⟡—

JAX IN TIME

M ax had only been back in her office for a few minutes when she heard the lock at the front door click and the knob turn. The intercom did not sound off with its usual buzzer and there was no opportunity to glance at the monitor. Suddenly a tall, thin, bald, black man appeared in the reception area.

"Jax, your rusty-old spook reporting for duty!" he said, offering a military salute.

"Spook, like in 'spy'?" Max said with a chuckle. She was well aware that a politically correct bone did not exist in Jax's exceedingly muscular body, a physique with "military" written all over it. Certainly, she knew that he was ex-CIA and had performed special assignments for Noble in the past, although she was not privy to all of them, including the last clandestine assignment for the president. And when Noble first recommended Jax, she suspected it was a way of keeping her safe. Most likely he induced Jax to take the job in preparation for his not-so-impromptu travel plans. But she had to admit, despite Noble's overly protective motive, that Jax was a perfect choice. She liked and respected him. He was well trained in the field and had a wicked sense of humor. In their business, sometimes the latter was more important.

Initially, when Noble had broached the subject of hiring her new associate, Max attempted to learn more about him, but she hit a brick wall. The records for Jackson Monroe were sealed. No longer having clearance, she was unable to access them. All she really had to go on was Noble vouching for Jax's integrity. In the end that was good enough for her.

As far as Jax was concerned, he was more than ready to try some spy-lite cases for a change. Sizing up Max was easy. It was widely known deep in the belly of the CIA that she was highly intelligent and resourceful and one of the best agents in the field. And the fact that she was easy on the eyes did not exactly hurt. Yes, Jax had sized up the situation and suspected it was going to be a fun gig.

"Any cases yet, Ma'am?"

"Jax!"

"Sorry! I'm just a southern gentleman at heart—Max."

"Funny you should ask! I have a case, but I don't have a client."

"Aren't we supposed to operate the other way around?"

"Someone made that very same point earlier." Max filled him in on what she saw in the park the night before and what little she knew about the senator and his apparent suicide.

"Perhaps the chief's right. Maybe it is open and shut," Jax challenged.

"My gut tells me otherwise—and my gut never lies."

"Noble warned me about that ever-reliable gut of yours." He chuckled. "I'm going in to set up my office. Anything else for now, boss?"

"Nothing now," she replied offhandedly; clearly her thoughts had traveled elsewhere.

Chapter 6

NO TIME TO GRIEVE

"Mrs. Spark, you have my sincerest condolences," the guard offered.

"Thank you. I'd like to go to my husband's office and retrieve a few of his personal belongings." She tried her best to be stoic.

"I'm afraid that's not possible. Access to the senator's office has been restricted while the investigation continues."

"But his case has been closed!"

"Ma'am, I'm not aware of that."

"The Capitol Police Chief notified me, himself, this morning," she insisted.

"Give me a minute." The guard left his station and walked across the rotunda.

Isabelle Spark stood by and watched while he appeared to be calling someone from another phone. She could not overhear the conversation, but it looked to be a difficult and lengthy call. She also suspected that he intentionally went out of earshot. After what seemed like an eternity, the guard finally returned.

"I was able to get you access to the late senator's office, but only long enough to retrieve personal items. And I can't let you enter alone. The police chief still wants the office cordoned off."

"What! Am I a suspect?" Isabelle was indignant. "Apparently, there is an inconsistency between a closed case and an office ban. I assure you the president will hear about this!"

"Please wait while I call another guard to escort you." The guard refrained from further conversation.

Moments later, a female guard appeared. "Mrs. Spark," she announced, "please follow me."

Isabelle was still reeling but walked with the guard through the winding hallways of the Russell Senate Office Building, until she arrived at her husband's office.

"I'll only be a few moments. I know exactly the personal items I want," Isabelle said, ignoring the other guard's instructions.

"Sorry, ma'am, but I can't let you go in there by yourself."

Isabelle was beyond distressed, but she fought to maintain a cool demeanor. She acquiesced and motioned the guard to lead the way. Inside, she set down a large, canvas gym bag that she had brought with her to carry away the personal effects of her dearly departed husband. With an eerie sense that her every move was being watched, she proceeded carefully to collect the personal photos in the various frames that graced the bookshelves and the credenza behind Sherman's massive mahogany desk. Then she began to collect the bits of paraphernalia scattered on the desk.

"Only personal objects," the guard reminded her sternly.

"Please, this is our family photo album." Isabelle now opted to plead.

"According to my orders, nothing with his writing can leave this office. I'm sorry." The guard tried to show a hint of empathy.

"It's just photos. You can look for yourself." Isabelle willingly released it into the guard's custody.

The guard, who had earlier showed compassion, now displayed annoyance as she hastily flipped through the pages. She handed it back to Isabelle in the same manner.

At that point Isabelle was a bit numb from the whole ordeal, but satisfied that she had at least won that round. Applying great patience, she collected several of the figurines the children had given their father and gathered up the baseball caps he had collected from his favorite teams. Finally, she took one last glance around the office. Content that she had collected Sherman's personal effects, she zipped up the gym bag and then walked across the room. Her final act was to remove the oil painting that hung on the wall—the family portrait was the one item she wanted above all others.

"Mrs. Spark, please, our time is limited," the guard urged.

It had become increasingly obvious to Isabelle that the guard was bored with her assigned detail. She promptly hoisted the gym bag over her left shoulder and grasped the sizeable picture frame under her right arm. "I'm ready," she announced and followed the guard out of her husband's office, never looking back.

<hr />

Isabelle sat on the floor of their living room, teary-eyed as she sipped a glass of wine. For the good part of an hour her eyes fixated on the gym bag that contained all the belongings she was allowed to take away. Suddenly, she cried, "Thirty years on the Hill and this is all I have to show for Sherman's sacrifices! Damn them!" She slammed her wine glass down on the coffee table, spilling droplets on the mahogany surface. Standing back up, she walked over to the family portrait that had been leaning against the overstuffed chair and stared down at it. Seconds later, she collapsed back onto the floor and sobbed uncontrollably. While succumbing to moments of despair, she caught herself fondling a large gouge in the left hand corner of the frame. "It must be in perfect condition for his funeral!" she shrieked, reviving her anger.

Chapter 7

CLIENT CALL

Ford Investigations had been in business for one week. Still, each time Max approached her townhouse, she would glance up and proudly view the shingle hanging outside the front door. Today was no exception. It still seemed surreal to her that she was operating on her own and without all the resources the government had to offer. *Noble was right. I need to play by a different set of rules,* she thought as she closed the front door behind her.

Buzz came the blaring sound of the intercom. Startled, she abruptly turned around and looked through the peephole. Standing on the stoop was a middle-aged, smartly dressed woman holding a sizeable leather-bound book. Max opened the door.

"Maxine Ford?"

"Yes, may I help you?" Max asked, thinking it odd that this woman would address her by her formal name. *No one calls me Maxine.*

"I'm Isabelle Spark."

Max felt her heart flutter as she controlled her composure. "Please come in," she invited, and then offered her a seat on one of the sofas in the reception area.

But before either of them had a chance to sit down, the senator's wife spoke.

"Notwithstanding the questionable police reports, I believe my husband did not commit suicide! The police have dropped the ball. I'm positive he was murdered!" Isabelle's voice was strong and unwavering as though the matter was indisputable. She took her seat.

Max sat across from her on the other sofa with the glass coffee table in between them.

"How can you be sure it wasn't suicide?"

"I know my husband! It's not in his character to contemplate suicide under any circumstances!" She placed the leather-bound book on the table and spoke with more calm. "I went to the Russell Senate Office Building to collect his belongings. The guard at the front desk resisted at first, not wanting to grant me access to Sherman's office. He said the case was still under investigation and his office had been sealed. That's not only odd, but totally inconsistent with the case being closed."

"Excuse me," Max interrupted. "I was also under the same impression that the case was closed."

"You can imagine my surprise. But the guard stepped aside and had a lengthy conversation with someone on the phone. Apparently the person acquiesced, except I had to be escorted and watched the entire time." Her indignant tone returned. "I wasn't allowed to take anything with his handwriting. The entire fiasco was humiliating and thoughtless."

"Very interesting," Max said, while thinking *that son of a bitch*, as she recalled her last visit to the Capitol police chief. "Please continue, Mrs. Spark," she urged.

"One of the items I took is a framed oil painting. It's our family portrait that my husband had hanging on the wall. He would often say that no matter how difficult the task became he'd always have his family with him."

Max detected a slight quiver in her voice. "Do you need a moment?"

"No, dear, I'm fine. Thank you." She cleared her throat and then continued. "I want to display that portrait at Sherman's celebration-of-life ceremony. I want him to know that his family will always be there for him." Isabelle finally caved in and began to sob.

Max gave her the time she needed to regain her composure.

"Please excuse me. This is very difficult." Isabelle recovered from her brief emotional spell and explained, "The corner of the frame was damaged, and it was essential that it be repaired before the funeral." She immediately reached inside her handbag and retrieved a letter. As she steadied her hand, she passed the sheet of paper to Max. "This letter was found taped to the back of the canvas as it was being reframed."

Max's instincts told her that the frame was most likely damaged by the senator intentionally, knowing that his wife was a perfectionist and would have had it fixed. As usual, she discounted the possibility of a coincidence. Excitedly, she unfolded the letter and read the words in silence, all the while sensing that the senator's wife was studying her face. She tried to remain expressionless. The first few lines were obviously Spark's personal declaration of love for his family and for Isabelle. Max quickly skipped to the next paragraph. Her name was scrawled in the very first sentence. She was stunned to read: *Should anything happen to me, deliver the family photo album to Maxine Ford.* It took Max a moment to absorb the statement, even after rereading it several times. Then she moved to the next sentence. *Tell her about Claus.* The rest of the letter was clearly personal. Max slowly folded the paper and returned it to Isabelle. The dumbfounded expression on her face must have telegraphed.

"I'm as confused as you must be as to why Sherman would want me to tell you about Claus—or what it has to do with his death." Isabelle went on to describe that six months earlier, a scientist by the name of Claus Veunet was scheduled to testify at her husband's committee hearing and that apparently Veunet died in a climbing accident a week before. "Sherman didn't give me any specifics about the man or about his testimony, other than to say it was pretty hush-hush. As a rule, he never talked about the investigations being conducted by his various committees, nor did I ask. But I sensed that day, something was really bothering him. Now, I have to wonder about another mysterious incident." Isabelle paused to collect her thoughts.

"Please continue." Max was eager for her to move it along.

Isabelle cleared her throat and then explained, "It happened several weeks later. Again, it was one morning at breakfast while Sherman was reading the morning newspaper. Without warning, he knocked over his coffee cup. I was surprised because he just stood up and left the room. It was so unlike him. But when I went to clean up the spilled mess, I noticed the newspaper was open to an article. It was about a scientist who had died in a fatal car crash."

"Do you remember the name?"

"The print was badly smudged from the coffee, but I could make out the first name. It was Luca. I think the last name started with D-U-E or D-O-E. It was too difficult to read. I do remember, however, the article stated he was Swiss. That's all I can recall."

Max sat back a moment to consider the significance of Isabelle's story.

Isabelle gave her the time to cogitate. Then she reached over to pick up the leather-bound book she had set down on the coffee table and handed it to Max. "This is the photo album Sherman wanted me to give you. He might have left a clue in there somewhere, but honestly, it's only family vacation photos." She clasped her hands in her lap and looked directly at Max. "Please find my husband's killer."

Max and Jax had agreed that before accepting any new clients, they would first run through the case together. Problem was, Max could never resist her dominant instincts. She would break their self-imposed deal before she ever left the starting gate. However, there was one thing she would insist upon—a pledge from the client. "Mrs. Spark, as I advise all my clients, I will get to the truth—but it may not be what you prefer. You must be prepared to accept the outcome." Max paused, waiting for some sign of tacit agreement, but none came. Then she said the words her new client was waiting to hear. "I will take your case."

"Oh, dear, thank you. I need to know what happened to Sherman."

"Please call me Max."

"Yes, Max, but you must call me Isabelle."

Now that that's settled... Max thought, and she quickly swung into action. First, she needed to discuss the messy business of fees. Happily, they were of no consequence to Isabelle. Then she needed to prepare her client for what lay ahead. "Isabelle, it will take time. You must be patient. However, the fact that the Capitol police have yet to arrive at any conclusion may strangely be our first lead. Please let me know if they contact you." Max noted an odd look on Isabelle's face. "Is there anything else you want to tell me?"

"There is something else that may be useful," Isabelle said with obvious hesitation.

Max's ears perked up, as she was about to delve into the weeds of her first case. Isabelle had her full attention.

"Sherman must have trusted you. Now I must do the same. The night of his death I discovered my cellphone was missing. I thought Sherman may have picked it up by mistake thinking it was his. So I tried calling him repeatedly but there was no answer. Then I remember him showing me how to use this Lookout Security program, so I was able to locate the phone." Isabelle paused for a second. Clearly, she was uneasy. "It was at a location far from where my husband's body was eventually found."

"Where was the phone?"

"Lookout Security located it at a place called The Bachelor's Mill."

Max gulped. "Have you told anyone about this?"

"No one, until now."

"Do you have a record of the calls that were made from the phone?"

Isabelle reached again into her handbag and grabbed a slip of paper. She explained that she had contacted her service provider, and they had given her a list of the calls that had been made the day her husband mistakenly took her phone. "There were four calls. I recognized the first two phone numbers; those were calls I made. But the other one is unfamiliar. Someone called that number twice."

Max noted the numbers, along with the times they were placed. "I'll follow up on these, but you'll need to tell the police so they can trace the phone."

All at once, Isabelle withdrew sheepishly.

"What's the matter?"

"I followed the instructions on the Lookout Security site and deleted everything on the phone and then disabled it. I'm sorry, Max, but I thought Sherman had lost the phone, and I was trying to protect the data. I had no idea that hours later my husband would be found dead."

"Isabelle, you need to tell the police exactly what you've told me, including erasing the data. But, for now, they don't need to know about your husband's letter, the photo album, or these phone numbers." Max waved the slip of paper. "Give me a little time to investigate and if anything, of importance turns up, I'll make sure the police are kept informed." She reached across the coffee table and clasped Isabelle's hands. "We'll find out what happened to Sherman. I assure you." Max could see the tension receding from Isabelle's face. It was clear that she understood. At the same time, Max's own energy was about to burst. It was time to get to work on her first case. She reassured her client once more and then politely escorted her to the door.

As Isabelle was about to walk out the front door and down the steps, Jax came bounding up past her, excusing himself along the way.

Chapter 8

A SIXTH SENSE

"Guess what!" Jax blurted out. "Senator Spark's death is still being investigated. They haven't closed the case yet! Max, your instincts were right on the mark!"

"Aren't you going to ask me whom you just passed on the steps?"

"Didn't you hear me? They must have evidence that Spark didn't kill himself!"

Max stared back blankly.

"Okay! Who was it?"

"Our new client, Mrs. Isabelle Spark."

That time Jax was the one to stare back, but with a shocked expression plastered on his face. Without saying a word, he walked over to the sofa and plunked himself down, unknowingly where the late senator's wife had sat. "I'll be damned! Noble warned me about your mystical occult-like qualities."

Max flashed a huge smile and then joined him on the sofa. "Sorry, Jax, I broke our deal. But I had no choice under the circumstances."

"Hey, it's your name on the shingle. But why would the senator's wife want you to take the case?" Jax was more than mildly curious as to the answer.

"She didn't! The late senator left her a letter with instructions to seek me out in the case of his death from unnatural causes. I can only assume that he thought I was still at the SIA. Apparently, or should I say, fortunately, he didn't get the memo. Hey, it must be my karma."

"Okay, then why would the senator want you to take the case?"

"It might have something to do with what happened many years ago, while I was still at the CIA. I was in charge of an undercover sting operation to expose a group of arms smugglers who were using an escort service in Georgetown as a front. Lucky me, I got my hands on the appointment books."

"The senator?" Jax eyebrows instantly shot upward.

Max grinned. It was widely known among the inner circle in Washington that the escort service in Georgetown was also a front for a pricey brothel. "We got the bad guys and brought down their operation. So I didn't think it was necessary to smear the reputations of quite a few of our Washington elite, including notable judges and senators. Besides, the books were simply an accounting of their activities and had nothing to do with our case. Shortly thereafter, while attending a cocktail party, I received several whispered 'thank yous' in my ear. The senator was one of them. I surmised the madam with a heart of gold told her clientele that I had returned the books to her. I guess I made quite an impression."

Jax, apparently fascinated with the story, remained unusually speechless.

"What do you think?" Max grilled, trying to jolt him back to the conversation at hand.

"You tell me. According to your own rules for taking a case: one, is your client believable? Two, can you get to the truth? And three, is it worth the risk?"

Max did not answer the questions, but handed the photo album to Jax. "The answers may be in here." She also filled him in on the phone numbers and the mysterious deaths of two scientists. "So, with all we know thus far, what—do—you—think?" she repeated emphatically.

"Looks like we have our first case, Madam Detective!"

Max flashed him a wink and then checked her watch. It was 4:30 in the afternoon in France. "I'm gonna give Veunet's wife a call to see what she can tell me about the accident."

"What about the phone numbers from Isabelle's phone? You want me to track them down?"

"No, I'll give them a go."

"Then I'll take a whack at identifying the second scientist to see if there's a connection between him and Claus Veunet."

"Great! Would you also take a look at the photo album? I perused it while Isabelle was telling me her lost-phone story, but it appears to contain only family photos. I must be missing something. There has to be a clue among the photos that the senator wanted me to discover."

"Looks like we've got our work cut out for us!" Jax stood up with the album tucked under his arm and headed for his office.

Max sat back for a moment longer taking in her new space, a space she and Noble had discussed sharing. But in the end he convinced her that she needed to go it alone. Especially if they were going to give their new relationship a fair chance. She could not help but wonder at that moment where he was. She wished he would call. Normally, he would have been the first person with whom she would discuss a case. A stimulating exercise, bantering about the options, was something they both enjoyed. Now, she was doing it with Jax, her new associate. *Enough!*

Max stood up with the slip of paper Isabelle had given her and marched into her office. But before calling France, she decided to check out the phone numbers, starting with the first two numbers Isabelle had identified as her own calls. They both checked out; one was to cancel a hair appointment, the other to confirm a dinner date with neighbors. The next two were oddly the same phone number with a 941 area code, but one call had been placed at 5:48 p.m. and the second call had been placed at 8:59 p.m. Both on the same day. The same day the senator's body was found in the park.

Something doesn't make sense. She sat tapping her fingers on the desk, trying to recall the night when she saw the flashing lights. Noble had just arrived. She was positive that when they walked to the park to see what was happening, it was sometime around 8:00 p.m. Noble's unexpected visit was to take her to dinner. He would not have arrived at 9:00 p.m. "How can a corpse make a phone call?" she wondered aloud, and then assumed, "There's only one way to find out." Max took a deep breath and dialed the number starting with 941, placing a call to Sarasota, Florida. The phone rang continuously without anyone picking up. She tried several other times to no avail. "I'll give it another try later," she uttered, continuing to speak to the air. At the same time, she assumed that if the call was connected to Spark's death, the phone had most likely been tossed.

Max then braced herself and called Veunet's wife but had to leave a message. She made sure that she introduced herself as the former deputy director of the SIA, and that they were investigating the death of Senator Spark. Max intentionally stumbled over the word *former* and threw in the *they*, hoping the international connection would do its usual thing of cutting in and out. Satisfied with her message, she stuck her head into Jax's office.

"No luck here. I had to leave a message with Veunet's wife and there was no answer at the 941 number, the one in Sarasota." She continued to lean against the doorway with a pensive stare.

"What's the matter?"

"I can't put my finger on it exactly, but something's bugging me. I'm gonna head over to the Capitol police station to have another talk with the chief."

"Go ahead; I'll hold the fort."

Chapter 9

———◦◦———◦———◦◦———

FRENCH CONNECTION

M ax tapped the Uber app on her smartphone and prepared for the car's arrival. Minutes later she was seated comfortably in the back seat on her way to the Capitol police headquarters. Normally it was a seven-minute drive, but now it was the dreaded traffic hour and the cars were bumper to bumper along Massachusetts Avenue. She checked her watch as the car inched along. Suddenly, her phone rang. The incoming phone number on her screen started with 33. The call was from France.

"Pull over, please. I'll walk from here," she instructed the driver.

Max stood at the corner of Fifth and C Street and took the call. "Mrs. Veunet?"

"*Oui*, yes, this is Antoinette Veunet. I just received your voice message. You said you were investigating Senator Spark's death. I'm confused as to why you would call me."

"First, my condolences for the death of your husband."

"*Merci*."

"Mrs. Veunet, Claus died a week before he was scheduled to testify at a committee hearing in Washington, DC It was co-chaired by Senator Spark."

"*Oui*, but what does this have to with the Senator's death?"

"I'm sorry to put you through this, but can you tell me what happened to Claus?"

There was silence on the other end.

"Mrs. Veunet?" Max heard her weeping from a continent away and waited for the widow to respond.

"*Désolé.* I'm sorry. It's still painful, even though it's been several months since Claus' death. To answer your question, he died in a horrible climbing accident. He and another man named Ernst went climbing the day before. Then Ernst wanted to have the opportunity to climb Lou Passo, another climbing route, before he departed the following day to return to his home in Lucerne. So they went climbing again on that Sunday—but Claus never came home." Antoinette began to weep again. "I don't know what else I can tell you."

"Again, I apologize for the intrusion, but how did you hear about the accident?"

"The police called me. They said another climber had reported seeing a body fall from the cliff. According to the police, one of the protection bolts dislodged, throwing him against the rocks." She paused and then uttered, "The impact broke his neck. They said his rope had been cut, but speculated that Claus himself cut it, knowing he would not survive."

"Mrs. Veunet—" Max was suddenly cut off from her question.

"Those bolts are inspected on a regular basis! I don't believe it was freak accident!"

Max did not think so either, but tried again with her question, "What about the man named Ernst?"

"All I know is that he was an avid rock climber like Claus. They met a few days earlier at a conference they had attended." Again Mrs. Veunet paused.

Max kept silent, imagining how difficult it must be for Antoinette to recount that day. But the questions were necessary. She had to push for answers. "Mrs. Veunet, please tell me about Ernst. Where was he at the time of the accident?"

Antoinette's voice became faint. "I asked the same question. The police said there was no evidence to indicate that he was climbing with anyone else." Her anger returned. "They said he was climbing alone!"

For the first time, Max heard doubt in her voice. "Do you believe that's what happened?"

"He knows I didn't like him climbing alone!" she blurted out. Then defeat laced her voice. "It's possible he used Ernst as an excuse. But he's never lied to me before—I don't know what to think."

"Excuse me, but I have a few more questions. Do you know a man by the name of Luca?"

"You mean Luca Doerfinger? He was a good friend of my husband, but I never met him personally." Antoinette was particularly confused by the question, but continued. "They were classmates at *École Polytechnique Fédérale de Lausanne*. Please, what does all of this have to do with Claus?"

"I believe Luca was killed in a car crash a few weeks after your husband's death."

"*Oh mon Dieu*! You think Claus' accident is connected to Luca's death?"

"Mrs. Veunet, I'm not sure what to think at this point," Max admitted, but she was careful not to imply that Claus may have been murdered, even though she suspected that to be the case. Max also needed someone in a position of authority to get the necessary answers. Not wanting to torment the poor woman any further, she asked only a few more questions relating to Claus' occupation. Max then assured Claus' widow that she would be back in touch. But before ending the call, she stressed, "In the meantime, it would be prudent not to discuss this call with anyone, including the *gendarmes*, until I have gathered more information."

It was clear that Mrs. Veunet understood.

Chapter 10

NEW SHERIFF IN TOWN

Max managed the rest of the distance by foot and hiked up Massachusetts Avenue to D Street in six minutes. After two minutes more of maneuvering through the narrow corridors of the Capitol police headquarters, she had finally arrived at the chief's office.

"Hey, Max."

"The chief in?"

"Yes, but please let me announce you this time." The secretary stood up and stuck her head in the door of the chief's office.

Max could barely hear the conversation but she certainly knew the subject matter.

Seconds later, the secretary turned around. "Enter at your own peril," she joked, and then invited Max to go in.

"Hey, Ray."

"What, Max? I assume this isn't a social call."

"What's going on with the Senator Spark investigation? You lied to me and said the case was closed."

"Max, stay out of it. It's not your case."

"Guess again! Isabelle Spark hired me to find out who killed her husband." Her huge smile appeared to annoy the chief.

"I can't believe you're actually licensed to do whatever it is you do?"

"Check this out!" Max flashed her identification card. "I'm a gen-u-ine private detective in the District of Columbia."

"You really left the agency to become a private dick—or is that a private jane?" The chief shook his head and then lightened up his tone. "My hats off to you, Max."

"Thanks, but what about the senator?"

"It's still ruled a suicide."

"You don't buy that? That's why the case is still open. Let's start with the time of death."

"Max, you're not going to make this easy, are you?"

"Never have. Time of death?"

"The coroner estimates between 6:00 and 7:00 p.m."

"What type of gun?"

"A Luger P08 with a six-inch barrel."

"That's a semi-automatic and the six-inch barrel is military issue." Max was getting an uneasy feeling. Something did not stack up. "An odd choice for suicide, I'd say."

"Someone wanting to off himself isn't usually picky."

"Ballistics report?"

"We pulled out a nine-millimeter slug, but it shattered the bone, along with any evidence we could identify from the mangled bullet. Other than that the gun was clean, except, of course, for the senator's fingerprints."

"Gunshot residue?"

The chief winced.

"C'mon, that's Forensics 101."

"I'll find out and get back to you."

"Thank you! Now that wasn't so hard. I'm going to like working with you on this case, Ray."

"Hardy-har-har," the chief countered. "Okay, Max, what do I get in return?"

Max filled the Chief in about the mix-up of the cellphones and how the senator must have inadvertently taken his wife's phone by mistake. "Mrs. Spark had no idea that her husband was dead, only that her phone was lost."

"Okay, so we'll trace it?"

"Sorry. She followed the Lookout Security protocol and erased the data. Then she deactivated the phone."

The chief frowned.

"But wait, before she disabled the phone, the Lookout Security program located the device at around 9:00 p.m. on the same day the Senator's body was found in the park."

"And?" the chief asked impatiently.

"It was at The Bachelor's Mill."

The chief broke out in laughter. "Certainly not a place I'd expect the senator to frequent."

"Especially if he was already dead."

"How long have you been on this case, Max?"

"Oh, about two hours."

"Okay," he huffed, "we'll share any unsecured information. But if I find out you're holding on me, your new career will end very quickly. I'm the new sheriff in town and you play by my rules."

"Ray, is this any way to start a new relationship? You have my word. As soon as I come across anything definitive, I'll turn it over."

"Max, when you start being cooperative—I start to worry."

"Enjoy your day, Chief."

Chapter 11

THREE FOR THREE

Max returned to the townhouse and settled back into her office after noticing that Jax had stepped out. Moments later, the doorbell rang. "Yes?" she asked through the intercom. "Flower delivery!"

From the monitor, Max could see the profile of young kid with shaggy hair. Behind him was a white van with the name "Nosegay Florist" scrawled across the side. Feeling at ease, she opened the door, but was taken aback by the enormous arrangement of flowers placed inside a vase large enough for the Tomb of the Unknown Soldier. The bouquet blocked the kid's face and before she could thank him, he had swiftly turned around and headed back down the front steps. "Have a good day, ma'am" were his parting words.

"Mmm," Max said as she placed the flowers on her desk. She unpinned the small envelope attached to the tag and read the card inside: *Congratulations, from your ardent admirer.* "How sweet, Noble," she said aloud, but questioned, "Why *edelweiss?*" Max then started to wonder whether they could have actually come from Stanton but held off from calling him for the moment. "Another mystery to solve, but not today!" Suddenly, the phone rang, interrupting her thoughts.

———— ·◦◦· ————

"Hey, how uncanny, I was just thinking about you. Where are you?"

"Can't say, but it's great to hear your exuberant voice. What gives?"

"Noble—I have my first case!"

"That was fast. Who's the lucky client?"

"Isabelle Spark."

"The senator's wife?"

Max could tell from Noble's voice that he was a bit stunned. "Yes, she believes her husband was murdered and wants me to prove it."

"I thought the papers reported it a suicide."

"The coroner hasn't ruled out foul play yet, so the case is still wide open. And there's definitely more digging to be done. I don't have any conclusive evidence, but it's out there and I'm going to find it." Max refrained from telling him about the two dead scientists or the photo album, and she certainly was not about to mention her phone call to a mystery person in Sarasota. Like Noble, she also played things close to the vest.

"Take it slow, Max," he cautioned.

"What do you think about edelweiss?"

He thought it an odd question, given the sudden change in topic, but he was certainly curious. "Why?"

"Oh, I was considering decorating options for the office."

"How clever! Using a flower with the German term for 'noble' in the name. You'll be surrounded by me every day." He chuckled, knowing that decorating was not her forte. "What going on with you?"

"Nothing." *Pooh, he didn't send them.*

Max appeared distracted and he did not want to stay on the line much longer anyway. "Sweetheart, congratulations on your first case. I'm really proud of you for going out on your own. But I pity the suspects you uncover."

"Thanks. And how's it going on your end?"

"Everything's fine. I'll call you in a few days. Right now I'm pushed for time."

"Okay. Be safe wherever you are. Love you."

"Love you too. Give my best to Jax."

Max hung up the phone and sat back to admire the bouquet. At the same time, she tried to envision where Noble was—all she saw was a blank canvas. The reality that she would also be forced to retain secrets was sinking in, something she still wrestled with. She shook her head and refocused on the flowers. *So if it wasn't Noble, who sent the bouquet?* Then Stanton popped back into her mind. "Oh, let it go. Too much self-contemplation for one day. I have a business to run."

"This is Max Ford, the former deputy director of the SIA. I'd like to speak with Senator Erog." She thought a little clout wouldn't hurt, given the situation.

"One moment, please," his secretary replied.

"Max, to what do I owe the pleasure of this call?" the senator asked jovially, hiding his uneasiness. He had wrestled with the SIA before and did not care for their sticking their noses into his various Capitol activities, whether or not they fit under their investigative purview.

"I'm investigating the death of Senator Sherman Spark."

There was silence on the other end.

"Senator," she prodded.

"Yes, yes. I understand Sherman's death was ruled a suicide."

"The police are continuing their investigation, so the case is not closed—"

Erog cut her off. "But why are you involve—" only to be cut off himself.

"Senator, the point of my call is to ask what is the main objective of your committee?"

"It's public record. We study a variety of climate-change initiatives and recommend funding allocations to the House Committee on Appropriations. Why do you ask?"

"Do you know a scientist named Claus Veunet?"

Again there was silence, which Max found more telling than if he had given a direct response. She gave him the time to grapple for an answer.

"Max, what does this have to do with Sherman?"

"Veunet died in a climbing accident days before he was scheduled to testify before your committee. A committee you and Senator Spark co-chaired. And now the senator is also dead."

Erog refrained from denying. He knew it would only feed her suspicions. "Yes, it was very sad. Veunet was a brilliant scientist and Sherman was a dear friend. I'll be attending his celebration-of-life ceremony later this week."

She did not buy into his sentimentality routine and continued to grill. "What about Luca Doerfinger?"

"Luca Doerfinger," he muttered to himself, but loud enough for her to hear. "I'm sorry, Max. I'm already late for a meeting. I really have to go. Great talking with you."

The dial tone reverberated in her ear.

"I would really love to play poker with that guy sometime." She smiled thinking how easy it was until, unexpectedly, her phone rang while it still rested in her hand.

⸻

"So, Madam P.I., how was your first week?"

"Stanton, you're my lucky charm. On Sunday I hung up the shingle you gave me and a week later my first client appeared."

"Fantastic, Max! You're destined to be great detective. What's the case about?"

"I've been hired by Isabelle Spark to investigate the death of her husband."

"The senator!"

"The one and only!"

The fact that Stanton was head of the president's Secret Service detail made it easier for her to confide in him. But Max refrained from revealing the details of the case until she had verifiable facts. For the moment, she thought it best to change the subject and turned to more personal issues. "Amanda decided to take the honeymoon cruise on her own and Noble decided to disappear as well."

"Hmm, interesting. You sure he's not sailing on the blue-blue seas?"

"Oh, stop!"

"You can't blame me for wishful thinking."

"Oh, I almost forgot to thank you for the edelweiss, my ardent admirer!"

"Hey, doll, I'll always be your admirer, but I didn't send any flowers. And if I did, they wouldn't be a flower that literally means *noble*. Are you sure they're not from him?"

"Yes! So if Noble didn't send them, and you didn't send them, who sent me edelweiss?"

Stanton let out a pleasant laugh and made light of the conversation. "You're the detective. I suggest you should start profiling jealous admirers."

"Very funny."

"Max, good luck on your case. And you know you can call on me if you need anything."

"Thanks, Stanton."

"Catch you later."

<hr />

For the first time in a long time, Max reflected back on the day she had met the Major. It happened to be the day after a horrific explosion took place in an underground encampment in Utah, during which she had been badly bruised, but it also took the lives of two soldiers. Max was conducting an investigation for the SIA. Stanton was later assigned to work with her as a team to reenter the encampment in an attempt to locate the notorious terrorist Simon Hall. Initially, sparks flew as they stepped on each other's turf. Then the sparks took on a new meaning. *There was no denying he's handsome, intelligent, and witty... and the sex was great.* She smiled as she evoked the memory. But for some unknown reason and in spite of all his attributes, she was never able to commit. She chalked it up to one of life's mysteries and was content with the way things were, until another horrible event occurred. It was the day she was kidnapped and splattered with the blood from the former First Lady's fatal wound and Noble rushed to her side. At that moment, while he held her in a comforting embrace, she realized that he was the one who had touched her heart. Denying Stanton as her lover was painful— losing him as a friend would have been unbearable.

Chapter 12

———◦◦═══◦═══◦◦———

TRADING HITS

T he senator leaned back into his office chair, clearly unnerved. Beads of sweat blanketed his brow. Then he heard the vibrating phone in the desk drawer and panic shot through his rotund body. "The timing sucks," he muttered. But having no choice, he opened the drawer and answered the call.

"Have you found him yet?" The voice was purposely distorted, but the gruffness was apparent.

"No. And we have another problem. Spark's wife apparently hired Max Ford to investigate his death."

"Shit! There's nothing to uncover—right?"

The senator suddenly had a sinking feeling that the conversation would not end well, but holding back would be lethal. "You don't know Ford. She's already thrown out the names of Claus Veunet and Luca Doerfinger."

"She's fishing with an empty hook. Find them and end this nightmare!"

"What do you want me to do about Doiron and his gang? They're still out there, propagating the fallacies of global warming."

"Leave them alone! They're too exposed. Half the scientific community thinks they're a bunch of geriatrics who've lost their stuff. That's good enough." The brusque caller paused and then, in a calmer tone, admitted, "However, there are two scientists running amok who could prove these guys actually know what the hell they are talking about."

"But now Ford complicates matters. It means we're in a foot race with her to find them."

"Then find them first!"

The phone went dead.

The senator hastily placed a call from the same secure phone and waited to hear the click on the end of the line. Then he spoke. "The Director is getting nervous. Find them soon or all will come tumbling down—and you're going with us."

"We're working on it."

"There's something else I want you to do."

Chapter 13

JUMBLED CLUES

When Max heard Jax coming through the front door, she sprang out of her chair and dashed into the reception area. "Luca Doerfinger!"

"What are you talking about?"

"Doerfinger! That was the name of the scientist who died in the car crash. Now we need to find out if there's a link between Claus Veunet and Luca Doerfinger. According to Veunet's wife, both were classmates at the École Polytechnique Fédérale de Lausanne."

"Impressive! Pronunciation and all. But how do you come up with this stuff so fast?" Jax shook his head in amazement. "I'm not even sure you need me on this case."

"Ah, Jax, of course I do. You're my right arm. Now cheer up; there's more." Max rapidly filled him in on the rest of her conversation with Veunet's widow and her subsequent conversation with the senator. "You can't believe how easy it was to get Erog to give himself away."

"Whatever's going on, it obviously has the co-chair of the committee rattled. But before you go flying into outer space, I have something to show you. Follow me." Jax headed into his office and sat down at his desk.

Max trailed behind.

"Pull up a chair and sit next to me." Jax opened to a page he had bookmarked in the Spark family photo album and pulled out one of the photos to show Max.

"What's that, Gematria? Or some other coded language? I don't understand." She was confused by the scribbling on the back of the photo.

"I'm not sure, but I found similar letters and numbers on the back of only three other photos. I remembered your telling me that the senator hid the letter to Isabelle behind the family portrait. As you suspected, he most likely damaged the frame deliberately, knowing that his wife would ultimately find his final instructions."

"Mmm, Senator Spark would have known that if anything unusual happened to him, everything in his office would have been confiscated except for personal items, which would have been handed over to his family. It's standard protocol for any investigation of a high-level official. Now it appears our senator had good reason to be suspicious."

"Exactly! So that got me to thinking. Why would he want you to have the family photo album?"

"You think the letters and numbers are clues as to why he was killed?"

"If these scribbles are in the senator's handwriting—they could be our first clue."

Max inspected the notations more closely. "It looks like the same handwriting from the letter he wrote to Isabelle. But I can't be sure. What's befuddling is that we still don't know exactly how Spark died, thanks to the snail-like investigators at the Capitol Police Department."

"True, but hear me out. I wanted to preserve the evidence in the event we end up having to turn it over to the authorities. So I wrote down what I found scrawled on each of the photos and then returned them to their original place. It's not going to be that easy to decipher, but I have a few wild guesses." Jax winked and then placed the photo back in the album. He then handed Max a sheet of paper. "Have a look. I'll explain the notations in parentheses as I go along."

Max studied the jumbled clues.

LD 5.19-5.16 *(CH)*
AM *(IT)*
JVB 10.13 *(GR)*
CV 4.8-4.2 *(FR)*

"Do you think they were written on the photos randomly and then scattered throughout the album?" she asked.

"I wondered the same thing, but bear with me. The first notation on the list, starting with the letters 'LD,' followed by the numbers five-point-nineteen to five-point-sixteen, which were written on the flipside of this photo, the one I just showed you."

Max re-examined the photo as Jax continued to explain the significance.

"As you can see, Mrs. Spark is standing on a river bank. I've been there. It's in Lucerne, Switzerland. The buildings behind her were a giveaway. The 'CH' scribbled in parentheses is my notation for Switzerland."

"Okay! You have my undivided attention."

Jax turned to another page in the album. "You can see for yourself that's the Duomo in Florence, Italy. This time, I assume it's of the entire family. On the other side of this photo were the initials 'AM.' Again, my scribbling 'IT' indicates the country."

"What are you doing? You said the initials read 'AM.'" Max asked as she watched Jax reach into the plastic casing to retrieve the photo.

"Look." Jax turned the photo over. "I wasn't about to write this gibberish down."

$$\text{Temp(year)} - \text{Temp(1850)} < 1.8\{\text{Log}[\text{CO2(year)}/\text{CO2(1850)}]/\text{Log}[2]\} \text{ deg C}$$

Max was baffled by the chaotic mix of letters, numbers, and symbols. "This case is getting weirder by the second. What's your best guess?"

"Considering we are looking for a bunch of scientists—I'd say a scientific formula. Now let's try to find one of the *Einsteins* who can tell us." Jax started to slide the photo back into its proper place.

"Hold on a minute. Hold it still." Max quickly snapped a picture with her smartphone. "Got it."

Jax then put the photo back in the album and quickly moved to the next page. "'JVB' ten-point-thirteen was written behind this group photo of the family at the Brandenburg Gate in Berlin, Germany." Without hesitating, he flipped to another page and said, "Here's the last photo. Obviously, it's of the Eiffel Tower and this time no one is in the picture. But the letters 'CV' four-point-eight to four-point-two were written on the back."

Max continued to study what appeared to be random letters and numbers.

Then while Jax was waiting for Max's brilliance to come to the fore, he headed out to the kitchen. "I'll go grab us a couple cups of coffee."

"Thanks," she answered. Her eyes remained fixed on the paper.

Moments later Jax returned with two steaming mugs. "Anything flash through that beautiful, analytical head of yours?"

Max glanced up. "Look at your notations. All the photos were taken in different countries, and some of them many years ago based on how Mrs. Spark was dressed. But look at the letters that were written on the photos of France and Switzerland." She gave him time to study the list, but then she couldn't hold back any longer. "It's so obvious!" she goaded.

Jax held up his hand, signaling her to let him have the honors. "I knew you'd get it! Of course, 'CV' refers to Claus Veunet. Obviously, the French scientist. And now we know that 'LD' has to be for Luca Doerfinger, the scientist from Switzerland."

"Exactly! And the second number next to their initials is definitely the day they died. We know that Veunet was scheduled to testify a week after his death. That must be the first number. So most likely 'AM' is an Italian scientist and 'JVB' is a German scientist. According to the number next to 'JVB,' he or she is scheduled to testify before the committee on the thirteenth of October."

"Which gives us only a few days to find our German," he stated hesitantly, "hopefully, still living and breathing."

Max's mind suddenly veered off in a different direction.

Jax could not help but notice. "Hey, what's going on?"

"How about another cup of coffee?"

Jax could tell she had more to say. "This better be good. I'll be right back."

Chapter 14

---○---○---○---

FRENETIC REASONING

Jax returned with two caffeine refills and eagerly asked, "Now, what gives in that head of yours?"

"Jax, all we know at this point is that Spark is dead for reasons unknown. Two scientists who were supposed to testify in front of his committee are also dead. It's not a coincidence. And although we don't know exactly what their testimony was about, it must have had something to do with climate change, since that was the main objective of the committee. So it got me thinking."

"Okay, shoot. I'm all ears."

"A few years ago, Noble and I worked a case. Remember Simon Hall?"

"Ooh, yeah, how could I forget? The notorious international terrorist who finally met his maker."

"Right, but while we were chasing clues trying to prevent him from taking down the nation's power grid, we discovered a whole cast of characters whose primary goal was to push for renewable energy. Ever heard of Agenda 21?"

"Wasn't that a United Nations doctrine having to do with sustainable development? Presumably, it established the protocol to protect our natural resources for a growing population."

"Simplistically, yes, but if you dig deep, you'll find that it implements drastic actions to take control of the population's use of the earth's lands and oceans. Although some have said the phrase *sustainable development* implies totalitarian control eventually leading to depopulation in numerous countries as a means to preserve the sustainability of the world's resources."

"That was a mouthful," Jax teased, but then, in a more serious tone, asked, "Are you inferring a systematic means to reduce the population?" He was having difficulty figuring out the connection to climate change.

"Their words—not mine. But at the head of the sustainable development parade was Gro Harlem Brundtland, the first woman prime minister of Norway, who published a report in 1987 titled *Our Common Future*. Around the same time a battle cry was sounded against global warming by Edmund de Rothschild at the 4th World Wilderness Congress when he stated that man-made carbon dioxide emissions, referred to as the greenhouse-gas effect, were the culprit for heating up the earth's atmosphere. Both events provided the basic premise of Agenda 21."

"Wasn't Maurice Strong, a Canadian, credited with being the architect of the document?"

"Yes, and ironically he made his billions in oil before sustainability became his mantra. Up until his death a few years ago, he was a rather mysterious figure. Even though he was courted by heads of state around the world and was a recipient of multiple awards, he had been called everything derogatory from the 'Father of America's Destruction' to 'World Enemy Number One' by critics who questioned his activities. Although his admirers commonly referred to him as the Godfather of the Environmental Movement."

"I thought that was Al Gore's self-endowed title."

"He may have assumed the role after Strong's death. But it's interesting you should bring up his name. In fact, it was the partnership between Strong and Gore that catapulted their mission. It surfaced sometime around 1992, before the first UN Conference on Environment and Development took place in Brazil."

"You're referring to the Earth Summit?"

"Yes, Gore had been an intimate in the movement from the beginning and was instrumental in the political process for the US to endorse the Summit. In fact, he led the US delegation. It was at the Summit where Strong first introduced Agenda 21 and made the case that no nation can achieve sustainable development on its own. He emphasized that it required a global partnership to achieve its lofty goal."

"How well was it received?"

"Extremely well, considering leaders from more than one hundred and seventy-eight countries attended the conference and signed the document adopting its tenets. President George H.W. Bush signed for the United States. Although it's been reported that Bush was reluctant until the eleventh hour when the then-Senator Albert Gore, Junior, convinced him to attend. Coincidentally, it was the same year Gore published his book *Earth in Balance*, the precursor to his subsequent book *An Inconvenient Truth*. But his influence didn't stop there. The following year, the newly appointed Vice President Gore provided the impetus for President Clinton's Executive Order 12852, establishing the *President's Council on Sustainable Development*, bypassing Congress."

"Why did he have to bypass Congress? You said that Bush Senior participated in the signing ceremony at the Summit."

"Agenda 21 is not a treaty and therefore is non-binding. However, Clinton's Executive Order mirrors Agenda 21. You following?"

"Keep going."

"Okay, now fast-forward to 2001. Are you familiar with the Chicago Climate Exchange, or CCX?"

"Vaguely, something about carbon trading in an effort to reduce greenhouse gases."

"Correct. Companies that produce clean renewable energy, emitting fewer greenhouse gases or GHG, earn credits."

"Meaning less human-made carbon dioxide, or CO2 emissions that are claimed to cause global warming?"

Max nodded her head yes. "But get this. These companies can then sell those same credits to other companies that produce too much GHG. Essentially, the polluters can buy their way out."

"Isn't that akin to selling your frequent flyer airline miles to infrequent travelers?"

"Cute, but the basis for cap and trade is to limit, or cap, the amount of emissions a company can produce. But it also allows for companies that need to emit more CO2 as a means of doing business to buy credits from companies that produce less than the approved caps. They created a tradable asset out of thin air."

"This is fascinating, but I don't see how it connects to the case. Where's this leading?" Jax was still curious to see how she was going to make the link.

"Hang in. It will all start to make sense." Max appeared convincing, although the wheels were still spinning in her head as she spoke. "The Joyce Foundation, a philanthropic group provided over a million dollars to fund a grant to improve the quality of life in the Great Lakes area, but the grant went astray from its original purpose and was diverted to a Dr. Richard Sandor, an economist at Northwestern University. The funds were used to determine the feasibility of a cap-and-trade market, which hardly improves life in the Great Lakes area." Max eased back with a slight smirk. "Get this. A young senator from Chicago sat on the foundation's board during that time."

"That young senator didn't happen to become a US president?" Jax did not expect an answer. He simply shook his head in disbelief.

"Back to Dr. Sandor. He was the one that founded CCX in 2003 when trading operations commenced." Max paused to flash a grin. "But Sandor had a little help—from none other than Maurice Strong."

"The Godfather!"

"Maurice Strong was one of the insiders who sat on the board of CCX and admits to being the one who helped Sandor set up the company from the beginning. CCX became a viable entity with over four hundred members, including major corporations, universities, and unions. Get this. It was predicted that the carbon trade market would reach ten trillion dollars."

"If I'm getting it right, the success of CCX was heavily predicated on the passage of cap-and-trade legislation in Congress."

"You've got it. But here's where it gets really interesting."

"As thought-provoking as this is," Jax interjected, "I'm still waiting for the punch line."

Max was beginning to enjoy the pace of the conversation, teasing Jax along the way. "We're getting closer," she snickered. "Now it's 2004, the former Vice President Al Gore and former Goldman Sachs executive David Blood founded Generation Investment Management, or GIM, based in London. Both GIM and Goldman Sachs jumped on the bandwagon and became two of the largest investors in CCX."

"I'm getting a little lost in the alphabet, but it's clear that anyone who got into the game early would be rolling in dough?"

"For a while. But then the much-needed passage of the cap-and-trade legislation in the Senate stalled and caused CCX virtually to collapse."

"Virtually—I don't understand?"

"The carbon traders were confident that as soon as carbon trading was priced in the market it would soar. Finally, one metric ton of carbon was priced at seven dollars. But in 2008 the delay in passing the cap-and-trade legislation butted up against the housing market crisis. The price of carbon plummeted to ten cents."

"I'm still confused to how CCX virtually collapsed."

"These are smart guys who hedged their bets. They anticipated the possible fallout and with Dr. Sandor at the helm, the insiders created a series of companies and then established the parent company Climate Exchange PLC to operate all of these entities. They weren't betting on any one company. They were betting on the Super Environmental Bowl, relying on kickbacks from the carbon trading."

"Max, please cut to the chase." Jax was eager to hear how it all came tumbling down.

"In 2010, the Climate Exchange PLC was sold for over six hundred and four million dollars, based on the currency rate at the time. Records showed that Sandor made ninety million dollars on the sale for his sixteen percent share. GIM and Goldman Sachs each owned ten percent. You do the math. And one more point while I'm on Gore. He's also a partner for another venture capital firm, Kleiner Perkins Caufield & Byers, that invested one billion dollars in forty companies that benefited from cap and trade. He states that all his profits went to another group he founded, the Alliance for Climate Protection."

"This is incredible." Jax was clearly flabbergasted as the web of players spun in his mind.

"So now you understand what ginned up the global-warming debate? And why the continuous push for climate-change legislation?"

"Clever how the prior administration used linguistic hocus-pocus switching from global warming to a natural phenomenon that cannot be challenged. But whatever term is used, this prominent public issue has turned into a cottage industry—unbelievable."

"You were correct about those entering the game early." Max agreed. "They did make billions of dollars, lining their own pockets. But they also adopted a holier-than-thou demeanor as they hid behind an emotional public issue to cash in."

"'Money doesn't talk; it swears,'" Jax noted.

"'It's Alright, Ma,'" Max sang.

"Impressive! You know your Bob Dylan."

"They were great lyrics and rather prophetic, but the recipients I mentioned are only a small percentage of the benefactors when you factor in a bloated bureaucracy of government employees, manufacturers, and questionable climate scientists who all rely on a global-warming crisis. Everyone was definitely drinking the same Kool-Aid."

"Then if man-made global warming is disproved, cap and trade would go poof, and the cottage industry would be demolished."

Max was pleased that Jax made the connection because she sensed they were honing in on a motive. "Precisely, and if man-made global warming is refuted, then sustainable development loses its luster. And right now trillions of dollars are invested in the ever-broadening green-energy push."

"This is hardly a Walden Pond support group." Jax chuckled, still astounded by the group of actors. "It's evident that the global-warming debate has been on steroids since 1992, but the issue doesn't appear to be melting anytime soon. What's most acute is that all their success is predicated on creating a global-warming frenzy!"

"Very interesting!" The proverbial light bulb went on. "Jax, remember Veunet's wife telling me that Claus worked for the University of East Anglia in Norwich, England for the Climate Research Unit just before he took a sabbatical?"

"So what? We already knew he was a scientist of sorts."

"Yes, but his research was to study climate models and provide key information to the Intergovernmental Panel on Climate Change. The IPCC is the geopolitical body under the umbrella of the United Nations."

"That sounds familiar! Wasn't their server hacked and emails released?"

"Yes, it was referred to as 'Climategate.' If I recall correctly, the accuracy of the Climate Research Unit models had been seriously challenged in their ability to predict global warming. It was around 2009 when the New York Times reported the hacking of the server at the university. Email exchanges between the CRU and the National Center for Atmospheric Research refuted a study the university had conducted recording the earth's temperatures over the last two millennia."

"I thought there was never any real resolution."

"Some unsavory practices did spawn the controversy, specifically exposed in one of the emails from Phil Jones, the Director of the CRU, where he admitted to manipulating the numbers. It was an effort to reconcile the fact that recent temperatures were not warming but actually cooling. Let me go to my notes." Max grabbed her smartphone and, after a few taps, said, "They did it by switching their global temperature datasets and created HadCRUT4 from the ashes of HadCRUT3. I don't understand this jargon, but the methodology was exposed in a rather dry piece that found its way virally onto the Internet—I think it was called 'The Problematic Transition to HadCRUT4 from HadCRUT3.' It enabled continued claims of *the warmest month ever* by artificially elevating temperature records amidst the widely recognized atmospheric temperature flatline."

"What possibly could be their motive?"

"It revealed itself further in the now infamous Columbus Day 2009 email exchange between Kevin Trenberth of the US National Center for Atmospheric Research and Michael 'Hockey Stick' Mann—give me a sec—here we go. Trenberth wrote, 'The fact is that we can't account for the lack of warming at the moment and it is a travesty that we can't...Our observing system is inadequate.'"

"Who's this guy Mann? And what's the hockey-stick reference?"

"Michael Mann is Director of the Earth System Science Center at Pennsylvania State University and probably the most influential mouthpiece for the IPCC. One of his claims to fame is plotting the flat temperatures for the last thousand years, along with the recent spikes in world temperatures on a graph.

It created the shape of a hockey stick, hence the nickname. In the end, the Climategate scandal became limited to the emails but it triggered the nucleus of the global-warming debate. Finally, the computer-driven climate models as effective predictors of future temperatures were put into question."

"So that would beg the question: what information would Claus have had that would interest the congressional committee?"

"The goal of the Committee on Climate Change Initiatives was established to monitor appropriation recommendations to the House for all climate-change projects. The real question is—why would someone be bumped off for their expected testimony? Unless, of course, the testimony was aimed to kill a bill or perhaps even an industry affecting billions of allocated dollars. You said they needed a frenzy! The climate studies from the University of East Anglia would have helped to bolster the IPCC's claim of global warming—until they were proven false. I'd say that would have qualified."

"You think Claus had the goods on them?"

"What if Claus was involved in the HadCRUT3-to-HadCRUT4 transition?"

"Aha! Now that would make sense." Jax went silent, obviously letting the thought sink into his understanding.

Then Max threw the knockout punch. "If Claus was mixed up in this scandal, then Luca Doerfinger would have known. They're both dead. Jax, we have to find 'JVB' and 'AM' soon."

"Hold your horses! You've mentioned some pretty heavy hitters. Who else do you think is in the batter's box?"

"Gore's motives would have meshed nicely with the tenets of Agenda 21. He and his compadres' continuous push for global warming only helped fuel the support for the sustainable-development mania. You have to agree they share common goals and effectively promote each other's cause." Max raised her eyebrows, suggesting that she had tapped into the elusive motive.

"Why this obsession with Gore? You don't think he might be connected to this case?"

"Who knows? He doesn't leave fingerprints. But he could very possibly be the bogeyman in the room, at least tangentially. Remember, Gore established his prominence in the global-warming market. And although he's not a climate scientist, the fallout could be personally and financially devastating."

"Max, I'm sure I don't need to remind you to be careful. We're ostensibly messing around with the United Nations—and a whole list of powerful people. This may extend way beyond the deaths of a senator and a couple of scientists."

"I'm not ready to go there quite yet. First, let's find 'JVB' and 'AM,' wherever they are. They may be the only ones who can answer the questions with any certainty."

"Hopefully it's not too late."

"Jax, I'd also like to know exactly how Veunet and Doerfinger died. I don't buy a simple climbing accident or a car crash."

Like Max, he did not believe in coincidences either. "This is becoming enormously intriguing. I'll start looking for the answers right away."

"I'll be in my office if you come up with anything. There's something else that's nagging at me," Max admitted, but didn't offer up any more than that.

Chapter 15

―――⌇o―⌇o――o⌇―

A GHOSTLY CALL

B ack at her desk, Max found the slip of paper Isabelle had given her with the list of telephone numbers. Her eyes immediately zoomed in on the number with the 941 area code. She thought it was worth another shot and dialed the number for a fourth time.

"Hello," announced a crotchety voice.

Max, half-expecting the phone to ring continuously as it had before, was startled when she heard a response. Seconds after she introduced herself the line went dead. "How rude!" Suddenly, her smartphone vibrated as a text message arrived. Printed on the screen was a different phone number. Highly curious, she dialed it straightaway.

"What do you want?" asked the same bad-tempered voice.

"I'm investigating the death of Senator Sherman Spark."

"Oh my God—he's really dead." The man's tone changed dramatically. "Tell me what you know?" he urged. His voice became more frantic.

Max sensed that he was genuinely shocked. She slowly described in detail the scene in the park and explained that the police ruled it a suicide but had not yet closed the case. "How well did you know the Senator?"

"We need to talk!"

"Where?"

"I'll text you the address. And don't call me again."

Max heard the click. She sat eagerly waiting to see where she would meet the mystery man. In seconds, she felt another vibration. The message read: *1481 main st sarasota fri 4pm.* "Sarasota!"

"Hey, does this look familiar?" Max asked as she stormed into Jax's office.

Jax, engrossed in his own research, said, "Give me a sec."

"Look!" she replied, thrusting her smartphone in front of him, flashing the phone number that displayed on the screen.

"Where the heck did you get that number?" His apprehension was notable.

"Ha! Just what I thought! It's a CIA operative's burn phone."

"What in the hell is going on?"

"I'm leaving for Sarasota tomorrow. You're in charge."

"Wait just a minute, Max! Answer my question."

Max relayed the conversation she had with the mysterious contact. She did not like the expression staring back and braced herself.

"This is getting far too dangerous. Three people are already dead."

"I'll be fine. As I see it, the senator called our secret-agent man sometime right before his death and then whoever killed him used the cellphone and redialed the last call the senator made. Most likely, the killer made that call from The Bachelor's Mill and then ditched the phone. That's about a 9-minute cab ride from Lincoln Park."

"And how do you know how far it is?" Jax quizzed her with a slight smirk.

"I'm a font of information. And I suspect Mrs. Spark didn't know it was a gay bar."

"I assume you didn't tell her?"

"Let's wait until we have a few more pieces of the puzzle before distressing the poor widow further. One thing we know for sure is that someone else was in possession of the missing cellphone. Jax, track down who owns the 941 number Isabelle gave me. The number I dialed before our spy hung up on me."

"I'll see what I can do. But we're getting in pretty deep and we haven't even started. What—it's been less than seventy-two hours?"

"Then let's watch our backs on this one."

"Max, you might want to tell Mrs. Spark to do the same."

"Agreed. Now I have to arrange for a flight to sunny Florida."

"Be careful," he cautioned again. "When ex-CIA finds it necessary to play cloak and danger, it means there's a lot more below the surface."

"Jax, work on the link between the scientists. That may give us our first real clue. And I'll go find out what our Sarasota spy knows, if anything."

"Will do, but be careful," he droned for the third time.

Chapter 16

GERMAN HAPPENSTANCE

O ctober was an unusual month of light rain and humidity in the nation's capital, but so were the preceding months of unusual heat. The forecasters were perplexed. But for the portly gentleman who had arrived only an hour earlier inside the beltway it felt like home. In spite of the drizzle, Jonas decided to brave the elements without an umbrella and walk from his Savoy Suites Hotel to what was purported to be one of the best German restaurants in town. Slowly, he wended his way through the puddles down Wisconsin Avenue until he arrived at the Old Europe Restaurant.

"*Wunderbar,*" he said as he entered through the rustic green doors of the establishment.

Without hesitation, the maître d' swooped in like a hawk and escorted Jonas to a table along the wall covered with oil paintings of the German countryside. "Sir, I'll send your server right over."

"*Danke,*" he responded.

Jonas had learned about the restaurant on his trip over from Berlin from the passenger seated next to him. He was excited to try what promised to be authentic recipes from the homeland. But before gazing at the menu, he shot his arm up in the air. Quickly, he caught the attention of the waiter who speedily headed his way.

"*Asbach Uralt soda, bitte,*" he ordered.

Minutes later, the waiter returned with a glass of brandy on ice accompanied by a splash of soda. It was the same refreshing cocktail that Jonas drank before every evening meal.

"*Danke.*" He thanked the waiter and then took a sip. "*Wunderbar.*"

The waiter remained standing by with paper and pen in hand, prepared to take his order.

Jonas shrewdly perused the menu and made his selection. "*Wildschweine mit bratkartoffeln, sauerkraut, brokkoli—und ein weiteres Asbach Uralt soda,*" he ordered.

The waiter wrote down one order of wild boar with roasted potatoes and a side of sauerkraut and broccoli. Then he said, "I'll bring you another drink right away, sir."

Jonas sat back and enjoyed his second refreshing cocktail as he listened to the musicians seated in the back of the room. An older woman with harsh features was strumming the guitar while a man half her size played the accordion. Seeing them dressed in traditional clothing and playing German folk songs gave Jonas pangs of homesickness. As he continued to sip on his brandy, he became unusually dizzy and confused until the pangs in his stomach turned into excruciating pain. He yelled, "*Hilf mir!*"

The waiter heard Jonas call for help and rushed to his table. He could see that his patron was in dire trouble. Frantically, he shouted to the maître d' to call for an ambulance. At the same time, the music came to an abrupt halt and the other patrons' conversations and forks came to a standstill. All eyes were on the heavyset gentleman hunched over the red tablecloth as he shattered the place setting.

From nowhere, red lights started flashing outside the restaurant window. The ambulance had arrived. The diners watched as the EMTs rushed past their tables and made their way to the ailing man. Soon after, the stretcher arrived. Then as though no disruption had occurred, the EMTs departed with Jonas, and the activity in the restaurant resumed without missing a beat. The sound of German folk songs filled the air.

Chapter 17

AND THEN
THERE WAS ONE

J ax worked through the night plodding through a wealth
of information, starting with what Max had learned from
Veunet's wife. Most important, both Veunet and Doerfinger
attended École Polytechnique Fédérale de Lausanne. Jax easily
discovered that the École was one of the top research universities
specializing in technology, engineering, and the physical sciences.
The main campus was located in Lausanne, Switzerland. So it
was a place to start.

He agreed with Max's conclusion that the numbers next to
the initials, written on the back of the photos were dates, except
for the equation on the back of the photo with the initials "AM."
The second set of numbers next to Veunet's and Doerfinger's
initials clearly coincided with the dates they died. That would
explain why Doerfinger had arrived in Washington a few days
before his scheduled testimony, thus making him an easy target.
But there were still two other scientists unaccounted for whose
lives could be in jeopardy. "AM," who apparently had not yet
been summoned and "JVB," presumably scheduled to go before
the committee the day after tomorrow.

He had to find them.

"Could all four scientists have graduated from the same school and possibly in the same year?" Jax questioned himself. He knew the graduating year for Veunet and Doerfinger from Max's conversation with Veunet's wife, and based on their ages it made sense. So he began to scour the Internet looking for the roster of the graduating class of '87 at École Polytechnique Fédérale de Lausanne.

"Perfect!" Jax blew out a puff of air as he saw both Claus Veunet and Luca Doerfinger listed among the graduates. With his adrenaline pumping, Jax expanded his research and focused on the missing scientists. What he discovered was that there had been a total of twelve graduates with the initials "AM," but only one with the initials "JVB." He continued his search until he happened upon a yearbook from their alma mater. He flicked through the virtual pages using his index finger on the touch screen and found what he was looking for. "Gotcha. Now what have you guys gotten yourselves into?" It took several hours more of working slavishly at the keyboard but the Internet rewarded him finally with results. "Jackpot!!" He hit a speed-dial button, hoping to catch Max at the airport before she boarded her flight. The second he heard the click on the phone line, he blurted out, "von—"

"Jax!" She abruptly cut him off, "have you seen the news this morning?"

"No, I've been focused on trying to identify the other two scientists. What's up?"

"One of them may be Jonas von Boehmer."

"Unbelievable—that's the reason I was calling you." Jax stammered, giving into unbound excitement.

Missing the intonation in his voice, she rattled on, "There's an article in today's paper. Evidently, he died of a heart attack yesterday. Given the report, he was dining at a restaurant here in Washington. Suddenly he became ill after drinking a cocktail. The manager called the ambulance that arrived minutes later. Once they got him into the ambulance, he went into cardiac arrest and died on the way to the hospital."

"Max, slow down. Now, gimme a minute." Jax grabbed his notes. "According to the numbers next to the initials JVB, he was scheduled to testify tomorrow."

"What the hell is going on? We now have three dead scientists and one dead senator!" Max shouted into the phone, cupping her hand over her mouth, trying not to attract attention.

"That's what we have to find out. How much time do you have?"

Max checked her watch. She had about forty-five minutes before she had to board. "I've got time. Gimme all you've got?" She was ready to hear anything that would explain the bizarre twists of their first case.

"I hope you're sitting down." Jax spoke fast for he had a lot of information to impart. "All the scientists graduated from the same school in 1987. That's how I discovered von Boehmer. So I researched each of the organizations where they worked and found another common denominator—it's definitely climate change."

"That would make sense. It confirms why they were supposed to testify at the Senate's Committee on Climate Change Initiatives."

"From what I can tell, Claus Veunet would have been the prime witness. As we already knew, he worked for the Climatic Research Unit at the University of East Anglia, where several of their top climate scientists are major contributors to the IPCC reports. Interestingly, Luca Doerfinger was an associate fellow at the Global Warming Policy Foundation, a London-based think-tank that has been a major force in disputing the IPCC's claims."

"I'm familiar with the organization. They're completely independent of outside corporate and governmental influences. If my recollection is accurate, their main focus is to analyze global-warming policies and their economic implications."

"Correct, but over the years they have become highly skeptical of the IPCC reports, considered the bible for climate change, which governments around the world rely upon."

"Tell me what you found out about von Boehmer?"

"He was an advisor to The Center for Global Food Issues, a project of the Hudson Institute, another think tank based in the U.S. But his role was more directed toward studying the environmental effects on food production and to raise the awareness among farmers. However, the director of the center at the time was Dennis Avery. He, along with an associate S. Fred Singer, co-authored a *New York Times* bestseller titled *Unstoppable Global Warming: Every 1,500 Years*. Interestingly, it's not what you'd expect. In essence, it disabuses the IPCC's claim that global warming is mainly caused by humans emitting CO2 into the atmosphere and expounded the more likely cause to be natural through solar-driven cycles."

"Good work, Jax. See if you can get in touch with Avery and find out specifically what von Boehmer was working on. Maybe we'll find a direct link to the others." Max glanced at her watch. "Keep going," she prodded, sensing there was more.

Although Jax had been battling the incessant announcements in the airport's background, he was eager to pass along the *pièce de résistance* of information. "Remember I told you I found the class yearbook for 1987? Well, I also discovered a class picture with our three deceased scientists arm-in-arm—along with a fourth person. The photo was faded, but the name under the photo was crystal clear. The name was Antonio Maieli."

"Mwah! Jax, I could kiss you! But why did you wait so long to tell me?"

"Don't get too excited. We still have to find him."

"Hopefully he's still missing," Max replied with a sound of dread.

"Remember, there were no numbers next to the initials 'AM,' only that bizarre equation."

"Perhaps a date to testify had not yet been scheduled or maybe he wasn't even supposed to appear before the committee," Max presumed.

"Get this—the day after Luca Doerfinger's death was reported in the newspapers, Antonio Maieli took a leave of absence from his job at NASA. He hasn't been seen since. One thing we can infer is that he was alive—at least before the Senator died." Jax tried to provide some solace.

"What were you able to find out about him? You mentioned NASA."

"Antonio's a mystery. He's the odd duck. I wasn't able to track down any family or close friends. However, his position at NASA had to do with chemically altering cellulose derivatives; something to do with polymers you'd normally find in wood or cotton. Evidently, he was trying to create a new synthetic polymer that could be used in the production of space gear, making it lighter or more resistant to the environmental factors—like on Mars. Pretty wild stuff, but absolutely nothing to do with climate change."

"Nothing! Jax there has to be something."

"There's one possible connection. I came across an article in the *Business Insider* written by guy named Gus Lubin. He wrote about a letter that was sent in 2012 to Charles Bolden, the NASA administrator at the time and signed by forty-nine NASA astronauts and scientists. According to Lubin, the co-signers were fed up with the agency's activist stance toward climate change and charged the agency with advocating the position that man-made CO_2 was a major cause of global warming, without empirical evidence. Here are a few poignant points that were highlighted in the letter itself. It said, 'the unbridled advocacy of CO_2 being the major cause of climate change is unbecoming of NASA's history of making an objective assessment...that man-made carbon dioxide is having a catastrophic impact on global climate change are not substantiated...With hundreds of well-known climate scientists and tens of thousands of other scientists publicly declaring their disbelief in the catastrophic forecasts...it is clear that the science is *not* settled.' I emphasize the word *not*."

"Interesting, but where's the link to Antonio Maieli?"

"I contacted the administration at NASA. Their records show that Antonio had a sponsor when he arrived in the US from Italy. His name is Harold Doiron. He also worked at NASA as an aerospace technologist working on the Apollo Program and was one of the scientists who signed the letter addressed to Bolden. But that was back in the seventies. Somehow Antonio connected with him."

"So what? Antonio had a connection with someone involved in the climate-change debate. I don't see the relevancy to what he might be involved in today."

"Wait, there's more. In 2012, Doiron organized a group called The Right Climate Stuff research team, of which he is the chairman. Its thirty-plus members comprise a core group of more than twenty retired NASA Apollo Program specialists. These astronauts, scientists, and engineers banded together and were joined by other accomplished researchers to perform an objective, independent study of climate science to determine if unrestricted burning of fossil fuels could cause harmful global warming."

"Any conclusions?"

"From what I've been able to gather, they're convinced the science is not settled as is specified in the NASA letter. They state that natural processes dominate climate change and the manmade CO2 impact appears to be muted. They believe that the government is overreacting and there is no empirical evidence to support catastrophic global warming."

"You know those conclusions sound an awful lot like Avery's. Could this be what it's about?"

"It's a brainteaser all right. But at this juncture we have no way of knowing exactly. We can only hope Maieli has the answers— then again, as I said we have to find him first."

All of a sudden Max was antsy to get to Sarasota. She noticed that her flight was about to board and needed to sign off. "Great work, Jax!"

"If our luck holds out, you might get something tangible out of our newfound spy."

"This has to be connected to Spark's death—I can feel it." Max heard the final call. "Jax, chew on this for a while. Let's say these scientists had proof that could dispel or at least muck up the water as to the degree of manmade global warming. Then the billions of dollars allocated for the individual projects would dissipate; the *taxpayer well* would run dry. And let's assume kickbacks were involved. I don't know about the other senators, but I suspect Senator Erog would take a pretty big hit."

"Max, you have a vivid imagination."

"There's something fishy about that guy. Check him out."

"Another infamous hunch?"

"You got it! Gotta go. Later, Jax."

Chapter 18

—⊶○⊷—

SARASOTA SETBACK

M ax's flight arrived at the Sarasota Bradenton Airport ten minutes late, but she managed to hail a taxi without delay. Hurriedly, she rattled off the address to the driver. Fifteen minutes later she was standing in front of Patrick's on Main Street. When she entered the restaurant she immediately identified the booth in the far left corner as instructed. Seated at the table under the dim lighting was a rather stocky man. As far as she could tell, he was dressed in a dark-blue blazer and jeans. What was obvious were his piercing eyes aimed in her direction. *Yup, that's my spy,* she thought.

As Max took her seat across from him, she asked, "Should I call you Sam? Or would you prefer Casper?"

"Sam," he replied in the same gruff voice that had echoed on the other end of the phone a day earlier.

Thanks to Jax's expert sleuthing, Max was armed with Sam's full identity. The private, unlisted 941 telephone number was traced to a Samuel Ames, a CIA operative Jax had worked with in the past. But he knew him as "Casper," a man notorious for being one of the spookiest spies and not as friendly as the name would imply. Max purposely invoked

Sam's code name hoping to throw him off guard—but he seemed catatonic in his motionless reaction. She also detected that he was a man of few words. The clock was ticking. She had only a short time to draw out whatever information he was willing to reveal.

When Max first sat down she noted that Sam had already ordered a bottle of wine and had poured a glass for himself. Now in a presumptive move, he poured a glass for her. Foregoing the usual polite toast, he continued to sip his wine and waited for her to open up the conversation. Max took her cue and spoke in a low, soft voice aware of the other diners.

"Three scientists died days before they were scheduled to testify in front of a committee on climate-change initiatives. The same committee Senator Sherman Spark co-chaired. I believe all their deaths are connected."

"How was Sherman killed?" he whispered back hoarsely.

"With a Luger. His death is presumed a suicide. But I don't buy it."

"The others?"

"Veunet died climbing Lou Passo in Provence. Doerfinger was killed instantly when his Lexus slammed into a guardrail."

"Any other cars involved?" Sam asked, attempting to hurry along the conversation.

"No. It was late at night. He had just arrived at the Reagan International Airport an hour before. After renting the car he headed to his hotel."

"And the other one?"

"Von Boehmer apparently died in an ambulance on the way to the hospital." Max waited a second, anticipating another question, but Sam remained silent as his eyes darted about the restaurant. She wondered whether he was even listening and then feared that perhaps he thought they may be in danger. Max refocused. "There's one other scientist missing and we believe he's in fear for his life and he's nowhere to be found.

His name is Antonio Maieli. I have a gut feeling he's the missing link and can tell us what happened to the Senator—and possibly the others."

With a blank face, Sam coolly asked, "What makes you think I can help?"

"You were the last person Senator Spark spoke with before he died. Did he tell you anything that can help me find Maieli before it's too late?"

Sam's eyes never stopped perusing the room. Either it was a habit from the old days or he knew Max was on to something. Either way, it was obvious that he was becoming uneasy. "Let's go. We've been here too long—I can't help you."

"Sam, this may be the only lead I have to find out what happened to Sherman Spark—your friend," she implored.

Sam ignored her plea. He slid out of the booth and stood up. His face was still straight-faced other than his roving eyes.

Max was deflated. She had reached the end of the line. Sam had been her one real hope. Flustered, she gathered her luggage and trailed behind.

Suddenly, Sam spun around, his face only inches away from hers.

A chill shot up her spine. Max could feel his breath as he began to speak.

"Pliny the Elder once said, 'In wine there is truth.' Perhaps the truth you're looking for is in the wine. Let's go. There's nothing else I can tell you." Sam turned and headed to the entrance.

Max again followed, but as she started to walk away an eerie sensation came over her. For some inexplicable reason, she turned and glanced back at the booth where they had first met. Resting on top of the table remained the two wine glasses and the empty bottle of Capannelle Solare they had shared.

Sam, seeming more agitated, waited at the front entrance holding open the door. "Ladies first," he said when she approached.

They walked to the curb together.

"Watch out!" Sam shouted—but it was too late.

Max hit the pavement hard.

Sam rushed to her side. "Are you okay?" he asked, not fully comprehending what had just happened.

There was no response.

Blood gushed from a gash above Max's left eye as she lay unconscious on the curbside. It was clear that her ankle was also badly injured. "Sully, grab me a towel and some ice!"

Jim Sullivan, the owner of Patrick's, called out to one of the wait staff. He was already on his cellphone calling the ambulance. Fortunately, he had seen the whole scene play out.

Sam was still crouched down next to Max, cradling her head in his lap. He tried to keep her head positioned above her heart to slow down the bleeding.

"Here." Sully handed Sam the ice wrapped in a towel.

Quickly, Sam placed the improvised cold compress firmly on Max's head.

"They're on their way," Sully announced. "And hey, I caught the plate number. It was JAF 428."

"Let's keep that between us," Sam asked.

Sam had been a good customer and a friend for years, and although he had been very secretive about his past, Sully never meddled. He trusted and respected him.

In no time at all the sound of the sirens could be heard blaring nearby. Sam knew the ambulance would arrive in minutes. "Sully, take over. I have to go. Make sure they take her to the emergency room at the Sarasota Memorial Hospital. Tell them to get in touch with Dr. Paul Yungst as soon as they arrive."

"No problem, Sam." Without questioning, Sully stooped down to take Sam's place and cradled Max's head. He could see that the wound was still bleeding profusely and continued to apply the ice pack.

By the time the ambulance pulled up to the curb, Sam had left the scene. Swiftly, one of the EMTs moved in to check Max's vitals. The other EMT wrapped her head tightly with a gauze bandage. Then, in unison, they placed her on the stretcher, giving extra care to her damaged ankle. Sully, as per Sam's instructions, gave them the name of the doctor to contact.

Max remained unconscious.

Seconds after the ambulance arrived, a police vehicle appeared. Two officers stepped out of the car. One of the officers hurled the first question out to the burgeoning crowd. "Who saw what happened?"

"I did." Sully was the first to step forward. He proceeded to tell them how a white car had come speeding around the corner on North Lemon and turned on to Main Street the moment the woman stepped off the curb. "The car hit her square on. It never attempted to stop," he explained.

"Do you know the name of the woman who was hit?"

"No, I've never seen her before." Sully answered, realizing he really had no idea who she was; certainly he was not going to mention her companion.

The police officer then asked the same question of one of the EMTs as he was about to load the stretcher into the ambulance.

"No officer, no ID," the EMT replied and then, in haste, returned to his patient.

Sully overheard the conversation and thought it odd because he remembered seeing a handbag and a small piece of carry-on luggage when the mystery woman arrived at the restaurant. At once, he scanned the area where she had fallen, but nothing was lying on the ground. He was positive he had seen the items, but then again a lot was happening. He admitted to himself that he could have been wrong.

The police officer redirected the questioning back to Sully. "Can you give a description of the driver?"

"Excuse me?" he replied, not hearing the question. Sully's thoughts were elsewhere.

"The driver. Can you describe him?"

"Um, a male." Sully shrugged.

"Make and model? Did you get the make and model?"

"I'm not sure. It could have been a BMW or an Audi. They all look alike these days."

"You didn't happen to see the license plate number?"

"No, officer. Just that it was a Florida plate."

In an obvious rush, one of the EMTs shouted out, "We're off! We're taking her to Sarasota Memorial!" Swiftly the ambulance doors closed, and it sped away with Jane Doe.

Chapter 19

<hr />

OUT OF A LIMB

"Maxine Ford? —Ms. Ford?"

"What?" Max punctuated, clearly annoyed at being disturbed in the midst of a dream. She forced her eyes open with great reluctance. Although her vision was blurry she could make out the silhouette of a person standing over her. She blinked several times, clearing her vision enough to reveal a tall man wearing dark blue scrubs. "Who are you? Where am I?" Panic set in. She scanned the room. Everything still looked fuzzy. But there was no doubt—it was a hospital room.

Recognizing her muddled state, the man spoke slowly. "Ms. Ford, I'm Dr. Yungst and you're at Sarasota Memorial Hospital. You've been in an accident, but you're going to be okay."

"My phone! I need my phone!"

"That can come later. Right now, we'll be prepping you for surgery. I'll need you to sign a consent form."

Max had no idea what he was talking about and her head felt like it was bursting. "Consent for what?" Irritation had displaced her panic.

"Ms. Ford, you need to stay calm. You have a severe laceration on your forehead and evidence of a concussion. We need to ensure that there is no internal bleeding. I also have one of the best plastic surgeons standing by to stitch up your head wound."

Max reached up and touched the bandage. She had no idea what it looked like, but it certainly explained why she felt like she had gone ten rounds with Ali.

"You also have several nasty breaks in your left ankle that will require my handiwork." Yungst smiled trying to make her feel more relaxed.

It didn't work. She was becoming even more restless. "Why am I here? Where are my clothes? I need my phone!"

"Ms. Ford, you've had a severe head trauma. I know this must be very confusing."

"How do you know my name?" she asked, speaking calmly for the first time.

"Your friend Sam. He's also a friend of mine. Trust me; you will get the best of care. But please, we must get you to surgery."

Hearing the name "Sam" jolted her memory. She remembered meeting him at a restaurant, but that was all she recalled.

Yungst handed her the form on a clipboard and patiently explained the information. "Please, sign right here." He pointed to the open space at the bottom of the page.

Despite the lack of clarity, Max was coherent enough to realize that the sooner she cooperated, the sooner she would get out of there. She relented. With blurred eyesight, she managed to scribble her name on the paper. "Doc, when do I get my phone?"

Yungst smiled thinking about her priorities. "You'll be in surgery for about three hours and it will take another hour for you to come out of the anesthesia. Expect to be groggy for the rest of the day. Your leg will also be in traction for a few days, but then we'll get you out of bed so you can practice using the crutches."

"Excuse me—traction—crutches. You don't seem to understand—I have to get out of here. This can't be happening!"

"Ms. Ford. You've been through quite a shock. Let's first repair your ankle. And then we can discuss your options. Are you ready?"

Max thrust her head into the pillow in a move of reluctant surrender. An action that hurt like hell.

⁕

"Ms. Ford? —Ms. Ford?"

"Who are you?"

"Dr. Yungst."

"Who?"

"Dr. Yungst. I performed the surgery on your ankle. I just came by to see how you are doing and to let you know that everything went extremely well."

"What time is it?" Max asked, still coming out of her daze.

"It's Saturday, shortly after noon."

"What?" Max shot up from the bed. "Ouch!" She fell back onto the pillow. She realized that she was in the midst of another dream, but this time the handsome doctor standing in front of her was not part of it, nor was her splinted ankle. And somehow she had lost two days.

"Ms. Ford, please relax. Rest will be your best friend."

Slightly embarrassed, Max began to feel her face flush. "Sorry, Doc. You caught me off in another world. And please call me 'Max.'" Then, staring at her dangling limb in the air, she asked, "What now?"

Yungst explained the surgery in infinite detail, making sure that his inquisitive patient would heed all precautions. "You broke two of the three malleoli, the bones at the base of the tibia and fibula bones that connect to the ankle bone, the talus." He used a foot skeleton and pointed to the location of the break. "The first was a medial malleolus fracture, here at the base of the tibia on the inside." He demonstrated how the tibia bone ran the length of knee to the ankle. He watched her face to measure her understanding and then continued. "The second break was a lateral malleolus fracture at the base of the fibula. This bone also extends from the knee to the ankle as you can see, on the outer side of the leg."

Max was listening but had had enough of the anatomy lesson. "Doc, cut to the chase!"

He scowled teasingly and then continued to demonstrate using the foot skeleton, attempting to maintain her attention. "Max, it was necessary to place a metal rod here and two metal screws here. This is referred to as internal fixation and will provide stability as the ankle fractures heal."

"I'm really not into heavy metal, Doc," Max kidded, allowing him a bit of slack.

"Actually, the rods and screws are not metal at all." He retaliated with a smile. "They're made of a combination of biodegradable polymer and hydroxyapatite, the same mineral that forms in natural bone. The rods and screws function as an internal splint but will dissolve over time. So, you won't be setting off any metal detectors."

"Okay, what now?" she goaded.

"Your ankle is wrapped in a synthetic posterior splint that will allow room for post-op swelling, but you'll still need to keep your ankle immobilized for a few weeks, giving the bones time to heal partially. Then we'll replace the splint with a removable boot cast so you can start putting weight on your ankle. It's going to take another six to eight weeks, so I'm afraid the boot cast will become your new best friend." Shocked at Max's sudden complacency, he took advantage and continued. "Let's give it a few days to allow the swelling to subside. Then we'll get you up out of bed so you can start using the crutches. Everyone is different, so we'll take it slowly." Her facial expression remained sullen. He was beginning to wonder whether she had heard him at all and risked asking, "Is there anything else I can do for you now?"

"My phone, please."

"Max, you really should rest."

"Phone, please."

"I can tell you're not going to be easy." He motioned for the key strapped around her wrist.

"Join the crowd. That's what everyone tells me." Max flashed a grin as she handed him the key. "By the way—who sent the flowers?" she asked hesitantly, spotting the bouquet of edelweiss on the nightstand.

"They came yesterday," he answered while he fumbled in her jacket pocket looking for her smartphone. But before handing her the phone, he made one last plea, "Try to get some rest, Max. I'll check back in on you later." He doubted that she was inclined to follow orders, but handed her the phone, the key, and the card that came with the flowers.

Max did not hear a word the doc said, distracted by the odd twinge she felt when he handed her the card. She stared at the wording. It read: *Be careful out there. It can be dangerous.*

"Are you okay, Max?"

"Fine." She looked up to reassure him.

Chapter 20

———◦○◦————○————◦○◦———

THE LETTER

Max clutched her phone to her chest and took a deep breath as she watched the doctor leave the room. She began to feel somewhat human again, as though she had just been given back one of her appendages. Already she resented the ridiculous hospital gown. Being held captive was another problem. And while the flowers were disturbing, at least now her smartphone gave her a link to the outside world. After a long sleep and the anesthesia having finally worn off, she was ready to swing into action. She placed her first call.

"I'm unavailable at the moment. Leave a message at the beep."—*Beep*.

"Noble, please call." She sighed and then hit the red *Phone* app.

"Hey, this is Jax. You know what to do."—*Beep*.

"Jax, call me!" she grumbled, having finally hit the apex of her frustration.

The second she ended the call, her smartphone rang. In a flash she hit the green phone icon without bothering to take note of the caller. "Noble!" she sputtered.

"Max, where are you? It's Isabelle!" Her voice was frantic.

"In a hospital. I had a slight accident, but I'll be fine. What's happening, Isabelle?"

"Oh my dear, it's all my fault."

"What are you talking about?"

"The letter, Max. They found the letter. Someone broke in and ransacked the house. Nothing was missing except the letter!"

"Isabelle, why didn't you destroy it?" Max asked with a measured tone, trying to calm her down.

It had no effect. In a weepy voice, Isabelle replied, "It was Sherman's last words before his death. I couldn't." The weeping suddenly turned to terror. "Now they know that you're investigating his murder. And they know about the album. I'm so sorry, Max. Please be careful."

It was not a time for recrimination. Max asked evenly, "Did you call the police?"

"No, I wanted to talk with you first."

"Wait ten minutes," Max instructed, "and then call the Capitol Police Chief Ray Tomson. Tell him everything. He'll be pissed off, but I'll take the heat. Okay?"

"Okay, but please be careful."

Chapter 21

QUID PRO QUO

Max was not accustomed to working with others outside of the agency, especially when she did not have the overriding authority. But she needed the chief. Their collaboration on cases in the past always paid off. She knew he was the only person who could get the conclusive evidence to prove that Spark had been murdered. She also knew that she would have to offer up some of the evidence she and Jax had uncovered—but not all of it—after all, it was still her case. She placed the call.

"Hi! May I speak with Chief? It's Max."

"I know it's you, Max. Let me see if he is available," the secretary said.

The silence on the other end of the line seemed endless until she heard an *ahem*, obviously meant to gain her attention.

"And to what do I owe the pleasure?" the chief asked.

"Ray, remember that quid pro quo? I have something for you."

"Why am I nervous?"

She ignored his needling. "Isabelle Spark will be calling you shortly. She's had a break-in and the thieves found a letter from the late senator to his wife. In the letter, the senator requested that should he die from other than natural causes, I should investigate his death. Ray, over the past few months, three scientists have died. All of them were supposed to testify before a committee Spark co-chaired. So the killer or killers now know I'm involved."

"What makes you so sure they were not accidents?"

"Trust me! There's a definite connection between the senator's murder and the death of these three scientists. You need to have the bodies of the scientists autopsied to find the true cause of death."

"What! Are you crazy? In any case, Spark's death was deemed a suicide."

"No way! I say he was murdered!" Max ignored his official line. "Ray, what about the scientists?"

He placated her for the moment. "Okay, tell me what you know about them?"

"Claus Veunet, a French scientist, died while climbing in Provence in April. A Swiss scientist named Luca Doerfinger died in May in a car crash after leaving the Reagan International Airport in a rented car he had just picked up. And a few days ago, Jonas von Boehmer, a German scientist, died after leaving the Old Europe Restaurant in an ambulance."

"Max, I have no jurisdiction. The French government alone would be impossible."

"You could at least call the French authorities to see what you can find out. And both Doerfinger and von Boehmer were killed in Washington."

"Sit tight, Max."

At once elevator music began assaulting her ear. She could forgive the chief for his abruptness as long as he was verifying her information. Several times she checked the wall clock to pacify herself. He had kept her on hold for almost ten minutes. Isabelle would be calling at any second. She needed Ray's okay first. Max heard a click.

"Doerfinger's body was released to the family over five months ago. By now, it's six feet under Swiss soil."

"What about the Hertz rent-a-car?"

The chief sighed. "I'll see what I can do to track it down. If so, we still may be able to test the brakes. But von Boehmer's body is out of the question," he said adamantly.

Max wouldn't let up. It took some cajoling, but Ray finally admitted that the corpse was still at the morgue, waiting for the next of kin to arrive to claim the body.

"Convince the family that you have evidence to suggest foul play. If I'm right, then we can be sure that Spark was also murdered. And any reasonable person would conclude that Veunet's climbing accident was staged."

Ray knew Max pretty well. Enough that her definitive tone told him she might be actually onto something. And he wanted to know what. "Max, I can't believe I'm going out on a limb for another one of your wild hunches!"

"When have I been wrong?"

"Anything else you want to tell me?"

"Nothing," she said with partial honesty. She had no clue as to her next step. And mentioning Sarasota would only complicate matters.

"Max."

She could tell from the tenor of his voice that the chief knew she was holding back—and she was. It was an ideal time to end the call. "Ray, sorry; gotta go."

Chapter 22

———◦○◦———○———◦○◦———

DOC ATTACK

Max checked her smartphone. Still no call from Noble. She tried him again, only to hear the annoying message telling her that he was unavailable. She also needed to speak with Jax but first she had some tough decisions to make. Things were happening too fast, at least in her mind. She needed to slow down the pace. There was a lot at stake and failure was not an option. But a major piece of the puzzle was still missing. Besides, it was apparent that her battered body was not going anywhere anytime soon.

Surrendering to her new work environment, Max lay in bed in the silly hospital gown and watched her leg suspended in the air. As she attempted to shift slightly in the bed, trying to get comfortable, she caught a glance at the bouquet of edelweiss. Odd thoughts of Sam reappeared. She visualized his piercing eyes staring at her right before they left the restaurant. But it was Sam's last words that resonated in her ears. She replayed Pliny the Elder's quote over and over in her mind, struggling to find the significance. Then the image of the wine bottle appeared. Then she recalled hitting the ground. Frustrated, she ran the events through her foggy mind once more.

"Son of a—!" She grabbed her smartphone and tapped the Chrome app. Hastily, she typed the word *Capannelle* in the search field and hit the *Enter* key. Within a nanosecond the screen displayed the website for a wine resort in Gaioli in Chianti, Italy. The name Antonio Maieli immediately flashed into her mind. "That's what Sam was telling me! Spark must have told him where Antonio was hiding out."

"Did you say something?" Yungst asked as he entered the room.

Max just nodded her head without taking her eyes off her smartphone.

"Do you feel like having a bite to eat?"

At the mention of food, her head shot up in Yungst's direction. "Is starvation part of my therapy?" she asked. "More important when can I get out of here?"

"Max, give it a few days. I told you we'll take your leg out of traction and see how you do on the crutches."

"I want to try now." She was adamant.

"It will hurt like hell. Especially when the blood rushes down to your ankle. Give yourself a little more time to heal."

"I guess then it will have to hurt like hell."

Yungst smiled as he shook his head. He had quickly figured out that the only way to convince her was to concede. "I'll have the crutches brought in. Give me a few minutes and I'll be back to help you."

"Thank you," she said, returning a cocky grin.

⁕

Max leaned back on the pillow, satisfied that she had won the first round. As she stared up at the ceiling she wondered: *Noble—Jax—why haven't you returned my calls?*

Out of nowhere, a man appeared in the doorway, breaking her train of thought. He wasn't wearing the dark-blue scrubs that everyone else seemed to favor; they were the putrid green you see on the people mopping the corridors.

Max's internal alarm went off. "Who are you?" she asked, noting he also did not reach for the latex gloves from the box attached to the wall. Standard protocol.

"I'm the doctor's PA and I'm here to give you a shot. It will help you with the healing."

"And what's my doctor's name?" she challenged.

The stranger did not respond. He continued to walk toward her fondling a menacing syringe.

Given the limited options for the moment—Max screamed.

"Hey, what are you doing here?" Yungst shouted, as he re-entered the room.

The stranger instinctually spun around and plunged the syringe into Yungst's neck as Yungst was about to fight back with the crutches.

The unknown assailant bolted out of the room.

Yungst collapsed on the floor.

Max screamed again for help. In a mad panic, she also pushed the call button.

One of the nurses rushed in. Seeing the doctor lying on the floor, she immediately hit the code-blue button. In no time, Yungst was rushed out of the room.

Max lay helplessly in the room alone until fear took over. "I have to get out here now!" She pushed on the call button again. It took several tries until finally a nurse appeared.

Staving off her uneasiness, she first asked, "How's the doc?"

"We got to him in time. Thanks to you, he'll be okay."

Thanks to me he could be dead. "Would you please fetch my bag from the locker?" Max handed the key to the nurse.

The nurse obliged and went to open the locker but was taken aback. "I'm sorry, but there's no bag in here, only the clothes you were wearing when you arrived," she explained, and then asked, "Is there anything else I can do for you?"

"No," Max responded, vaguely hearing the nurse say something as she walked out of the room. Left alone again in the sterile surroundings her mind began to spin as she desperately tried to remember. *I remember the taxi driver at the airport asking if I needed help with my carryon luggage. I remember carrying it into a restaurant named Patrick's. I remember carrying both my shoulder bag and luggage out. I remember—* "Sam!" Feverishly, she paged through the recent numbers she had called on her smartphone, looking for the one that started with the area code 941. "There it is." She hit *redial* and heard the click. "Sam!"

The phone went dead

Max rapidly typed a text message to the same number. All it said was *SOS*.

Instantly, her phone vibrated with an incoming message; it read: *This number does not accept text messages.* "Shit, now what?"

For the next half hour, it was pandemonium. The police arrived, including Sarasota's female brass hat, Chief Bernadette DiPino. The hospital administrator also dropped in. And the nurse on duty showed up with drugs, thinking they would help to calm Max's nerves. Little did she know that Max was about to kick into high gear. Max refused the medication and spirited the nurse out of the room. After the administrator assured her that Dr. Yungst would be fine, he remained standing by to listen in while Sarasota's finest questioned her.

"Can you describe the man?" Chief DiPino asked.

Max complied, giving her a fairly accurate description. Following suit, she answered the rest of her questions wanting to move things along. She had questions of her own that needed answers, none of which would be discovered lying in a hospital bed.

"A police officer will be posted outside of your room, ma'am," the chief assured her. "We're searching the hospital as we speak, but I suspect the assailant has already escaped. I'll keep you posted."

Just then, a familiar face peered into the room.

"He's okay. He's a friend," Max assured, while taking a deep, thankful breath.

Based on Max's okay, her guest was allowed to enter without being searched. But he stood off to the side waiting for the chief to wrap up his questioning. Once everyone had vacated the room, leaving her alone with her visitor, Sam stepped forward.

"Looking for these?" he asked as he set her carry-on luggage on the floor. He unzipped her shoulder bag and pulled out the corner of the pearly handle of her Browning automatic. Immediately, he slipped the gun back inside and zipped up the bag.

"Thank God it was you, Sam!"

"Do you mind telling me what the dickens is going on around here?"

Max filled Sam in on the second attempt made on her life and on the doctor's misfortune. "I obviously have to get out of here. Can you help me?"

"Right now—you're probably in the safest place on Earth."

"Given the fact somebody has already tried to kill me twice in less than forty-eight hours—I doubt it."

"Seriously, the president's in town for a speech and the city's in lockdown. The security at the airport is tight as a drum. You're better off staying right here for now," he insisted.

"Fantastic!" She turned gleeful without a pause.

Sam was confused. "Huh?"

Max caught his expression but ignored him for the moment and hit another one of her speed-dial numbers.

"Stanton!"

"Hey, Max what's up?" He was certainly thrilled, but surprised to hear her voice.

She hastily filled him on enough details so he would help her get to Italy.

"Have the local authorities given you any protection?"

"There's a cop standing guard outside my room."

"Give me about twenty minutes to organize things here. Once the president begins his speech, I'll be able to break away."

"Thanks, Stanton. See you soon." She hung up. "Problem solved!"

Sam knew Stanton was the head of the president's Secret Service detail, and if the president was in Sarasota, so was he. As he stood by listening in on the conversation, he was most thankful that Max had left his name out of the discussion. "You have very interesting friends in rather high places." Sam flashed a rare smile. "I guess you won't be needing my services anymore."

"You and Pliny have been a great help. Thanks, Sam."

"See ya, kid." He turned and left the room.

Chapter 23

---◦————◦———◦◦———◦◦---

ARRIVEDERCI

"What a mess I've gotten myself into!" Max leaned back against her pillow and tried to conjure up more pleasant thoughts and suddenly the image of Stanton appeared. There was no doubt in her mind or her heart that she was deeply in love with Noble, but she still had feelings for Stanton. He would always be a part of her life. Thankfully, Noble understood. He knew they were good friends and he was cool with their relationship. He also knew that Stanton was an honorable guy and would respect Max's choices. One thing for sure: Max could always count on Stanton to come to her rescue. But for the time being, she would have to hang tight a bit longer. Stranded for the moment, she decided to try again to reach the guys. First, Noble.

"I'm unavailable at the moment. Leave a message at the beep."—*Beep.*

"Aargh!" Max muttered. "Noble, call me!" She abruptly ended the call and then tried her luck with Jax.

"Hey, Max! Where the hell have you been?"

"Excuse me. Why haven't you returned any of my calls?"

"I tried, but your phone has either been turned off or your voicemail box is full."

Suddenly, Max realized that during her anesthetic fog she had never thought to check her voicemail, only check her phone app to see if a new message had been received. She just waited for the calls to be returned.

"Sorry Jax, it's been a crazy couple of days." She took it slowly and told him what happened with Sam, about her injury, omitting the gruesome details, and about the doctor. She left out the flowers for the moment. That was one mystery she still wanted to solve on her own. "And I think I know where Antonio Maieli is hiding out—and Jax—the killer may come after the photo album."

"What are you talking about?"

"Listen." Max filled him in on her conversation with Isabelle and then cautioned him to watch his back. She noted the total silence on the other end of the phone and could only imagine how Jax was processing all that she had thrown his way. But he had to hear the rest. She spewed the words, "So I'm waiting for Stanton to show up," and then quickly bit her lip and prepared for Jax's retort.

"Stanton! What the hell has he got to do with this?"

"He's going to help me get to Italy without raising any flags at the airport."

"This is a really bad—" Jax stopped in mid-sentence.

She waited for him to continue but he remained silent. "Are you still there?" she prodded.

"Give me a minute—I'm thinking."

Max eagerly checked the wall clock, wishing Stanton would arrive.

"Stay where you are!" Jax ordered. "The police have given you protection and you're in no shape to travel. I'll make arrangements and go look for Maieli myself."

"Absolutely not! You think I'm going to give you a choice assignment and let you fly off to Italy? Remember, it's my name on the shingle!" she teased. "Seriously Jax, I have to follow through on this one. Besides, you'll be much more valuable in Washington. You need to decipher who's behind all the killings."

Jax remained silent. Then he relented. "You win. At least on that point—we may be getting a little closer. I've left messages for both Doiron and Avery and I'm waiting for them to return my calls. But I also checked out Erog at your suggestion. At first I wasn't sure what to look for until I remembered the one link between the three scientists was climate change. Get this: Erog's wife and two sons are on various boards whose companies are into green energy. In fact, the same companies Erog himself served on before he was elected to the Senate. And the same companies that received stimulus money. Not sure about conflict of interest, but it certainly raises suspicion."

"It could be a possible motive for Spark's death—if Spark knew. But it doesn't explain the deaths of the three scientists."

"What if Spark had to give Erog some inkling as to the testimony to get him to agree?"

"Then Erog may have thought it would jeopardize his personal enterprises as well as his position on the committee."

"Especially if he was peddling his clout."

"It could be a likely scenario but keep digging. Jax, also check back with the chief. I was able to convince him to have von Boehmer's body autopsied. He's also going to try to track down Doerfinger's Lexus. Get this, he even promised to follow up with the police investigation in Saint Léger du Ventoux."

"Another one of your miracles?" he jested and then acquiesced. He had met his match and lost. "Will do, Boss—reluctantly. But please be careful. And call me as soon as you arrive."

"Promise." She hit the red phone icon.

Max was getting restless waiting for Stanton. But in the meantime, she needed help to get out of her hospital garb and into her street clothes. She knew she had little time to spare. As she was about to hit her call button, she caught Yungst standing in the doorway.

"You look like hell, Doc," she ribbed, trying to make light of the whole situation.

"I could say the same for you." He smiled.

"Seriously, how are you feeling?"

"I'm fine Max, considering your visitor was running around with a curare-filled syringe."

"What do you mean?"

"The toxicology report showed over a hundred milligrams of pancuronium bromide. It's a pretty nasty drug. Basically, it causes the muscles to relax totally, paralyzing the diaphragm and lungs. Needless to say, causing a person to suffocate."

Max shivered. "Yeah Doc, I'm aware of the drug. Thank God you're okay."

"Thanks to you, I'm still kicking. It's good to be alive." Yungst tightened his expression and then steered the conversation away from himself. "The nurse tells me you've decided to leave our lovely establishment. With or without my okay."

"For your safety and others, I think it might be a good idea."

"Max, I really don't want to know what you've gotten yourself into. But if you ask for my medical opinion, leaving the hospital in your condition is a bad idea."

"Doc, I almost got you killed. And the longer I stay here, I'd be placing other lives in jeopardy as well."

Yungst exhaled, puffing out his cheeks. "I thought I'd give it a shot—no pun intended." He chuckled and then said, "So, are you ready?"

Max nodded as she pointed to her dangling limb.

Carefully, Yungst lowered her leg, freeing her damaged ankle from the sling and laid it on the bed. He could see that she was trying to be stoic but caught her wince. "Here." He handed her two bottles of pills. "This is Percocet. Take one every six hours for pain as needed. The other is Promethazine. You can take it in conjunction with the Percocet if you become nauseous. Max, try to keep your foot elevated as much as possible and ice it whenever you can. It's best to use the crutches and not put any weight on your ankle for at least another week. But against my better judgment, I'll give you this walking boot to be used when absolutely necessary. By all means, don't leave the stitches in for any more than two weeks." Slowly, a sympathetic smile crossed Yungst's lips as he placed his hand on her shoulder. "Other than that, I wish you well. Seriously, please be careful out there."

Max returned the smile, genuinely grateful for his care.

Suddenly Stanton appeared in the doorway and her pain was replaced with relief.

"Is there anything else you need?" Yungst asked, noting the expression on her face. He assumed the official-looking visitor was the one to help her leave the hospital.

"No, thank you. You've been great Doc, really."

"Then I'll go sign your release orders. But promise me, you'll see a doctor no later than two weeks. Seriously, you'll need the stitches taken out."

"Promise."

"Sure you will." Yungst turned to leave but as he was about to walk out of the room, he looked back one last time. "Good luck, Max," he said, displaying a bit of regret.

⋅⋗⋖⋅

"You look like hell," Stanton said, as he leaned against the doorframe, brandishing a friendly smile.

"Why do people keep saying that?" Max pouted, and then with sincerity she admitted, "It's so good to see you." She eased back into her pillow.

Stanton walked over to the bedside and touched the bandage on Max's head and then kissed her forehead gently. "Well doll, you've really gotten yourself into a fine mess. And you've been a P.I. for how long?"

"Not you too. I've already received a lecture from Jax, and God knows where Noble is, but I expect he'll give me an earful as well. Enough!" Max knew it was time to get the hell out of there and abruptly ended the teasing repartee. "Stanton, please grab my clothes out of the locker." She handed him the key.

He handed over her clothing and asked, "Need any help?" A devilish grin crossed his face.

"No! Turn around," she ordered. Max tried to get dressed the best she could, but found it difficult to pull the left pant leg over her newly donned cast and surrendered. "Stanton, turn around."

He immediately saw her predicament and the devilish grin returned. However, with some extra tugging, he managed to slide the pant leg up to her thigh.

"I can finish from here, thank you."

"Okay, princess, now let's get you out of here."

Chapter 24

BOTCHED ATTEMPT

It was late into the night and the senator was alone in his office. His corpulent figure cast an ominous shadow on the wall illuminated by the only lamp turned on. The corridors outside were empty and eerily silent. He was restless, repeatedly wringing his hands, waiting for the dreaded phone to ring—not the one on the desk, but the one in the drawer. Finally, the call came, breaking the deafening silence.

He grabbed the receiver. "It's about time!" he groused.

"She's gone," the caller said.

"What do you mean she's gone?"

"There are cops swarming all over the place. Somehow she slipped out of the hospital. I'm checking all the airports now, but security is really tight. Evidently POTUS is in town."

"She wasn't supposed to leave the hospital alive. For Christ's sake, she was in traction. How could you let that happen?"

"A doc walked in as I was about to send her nighty-night. I had to get out of there pronto."

"You botch this one—we're all going nighty-night. I promise you it won't be painless. Now find out where she's headed and finish the job!"

Chapter 25

BUON VIAGGIO

The doc was correct. It did hurt like hell. The moment Stanton helped her up onto the crutches, she could feel the blood rush to her ankle. But she had little choice. Now buckled into her seat, waiting for the plane to take off, she once again had little choice. So she spent the time mulling over the bizarre events that had taken place over the past three days. *Any sane person would think they're figments of my wild imagination—except for the fact they actually happened.* She gave into a slight shudder at the thought. Then Stanton popped back into her mind.

As promised, he arrived bringing reinforcements. And once he confirmed the hospital floor was secure, they moved into action. Stanton had prearranged to use the helicopter landing pad on the roof of the hospital to whisk Max away to the Miami International Airport—in none other than the president's private helicopter. He saw it as divine providence with the president being occupied delivering a speech, followed by the usual luncheon. After all, he needed only to borrow Military One for a short time, and the copter was sitting idly on the tarmac. He would have three hours before the president would need transportation to Tampa International Airport. It was a calculated risk, but he deemed it a worthy cause.

Stanton in his wisdom, arranged for a direct flight to provide Max with both ease and safety, for which she was grateful. His actions also included clearing her to carry a firearm. The accompanying cast and crutches provided her with additional privileges, making the boarding process manageable. The first-class seat was a nice added touch. And for the first time since her flight to Sarasota days earlier, Max was finally able to relax. *Thanks, Stanton, you covered all the bases.* She readjusted herself into a more comfortable position as the plane lifted off from the runway—and then finally it hit her. In nine hours and fifty-five minutes she would arrive at the Fiumicino airport in Rome, Italy to begin her hunt for a missing scientist.

<hr />

"Would you care for breakfast?" the flight attendant asked.

"Breakfast?" Max was clearly confused coming out of her slumber.

"We'll be landing in about an hour."

She realized that she had slept through most of the flight, but in a way she was relieved. She still had a mission to accomplish and needed to be sharp. "Yes, please," she responded and moved her seat into an upright position. After devouring her meal, her next order of business was to find a flight attendant to help her to the lavatory. She reached over and pushed her call button. Seconds later a smiling attendant appeared. With some effort and a lot of discomfort, Max managed to get out of her seat and sling her handbag over her shoulder. Then with the attendant in tow, she hobbled along on her boot cast, opting to forego the crutches. Fortunately, the lavatory was only a few rows away.

"Thank you," Max said as she managed to wiggle into the toilet on her own. "Egad!" Not until that moment had she thought to look at herself in a mirror. With all the commotion, she had forgotten that her head was still wrapped in gauze. Gingerly, she unwrapped the seemingly never-ending cloth until she reached the end. Then she took a deep breath and stared back at her reflection. Above her left eyebrow was a row of stitches in a nimbus of black and blue. "*Que sera sera.* Nothing I can do about it now," she sighed and then tossed the gauze into the trash bin. She was glad for the few bare essentials in the toiletry kit, compliments of the airline. Starting with one of the prepackaged facial cloths, she carefully cleansed her face and then brushed her teeth. She ran a comb through her hair and tossed it back up into a bun. As a final act of vanity she put on some lip gloss. Then she leaned back against the lavatory wall and reexamined the results. "This is as good as it gets!" She was semi-pleased, but more important, she was beginning to feel like her old scrappy self.

The plane had fortunately landed on time, but Max found the disembarking slightly more cumbersome than the boarding. But the wheelchair waiting in the gangway made it doable, coupled with the airport attendant steering her through customs at warp speed. While she imagined he drove his car the same Italian-devil-may-care way, she was thankful he had succeeded in delivering her to the driver waiting outside without incident. With his help, she managed to slide into the back seat of the Audi. The driver attended to her luggage. In no time she was on her way. And hopefully, closer to finding Antonio Maieli.

The driver effortlessly maneuvered the car through the winding hills of the Tuscan countryside almost as deftly as the airport attendant wielded the wheelchair. Relieved to be on solid ground and once again being left little choice, Max sat back and marveled at the unfamiliar scenery. There appeared to be endless rows of majestic cypress trees lining most of the roads surrounding the hillside towns. Staring at them out of the black reflective window was almost hypnotic, until she felt a sudden tightness in her chest, along with the staccato beat of her heart. Instinctively, she grabbed the left side of her bosom. Then came the Eureka moment. *It's not a heart attack you damn fool.* She knew full well what it was—it was the sudden confrontation with harsh reality. *I've traveled all the way to Italy on a hunch? What am I—nuts?* Uncharacteristically, she began to question her own instincts, wondering or rather hoping her self-doubt could be attributed to the anesthesia. A second later the onset of uncertainty turned to impatience, forcing herself to refocus. She glanced at her watch. They had already been on the road for over two-and-a-half hours. By her estimate, the time of arrival should be momentary. Evidently, she was correct. Minutes later, the driver turned off the main highway and ascended up a steep, narrow, paved road.

"*Signorina, siamo arrivati,*" the driver announced.

Max assumed as much, having just passed the gigantic bronze angel-like statue holding a ribbon displaying the emblazoned word Capannelle. She also saw on top of the hill, above the towering piece of metal, a large stone building that she suspected was the winery and hotel. The driver continued to follow the hotel signs leading the way until he pulled into the circular driveway. The car came to an abrupt stop.

Before tangling with her luggage and crutches, Max reached into her handbag for the envelope of euros Stanton had given her and proceeded to hand the driver four crisp bills in hundred denominations, the prearranged fare. Separately, she tipped him an additional fifty euros for his service.

"*Grazie* Signorina; *molto generoso.*"

Max was aware that Italians were unaccustomed to receiving large tips American–style and that sometimes it was overkill, but she thought under the circumstances it was warranted. She was also hoping for a little assistance. It worked.

The driver leaped out of the car and rushed to open the passenger-side door to help Max steady her crutches on the gravel driveway. He then retrieved her luggage and pointed to the sign marked *Guests*. Allowing her to proceed, he walked closely behind as Max maneuvered her way along the cobblestone path. After rounding the corner, they walked onto a large terrace. Both were taken aback by the breathtaking views overlooking the charming village of Gaiole. To her right she entered the stone building and walked into a stunning living room. It was elegant but rustic at the same time. Nothing one would expect in a hotel. She began to wonder whether she had intruded upon someone's private residence, but she was sure she saw the sign for Guests.

The driver placed her bag on the floor next to the sofa. "*Va bene.*"

"Yes, thank you."

"*Buonasera,* Signorina," the driver said, as he bowed and then departed.

Max let out a huge sigh of relief. She had finally arrived thanks to Stanton, who had also arranged for a private car to drive her to Capannelle, and provided her with an untraceable amount of euros. Now only Jax and Stanton knew where she was—and of course, there was Sam.

Chapter 26

———o0o——o——o0o———

A NIGHT IN THE VINEYARD

"Anyone home?" Max called out.

On cue a beautiful young woman bounded into the room. "*Benvenuto*. Welcome. I am Valentina."

"My name is Max Ford. I have a reservation."

"*Si*, Signorina, we were expecting you. Please follow me." Valentina picked up Max's luggage and carried it into an adjacent room on the other side of the sofa from where they stood. "We have several beautiful rooms upstairs and outside in the other building, but this one will be more comfortable for you, madam."

"This is lovely. Thank you."

"The person who made your reservation also arranged for your lunch and dinner meals to be served in the hotel. Normally we serve breakfast only but we are happy to accommodate you under the circumstances. Also, we lock up the house at seven-thirty when the staff leaves for the night. Only the guests have access. Would it be possible to serve your dinners at 7:00?"

"Of course. I don't want to be a burden." *Oh, yes, Stanton, you thought of everything.* Max smiled as she listened to the delightful woman pass along further instructions in her melodic Italian accent.

Valentina began by familiarizing Max with the layout of the house. "Directly from the living room, past the French doors, you will find our tasting room, a small library, the dining room and our kitchen," she explained with pride. Then she proceeded to inform Max about the breakfast hours, the pool, and the evening cocktails normally served at six o'clock on the terrace. "Next to your phone you will find a number where the office manager can be reached after hours." Valentina discerned that new guest understood all she had conveyed. "Signorina, please let us know if there is anything else we can do for you."

"Thank you very much. I'll be fine—" Max started to ask Valentina if they had a guest registered by the name of Antonio Maieli but resisted. She had no idea what danger may have been lurking. Thoughts of the doctor resurfaced and then her thoughts trailed off. *I have to find Antonio Maieli on my own. Then what?*

Valentina noted her expression and quietly left the room.

At the sound of the door closing, Max checked her watch. She had about forty minutes to unpack, acquaint herself with her foreign surroundings, and place a call to Jax as promised. She decided to use the cocktail hour as an opportunity to scour the guests firsthand, in hopes of finding her missing scientist.

"Where are you?" Jax sounded tense, as though he had been sitting by the phone for days, waiting impatiently for her to call.

"I'm at Capannelle—I just arrived—are you all right?"

"Yes, I've been worried sick about you. Thank God you arrived safely."

"You needn't worry. Stanton planned everything to a T. I arrived without a hitch."

"Are you alone?"

"Of course I am. Why?"

"I thought it was in your best interest that I—never mind." He quickly reverted to another topic. "I'm still waiting for a call back from Harold Doiron."

Max thought Jax was acting rather strangely but chalked it up to his concern for her. "What about Dennis Avery? Did you hear from him?"

"I did, and it was a rather interesting conversation. Let me grab my notes."

Max sat patiently waiting for Jax to resume the conversation. She could hear papers shuffling in the background. In the meantime, she checked her phone to see if Noble had called. "Aw, why haven't you called?"

"Did you say something?"

"Yes, to myself. And Jax, remember I'm six hours ahead of you and it's been a long flight."

"I'll make this quick. First, Avery told me that Jonas had asked for time off to work on a special project with a group of scientists."

"I think we have a pretty good guess who they are."

"Jonas wouldn't tell Avery exactly who the scientists are or what the project was about, other than to say it would blow the heat out of the global-warming theory. Avery did acknowledge that Jonas sounded troubled as though he was almost afraid to provide any additional information. In fact, he himself seemed quite distraught over the death of Jonas, but I also got a sense it was in part due to the loss of what Jonas' scientific findings may have revealed."

"Very interesting. Then Avery must have had an inkling as to what Jonas was up to?"

"I thought the same and probed a bit further. That's when I got quite an earful. We already knew that Avery offered scientific evidence that humans emitting CO_2 into the atmosphere have little effect on climate change. But he told me that by studying the physical evidence from two millennia of recorded history, he posits that climate naturally cycles between warm and cold. And argues that a 1,500-year solar-driven cycle is what controls the earth's climate."

"Jonas was obviously aware of Avery's position. Perhaps he set out to provide the added proof."

"Everything points to that being the case because he mentioned specifically that the climate models are ineffective in measuring huge correlated variables such as clouds and shifts in ocean currents."

"Claus worked with the climate models. That cinches it. Claus and Jonas must have been working together." Max was beginning to concoct her own theory. "I trust there's more?"

"Yes, Avery talked about something called the Pacific Decadal Oscillation and how the Pacific Ocean currents experience huge shifts in temperature. He cited an example how the Gulf of Alaska and the Columbia River actually reversed their population of salmon due to the shift in water temperatures. I found it quite intriguing."

"Wait a minute. I just read something online in *The Conversation* about the Atlantic Ocean entering into a cool phase. It was called the Atlantic Multidecadal Oscillation. The article detailed how it could potentially threaten drought and consequent famine to some parts of the world but would also mean fewer hurricanes hitting the U.S."

"So there is no such thing as ideal climate. Bummer!"

"I guess, Jax, it depends on where your sun shines."

"Cute, but get this. In spite of all the hoopla from the *parched-earth society*, Avery explained that climate has historically been most stable during the global warming phases. He said it's during the 'little ice ages' defined by periods of long winters and short summers that we can expect to be plagued with more floods, droughts, famines, and storms. Reading from my scribbled notes, his exact words are 'they ask society to renounce most of its use of fossil fuel-generated energy and accept radical reductions in food production, health technologies, and standards of living to save the planet.' He emphasized that 'science is the process of developing theories and testing them against observations until they are proven true or false.'"

"It didn't bode well for Galileo," Max quipped.

"What, now, you're a mind reader? Avery also mentioned Galileo. He said, 'he may have been the only man of his day who believed Earth revolved around the sun, but he was right!' Avery reasoned that absent proof that CO_2 is emitted into the atmosphere at dangerous levels, public policy should not be focused on 'banning autos and air conditioners,' but focus on adaptation. Frankly, he's stumped as to why humans armed with air conditioning fear global warming. He told me that history, science, and our own instincts tell us that cold is more frightening than warmth. He believes the climate event that deserves our real attention is the next Big Ice Age."

"Is it time to get my furs out of storage?"

"No, you've got some time. It's thousands of years away. Although Avery believes it will be a time when human knowledge and high-tech farming will be most needed. On the other hand, he reasons that a warming trend produces a more stable climate, crucial for farming. From my conversation, he's apparently confounded as to why the public is panicking over what he calls 'the finest climate the planet has known in all its millions of years.'"

Max absorbed most of what Jax had revealed and she was beginning to formulate her own opinions, but that never stopped her from playing the devil's advocate. "How can Avery be so sure that manmade CO_2 emissions have only a negligible effect on global warming?"

"Actually, I asked him that same question. He cited six shortcomings of the Greenhouse Theory."

"Can you give me the short answer?"

"Patience, Max, this is cool stuff."

"Jax!"

"You win. You can read it when you get home if you're so inclined."

"The way this is shaping up I may never discuss the weather again. Did he say anything else that may help us solve this case?"

"One final point. He seemed most dismayed that despite the evidence, the intelligentsia and leaders from around the world continue to spout the dangers of CO_2 emissions."

"Hey Jax, you're pretty good at this scientific mumbo jumbo." Max was impressed.

"Forgetting the dogma I received during my crash course, somehow this information got three smart guys killed. Max, the pieces of the puzzle are all there. I just haven't put them together."

"We discussed earlier how extremely profitable it has become to say the earth is warming to a dangerous level."

"You're on your Gore kick again! I can feel it."

"No, I'm not. But you have to conclude that someone or some group has an amazing ability to blag and figured out how to convince humanity that it's responsible for global warming. You can always count on the guilt-factor setting in and the lemmings to follow the usual mania. Savonarola comes to mind!"

"Max, you're being cynical."

"Call me skeptical, but Bret Stephens made a similar, more articulate statement in an op-ed he authored. One sec. Let me look it up." Max held her smartphone in front of her and searched for the article on her browser. "Still there?"

"Waiting breathlessly."

"Here it is. Now it's my turn to dazzle. In the *Wall Street Journal's* op-ed page, Stephens wrote a column titled "Liberalism's Imaginary Enemies," where he referred to global warming as a cottage industry. He writes about how its survival is dependent on being believed. He stated, 'because mindless repetition has a way of making things nearly true, and because dramatic crises require drastic and all-encompassing solutions. Besides, the thinking goes, falsehood and exaggeration can serve a purpose if it induces virtuous behavior.'"

"I think Avery would agree that statement hit the ball out of the park."

"Hold on! There's more, and this is a real tongue-twister. Stephens said, 'Dramatic crises for which evidence tends to be anecdotal, subjective, invisible, tendentious and sometimes fabricated are trumpeted on the basis of incompetently designed studies, poorly understood statistics, or semantic legerdemain.'"

"Man! One thing for sure—this case is mindboggling."

Max felt the same frustration that she sensed Jax was feeling. "Then maybe it's time to follow the old adage and follow the money," she suggested. "Senator Erog now comes to mind."

"There's no denying that a cozy relationship exists between the global-warming proponents and those doling out extraordinary sums of taxpayer dollars. Whether it comes directly from appropriations or from grant money parceled out from government agencies, it all comes from the same pot."

"However you slice and dice it, governments should not be in the business of promoting scientific research to fit a narrative. It's apparent that much of the public is being blindly led down a path of presumed evidence. Not sure where this will lead us, but go back and check out Erog more thoroughly. He's probably only the puppet, but I'd like to know who's pulling his strings."

"I'll get right on it! But to punctuate your last point, I recall an article I read recently in the *National Review* written by Henry Payne. He said, 'with a clear public-policy outcome in mind, the government/foundation gravy train is a much greater threat to scientific integrity.'"

"Jax, from what we learned about this case thus far—that was also a home run. I think Stephens and Payne are sharing the same bat. But give Erog another once-over and check out his connection to the IPCC." Max checked her time. "I gotta go. It's cocktail hour."

"By all means don't let me keep you from your libation."

"Seriously, this may be my first opportunity to spot Maieli. I have to keep him safe and find out what the hell is going on. You have to find the killer and prove Spark didn't commit suicide. Let's keep our focus."

"Got it. Stay safe. And Max, please keep me posted."

"You too. Let me know if you hear from Doiron."

* * *

Max pulled herself together and managed to hobble outside to the terrace. The fresh air was intoxicating despite the unseasonably warm October evening. She marveled at the stunning hillside as the sun sat low in the sky, assuring a spectacular sunset. The thought of a perfect film set entered her mind. After taking in the view a moment longer, she headed toward an empty chair off to one side. Once seated as comfortably as possible, she began perusing the myriad of guests milling about, sipping from their wine glasses, waiting for the colorful hue to disappear over the horizon.

First, Max eyed the couple in the opposite corner and decided that given their age differences and their overly caressive moves, his companion was not his wife. There was another couple, each one holding a wine glass in one hand and a smartphone in the other. Little conversation was taking place. *Definitely married,* she thought. Two other couples were standing nearby chatting in English, but one couple spoke with French accents, the other with a German inflection. Standing next to the wall bordering the terrace stood a rather tall man by himself. He seemed to be looking out toward the vineyards. She was able to catch only a glimpse of his profile, but she couldn't help wonder whether he was Maieli.

Just then a young woman walked out onto the terrace carrying a tray of glasses and a bottle of wine to offer the guests refills or fresh glasses for the new arrivals. Following directly behind her was another tall, slender gentleman. Max tried not to stare, but she began to wonder whether he might be Maieli. As he walked over in her direction, she breathed in deeply to ready herself. But after closer inspection she concluded he was much younger, although he bore a resemblance to the fourth man in the faded photo Jax had emailed her—the one he found in the yearbook for École Polytechnique Fédérale de Lausanne.

"Signorina Ford, my name is Manuele Verdelli."

"How do you know who I am?" Max instinctively went on guard.

Manuele realized that he must have startled his guest. He pointed to Max's cast and smiled, quickly adding, "I'm the sales manager of Capannelle. I was the one who received the call from Major Stanton asking me to make the arrangements for your stay. I hope they're satisfactory?"

Max relaxed, forcing a smile. "Yes. I've already met Valentina; she's charming. And thank you for the special accommodations."

"You're most welcome, but it was Valentina who volunteered to help with your meals. But please don't hesitate to let me know if there is anything else we can do to make you more comfortable." Manuele nodded farewell and then left to circulate among the other guests.

As soon he departed, the woman serving wine appeared. "Signorina, would you care for a glass of chardonnay?"

"Yes, thank you."

As the woman handed Max the glass of wine *oohs* and *aahs* began to emanate from the guests. They sun was about to set. Then as quickly as the pinkish-orange glow disappeared below the horizon, the guests and the woman dispersed as well. Max sat alone. No Maieli. Only a full glass of wine. She decided to steal the solitary moment, her first in days, to enjoy the fresh air, the refreshing beverage, and the reflective thoughts. The time appeared to drift by seamlessly until she glanced at her watch.

After one last sip of her wine, Max edged herself out of the chair and shuffled back to the main house. She would, regrettably, have to wait for another chance to meet Maieli.

———————— ·◦❀◦· ————————

When Max entered the living room, Valentina promptly appeared around the corner with a tray. "Tonight I can offer you *tagliatelle Bolognese*," she announced in a chipper voice. "Then perhaps a grilled chicken breast with rosemary and roasted potatoes?"

Max suspected it was a rhetorical question. But she was more than happy with the selection, given her last meal was a horrid array of breakfast foods on the flight over. "It sounds delish. Valentina, I know you are giving up time to take care of me. I really do appreciate the attentive service."

"It's my pleasure, Signorina. I'll leave you with a glass of our chardonnay and some *parmigiano* to start. With your meal I will pour an exceptional 2010 Chianti I hope you will enjoy." Valentina placed the tray of cheese and the glass of wine on the table and then left to prepare dinner.

———————— ·◦❀◦· ————————

Max sipped the wine and picked at the cheese as she thought *You gotta love Italians. They don't ask if you want wine. They simply describe the wine they are serving. I could get used to this lifestyle.* Promptly at seven o'clock her dinner was delivered. Without difficulty, the sumptuous meal and additional glass of wine went down easily, but Max soon found herself fighting to keep awake. She gladly called it a night, wanting to be rested and ready to scan the guests once again at breakfast. She needed to find Antonio Maieli—and soon.

Chapter 27

———⁓⧫⁓——○——⁓⧫⁓———

COLORE DEL SOLE

M ax took her first whack at trying to get ready by herself, including her first shower in days. As anticipated, it took longer than usual but she managed. She had hoped to spot Maieli at breakfast and decided to take the time needed not to look like a war casualty. The fact that she was famished helped to move things along. After one last glance in the mirror she readied herself and headed off on her mission.

When Max walked through the tasting room she eyed an empty seat at the end of the enormous table in the adjacent dining room. Valentina had explained earlier that the 17th-century convent table was precisely 20 feet long. That morning it was beautifully laid out with place settings for each of the guests. Max was somewhat dismayed to discover that many had already eaten and departed. But a few remained. Preoccupied as she scanned the remaining guests, she neglected to see the one step going into the room. One of her crutches hit at the wrong angle and she began to stumble forward. Fortunately, one of the guests swooped in and caught her before she was about to land on all fours.

"Signorina, are you okay?" the gentleman asked with a mild Italian accent.

"Yes, yes, thank you. I'm still getting accustomed to these wretched things." Max held up the guilty crutch, signaling the incident as no big deal. "Please don't let me disturb you," she said, giving the kind gentleman a way out.

"Va bene, ciao," he said and returned to his seat at the table.

Could that be Antonio Maieli? Then she noticed two other gentlemen seated at the opposite end of the table, one looking vaguely familiar. She managed to ease into her chair and then focused on the two of them. Fortunately, she was not too far from earshot. Minutes later Giuliana the chef arrived to take Max's breakfast order. After responding "yes" to almost everything that was offered, Max sat back and sipped her coffee. Trying to be unobtrusive, she managed to eavesdrop on the conversation taking place at the end of the table.

When Giuliana returned with an assortment of fruits and pastries, Max whispered, "Excuse me, but I've forgotten that gentleman's name?"

"Si, Signore Antonio Di Stefano," she replied.

"Yes, of course, Di Stefano. And the gentleman he is with?"

"Simone Monciatti, *il enologist.*"

"Ah, your winemaker. Thank you."

Giuliana retreated to the kitchen, thinking nothing of the guest's inquisitiveness.

Max's interest, however, was piqued straightaway. Continuing to appear disinterested, she only heard sporadic statements as she listened in on their conversation. But she clearly heard Simone say something about *cambiando il colore del sole.* Relying on her rusty Spanish and knowing that many words were similar in Italian, Max concluded that they were talking about the color of the sun changing. *Just my luck. They both happen to be speaking fluent Italian.*

It was obvious, however, that as the conversation progressed the two men became more animated. The man identified as Antonio, in a somewhat higher octave, asked Simone the winemaker something Max could not decipher, but Simone's response was unmistakable—he said, "global warming." The statement was so matter of fact that it spurred the conversation into rapid-fire mode. With Italian words and English phrases being flailed back and forth, Max was totally lost in translation. However, throughout the foreign dialogue, she was convinced more than ever that the guest was indeed Antonio Maieli. Max grabbed her smartphone and searched for the photo Jax had forwarded to her. *There it is.* She studied the photo and then studied Antonio, trying not to be obvious. But it was obvious— he was the missing scientist—a revelation that would have to wait a bit longer because it appeared they were about to depart.

Simone glanced at his watch. Then both men shot up from the table and quickly hugged each other.

Simone said, "*Dopo*" as he headed down into the wine cellar.

Antonio replied, "*A presto*" and took off in the direction of the parking lot.

Max thought that an American onlooker would have concluded that the two men had had a heated disagreement, but she knew from her Italian acquaintances that it was more likely a simple conversation among friends. One thing she concluded—the two men had agreed to continue their conversation at a later time. Now she would have to delay another opportunity to approach Antonio. But at least she had found him.

Momentarily satisfied, Max finished the few morsels of egg left on her plate and gulped down the rest of her coffee. *What now?* was her immediate thought. She decided to return to her room, rest for a while, and then plan her next move.

Clack, clack, clack, the door knocker resonated from the other side of the door. "Signorina Ford—Signorina Ford," echoed a voice.

Gradually, the raps on the door aroused Max out of a deep sleep. Hearing the repeated sound of her name finally stirred her to consciousness. "Excuse me!" she shot back as she glanced at the clock on the nightstand. It was 7:15 p.m. Shocked that she had slept the entire day and foregoing her modesty, she responded in a groggy voice, "Come in, please."

Valentina stuck her head in the doorway. "*Mi scusi*, Signorina, would you care for dinner tonight?"

"Silly me. Somehow I managed to sleep the entire day," Max offered unapologetically, but then realized that she had delayed Valentina from leaving for the night. "Please, please come in. I'm terribly sorry to have kept you."

Valentina entered the room carrying a dinner tray. "It's not a problem. For tonight I thought you might care for something light. I hope *capellini* with fresh *pomodori* and *basilico* will be to your liking?"

What's this—Italian penicillin? she thought, until she noted the tray also included a plate of prosciutto, pecorino cheese, and fruit. And of course, a glass of red wine. "It's fine, Valentina; thank you."

"Signorina, is there anything else you would like before I leave this evening?"

"No, that's all; thank you. Have a lovely evening. And Valentina, please call me Max."

"Si, Signorina—I mean Max." Valentina smiled and offered a final good night. "*Buonanotte.*"

As soon as Valentina left, Max stood up and attempted to head to the bathroom to freshen up, but immediately lost her balance and fell back onto the bed. It was apparent that a combination of jet lag, a broken ankle, and a gash on her forehead were all taking their toll. The fact that someone had tried to kill her had become a distant memory. And once again her insatiable appetite rose to the occasion, something else she attributed to her body's plight. "Max, get a grip!" she admonished herself, realizing she could not fight the obvious. *Dinner first, and then a good night's sleep. Tomorrow all will be well.*

Chapter 28

THE SNARE TACTIC

M ax's wish was not granted. She had a fitful night of tossing and turning. Patchy visions of a white car, blue scrubs, a syringe, Sam, and a missing scientist permeated her nightmares, among other flashbacks deep in her psyche—a place she would not enter. Semi-catatonic, she noted the time.

"Dammit!"

It was 10:15 a.m. The breakfast hour had passed and the prospect of befriending Antonio was gone. At least she was not hungry, but she needed a clear head to come up with another plan. Max reached over and picked up the phone to request a much-needed double espresso. Satisfied help was on its way, she sat up and edged herself out of bed. After gaining her balance, she managed to shuffle over to the window and fling open the drapes to let in some light.

"Oh, my!" Unexpectedly, a burst of sunlight blanketed the room. After readjusting her eyesight from the blinding glare, she was amazed by the stunning view of the hillsides off in the distance. The morning light offered an entirely new view of the landscape and inspired a completely new attitude. "It will be a beautiful day after all," she voiced aloud, noting the blue skies devoid of any clouds and a possible strategy that was coming into focus.

Both the view and the espresso worked wonders to clear the cobwebs from her mind and lift her spirits. She was now ready to face the task at hand. No doubt she had missed breakfast. But she reasoned that if she could get herself ready in time to sit out on the terrace before the guests departed for their luncheon venues, she might have a chance to snag Antonio for a brief introduction—the one where she would introduce herself as the accidental tourist.

The timing was perfect; it was 11:45 a.m. and there was not a soul in sight. Max plunked herself down in the same chair she had occupied the night before, guarding the entrance and waiting for the hungry guests to stroll out of the house. As luck would have it, Valentina was the first to appear, carrying a perfectly timed cappuccino. While Max sipped on the warm brew, Valentina discussed the lunch choices for the day. As they were about to conclude, none other than Antonio came jogging in from the parking lot. Based on his attire, he appeared to have gone out for a run.

"*Buongiorno belle ragazze,*" he imparted on his way into the house.

"What did he say?" Max asked, noting Valentina's expression.

"He said, 'Good morning, beautiful young ladies,'" she replied, blushing a tad.

"Hmm, it must be the jet lag, but suddenly my appetite has become voracious. Would you mind making that a large platter? And I agree, a glass of chardonnay will go well with the meal, but make it a bottle?" Max winked.

"*Subito!*" Valentina replied without questioning the order, and then left for the kitchen.

I hope that means right away, Max thought. Then her mind trailed off. About twenty minutes later, Valentina reappeared with the requested oversized platter of prosciutto wrapped in melon, salami, various cheeses, and fruits.

"Yummy! It looks delicious." Max was obviously delighted with the selection.

Once Valentina placed the platter down on the table along with a bread basket, she opened the bottle of Chardonnay. First, she poured a sip for Max to taste.

"Perfect," Max replied, but it was not in response to the wine. As luck would have it, Antonio walked out through the French doors and was heading toward the driveway, waving politely in their direction.

"Will that be all?" Valentina asked, ignoring the handsome guest.

"One moment." Max held up her index finger to stall Valentina as her eyes darted in a different direction. "*Signore*, would you like to join me for lunch?" she called out. The long-awaited opportunity had finally presented itself. Plan B was in full throttle.

"*Non ho capito*." Antonio, confused by the request, turned in his tracks and headed over to the table. "Was that an invitation?"

"I can't possibly consume this lavish lunch on my own." Max caught the expression on Valentina's face but continued with her audacious attempt. "Signore, if you don't have other plans, I'd be pleased to have you join me."

"I've heard you American women can be quite forward," Antonio quipped, but he could see she was not to be deterred by his comment. He replied at once, "Signorina, it would be my pleasure."

Valentina took her cue without hesitation and scurried off to the kitchen to fetch an extra plate and wine glass.

Antonio, gladly accepting the invitation, pulled out a chair at the table. No sooner did he sit down than Valentina reappeared with an additional place setting.

"Will there be anything else, Madam?"

"Thank you. That will be all." The glint in Valentina's eye was obvious. Max knew she was on to her ploy.

"Yes, Madam." Valentina excused herself and returned to her other duties, but she considered it odd that Signore Di Stefano would accept the invitation. She had observed him over the past few weeks and found him to be rather reclusive, other than the times he would spend with the winemaker, Simone. *Ha, he must have considered a single lady with a broken leg and stitches across her forehead nothing to fear.* She snickered.

⚬

Antonio reached for his napkin and commented, "Signorina, this is very generous of you."

"My name is Max Ford, but please call me Max."

"Then you must call me Antonio."

Ah, he's being cautious not to use his surname, Maieli, she mused. *But it's all coming together.*

"What kind of name is Max for such a beautiful woman?"

"It's short for Maxine." She feigned flattery but felt that no further explanation was necessary—like telling him Max was an ideal name for an undercover CIA agent.

"May I ask what happened to you?" he quizzed, literally eyeing her from head to toe but staying within the boundaries of a proper Italian gentleman.

"I just wasn't watching where I was going. Call me a klutz." *Or, perhaps I should tell him I was hit by a speeding car that most likely was driven by the same person who's trying to kill him. Nah.* Max put her kidding thoughts aside and quickly changed the subject. "What brought you to this paradise?"

Antonio reached for the bottle of wine and asked, "May I?"

"Yes, thank you."

As he topped off both of their wine glasses, he explained, "My father and Dottore Franco Della Piane were colleagues as young men while working in New York. I had heard stories over the years about Capannelle and decided that one day I should visit. So here I am."

"Dottore?"

"Yes, he's the chief executive officer for Capannelle. He is a wonderful, gentle man and has been like an uncle to me. Do you know the history of Capannelle?"

"No, please tell me."

"The original owner of this 17th-century farmhouse was Raffaele Rossetti. But in 1997 Capannelle was purchased by the famed James B. Sherwood, founder of the Orient-Express Group, later rebranded as Belmond. The hotel chain includes several of the most exquisite hotels throughout the world. The tourist guest rooms at Capannelle are no exception as they are reminiscent of the same quality."

"I had no idea." Max listened between Antonio's bites of prosciutto and cheese, alternating with small pieces of bread. She herself followed the process, picking up certain foods and slicing others.

"Do you know anything about Gaiole?" Antonio was clearly enjoying his role as tour director.

Max played along. "Other than it's down there," she kidded, pointing toward the valley below.

"Well, today Gaiole is a picturesque village nestled in a valley in the Tuscan region of Italy, as you can see. But she wasn't always so tranquil. As a matter of fact, it was during the twelfth century when her town square became a thriving marketplace for the surrounding castles and hamlets. Then in the thirteenth century, three villages formed a league, called *Lega del Chianti*, consisting of Castellina and Radda with Gaiole designated as the capital. These villages became the *heart* of the Chianti region."

"This is fascinating! I've seen you in discussions with the winemaker. I assume you know everything about Chianti as well?" she asked lightheartedly, even though the question was calculated.

Clearly enjoying his role, Antonio continued. "Oh, you mean Simone. He's an interesting guy and he's been a winemaker for over thirty years. He not only produces wonderful wines but he has many captivating anecdotes to go with them. In fact, I learned from him that we have Baron Bettino Ricasoli to thank for making Chianti famous, not only as a region, but as a wine. The Baron's formula using a blend of *Sangiovese* and *Canaiolo* red grapes, mixed with a blend of *Trebbiano* and *Malvasia* white grapes, created Chianti. When the grapes are grown within the region of the Lega del Chianti that I mentioned before, they are given the designation of *Denominzaione di Origine Controllata e Garantita* or more simply referred to as DOCG."

"So Capannelle wine is classified as DOCG?" Max continued to feign interest.

"Brava! You've tasted her wine, so I'm sure you would agree that if Gaiole were to be considered the heart of Chianti, then the Capannelle Winery would be part of the soul of Chianti Classico."

"Antonio, you expressed that so beautifully!" *Extolling his knowledge so profusely might be overkill*, she considered.

"You don't have any idea where you are—do you?" A sudden curiosity about his new lunch companion bubbled to the surface.

"Not really." Max attempted to play out her role as the stupid tourist, but evidently she was not convincing enough. She took another sip of her wine, wondering what the next series of questions would entail.

"Okay, mysterious lady. What gives? Why are you here?" Antonio's tone had gone from playful affection to mild suspicion.

Max picked up on his changed demeanor. But also deemed it was too soon to be forthcoming and decided to be a little more creative. "In all honesty I needed a break from some personal stress in my life—and when this unwelcome break happened," she quipped, pointing to her leg, "it was time to get the hell out of Dodge."

"Dodge?" Antonio crinkled his nose.

Max chuckled realizing it was American lingo. "It means to get out of a bad situation." She opted to leave out the word *dangerous* from the true explanation and continued with her tale, staying as close to reality as possible.

"Fruit?" he asked, taking it upon himself to place several pieces of peaches on her plate. "Please continue," he urged, showing a heightened interest.

"It was rather an impetuous decision, but hours before my accident I had met with a friend who happened to recommend Capannelle as a place to visit. It seemed like the perfect place to recuperate, both physically and emotionally. So, voila, here I am." She hoped that Antonio would be a gentleman and not pry further into the emotional reference. However, if he did, she was sure she could come up with something believable. But thanks to her acting abilities he seemed more relaxed following her not-so-true confession. At that point, she reasoned it was best to lighten the conversation. "I certainly made the right decision. See, I've already met a new friend."

"You're very lovely when you smile," he complimented, adding, "A woman like you should know only happiness." Antonio raised his glass and offered a toast, "*Per mia fortuna*—to my good fortune."

"You flatter me." *This is heading in the wrong direction*, she thought. *Change of plan*. "Antonio, I hope you don't mind, but yesterday at breakfast I inadvertently overheard a rather heated discussion between you and Simone. He said something about the color of the sun changing. I found it an odd statement, but given the language I couldn't understand his response." Max assumed her comment seemed innocuous and hoped it would change the dialogue.

"We were speaking of climate change," Antonio replied. "Simone believes that man-made CO_2 emissions are contributing to global warming. I was trying to convince him it had little effect on the overall climate."

"Please go on." This time around Max's interest was genuine, but she opted to tread with care.

"From basic physics and chemistry we know that the sun emits light energy that produces heat that warms the earth. It's also true that CO_2 in the atmosphere can trap that heat, further adding to an increase in temperature. And while the vast majority of climate scientists agree there has been a period of global warming and that the anthropogenic increase attributed to it, the degree of impact is literally up in the air."

"Excuse me, anthro what?"

"Anthropogenic. It's the name for environmental change that is caused by human activity that emits CO_2 into the atmosphere. 'Greenhouse gases' is probably a more familiar term, but anthropogenic global warming, AGW, is the same thing."

"You're basically talking about pollution?"

"Notwithstanding the US Supreme Court's ruling that the EPA can declare CO_2 to be a 'pollutant,' CO_2 is a colorless, odorless gas designed by our Creator to be an essential compound for the existence of all life on Earth."

"Whew! Okay, as in the use of fossil fuel?"

"Exactly! But there is no scientific proof that anthropogenic CO_2 will cause harmful global warming. Frankly, the claims are based on pseudoscience. The heavy reliance on computer-driven climate models and the inability to conduct repeatable experiments alone prove how it's being exploited. The models fail to include cloud cover and don't even take into account something as obvious as the amount of warmth buildings absorb. I'm not a climate scientist, but you have to wonder whether the field of climate science is being turned into a smoke-and-mirrors road show to fit a political narrative. Science is about *what is*, not about changing the climate system."

"I seem to recall hearing that ninety-seven percent of climate scientists believe global warming is caused by your anthropogenic CO_2?"

"The number was originally disclosed by John Cook, a Climate Communication Fellow for the Global Change Institute at the University of Queensland. He's also a blogger for a site called *Skeptical Science*. But he has been discredited by various sources and many other surveys put the number closer to three percent. The internal temperature of the entire scientific community is lukewarm at best when it comes to anthropogenic global warming. The reality is—there is no scientific consensus."

"So I gather you don't believe anthropogenic global warming, greenhouse gases, manmade CO_2 emissions, or however you refer to the current position on climate change as a major factor? You called it pseudoscience." Max appeared to seem somewhat surprised.

Antonio snickered. "Sometimes I think the terminology is meant to be deliberately confusing. Look, I have confidence in the traditional practice of science. It must be absolute and adhere to strict guidelines. I don't believe that's what's happening in this case." He wavered. In a fleeting moment he wondered whether he was exposing too much, but in the same span of time he deemed Max to be hardly a threat.

"Please continue," she urged, noting his hesitancy.

"All I was saying is that climate change is a natural occurrence. Our role is not to mess around with mother nature, but to understand her and plan accordingly."

"In what way?" Max noted his earlier reference about not being a climate scientist, but it was clear he knew his way around the study of science.

"For example, in Simone's case he's building more irrigation systems to mitigate what he thinks will be increasingly higher temperatures. He's already forecasting that in the future the higher temperatures will mature the grapes more rapidly, producing wines that will have more dried spices and pungent flavors."

"Wouldn't that be a positive approach? You mentioned it was prudent to plan accordingly. There's no question that the concern over global warming gave birth to a revolution of new green-energy companies and jobs throughout the world to combat the effects." Max held back, careful not to display too much of her own acumen.

"What it spawned was an exorbitant amount of increased taxes globally, which was foisted on corporations and taxpayers. It gestated from a political agenda, not from scientific examination. But what if Simone is wrong and the world isn't getting warmer, but in fact is—" Antonio was wound up until he stopped in mid-sentence and switched gears. "I'm sorry, this must seem like a boring subject, especially for such a beautiful lady on this glorious day?"

"In all honesty, I find it quite intriguing. Particularly your knowledge of science!"

Antonio suddenly tensed up, realizing he may have said too much.

Back off Max. You're pushing too hard, she cautioned herself. Like it or not, she would have to wait before she could get him to talk about NASA or the other scientists, and hopefully provide an inkling as to why he was hiding out in fear for his life. She could not afford to have him panic at this point.

"Excuse me for being a bit too animated," Antonio interjected, "although you Americans always think Italians are arguing when we're only having lively discussions." He was clearly ready to change the topic of conversation.

"You seem to know an awful lot about we Americans," she retorted. "Not to mention, your English is excellent. Have you spent any time in the US?"

He did not answer the question, but asked one of his own. "Would you like to join me in the village for dinner?"

Max was speechless, stunned by the invitation but at the same time relaxed. She was thankful she had not spooked him.

Antonio took her silence to mean that she needed more information and made his pitch. He rattled on about the lovely little restaurant in the piazza and how it would give them an opportunity to get to know each other better.

At that same time Max was listening to Antonio's proposition, a glare kept bouncing off the glass from the French doors catching her attention. *Odd? It seems that someone is staring at us from inside—but watching Antonio or watching me?*

"I can call us a taxi!" he emphasized, noticing she had become distracted and uneasy. "Max, did you hear me?"

"Yes; can I think about it?"

"Take all the time you need, at least for the next few minutes. I need to use the restroom, but I'll be right back." Antonio wagged his finger, indicating that *no* would not be an acceptable answer. Confident he would get his way, he stood up and walked into the house.

Max observed Antonio while he strolled toward the French doors. At the same time, a cloud hovered over the sun and she saw the face again. "Oh, my God," she gasped.

The out-of-place figure brushed past Antonio and headed in Max's direction.

"What the hell are you doing here?" she whispered, although there was no one else around to hear. Not waiting for the answer, she ordered, "Leave, now!" Max shoved her room key in his hand. "It's the first door on your left. I'll be there as soon as I can. Now please go!" she pleaded.

He obliged with great reluctance.

"Hey, are you okay?" Antonio asked, noticing that Max seemed a little flushed. "You look like you've seen a ghost."

"It's been a lovely lunch and a wonderful conversation, but the combination of the chardonnay and sun are taking its toll. And I feel a little jet lag coming on."

"Are we still on for dinner?"

Max hesitated for a moment and then replied, "Antonio, dinner would be lovely, but is it possible to get a rain check for tomorrow?"

"Are you sure you're all right?" He appeared genuinely concerned.

"Really, I'll be fine after a good night's sleep."

"Dinner, tomorrow—promise?"

"Yes, I'll look forward to it."

Max stood up with Antonio's help and then he leaned in for the Italian two-sided air kiss, minus the air. "Let me help you," he offered and then held open the French doors for her.

"Thank you. I can make it from here," she insisted.

Antonio backed off and headed up the stairs to his room.

Max hobbled to her door and then waited to hear the sound of Antonio's door closing. Then, she entered her unlocked room.

Chapter 29

AN UNIVITED GUEST

"Darling, I had no idea how badly you had been hurt." Noble rushed to her side and attempted to hold her in his arms. Max pushed back.

"Why the hell are you following me? You don't trust me to handle a case on my own?"

He scanned the bruise on her forehead and the boot cast. "It's clear you're in need of some assistance." He could see the ire building up from her facial expression. "Honey, will you relax! I told you I was working on something for the president."

"In a winery—in Italy?" Her question dripped with sarcasm as she limped over to the side of the bed and sat down.

Noble remained standing. "Wait a minute—I thought you were supposed to be investigating the death of Senator Spark?" He threw it back in her court.

"I believe the person who killed the senator also killed three scientists who were working together. I'm looking for the person who can tell us what happened. His name is Antonio Maieli."

Noble's eyes bulged. "Who did you say?"

"Antonio Maieli. What's the matter?"

He hesitated. But having no choice, he opened up. "Max—we're looking for the same person. That's why I was in Italy." He was shocked by his own words.

Max followed suit, but sat quietly waiting to hear more.

"I was heading down to Sicily when I learned about your accident," he replied evenly, and then asked in a hastier tone, "Have you seen him? We don't have a lot of time!"

Max's sixth sense kicked in; it was an inexplicable turn of events. She challenged him. "Why?"

"Do I really have to repeat myself?"

Hearing the seriousness in his voice she relented. "You just passed him at the French doors on the way to my room. He's registered under the name Antonio Di Stefano."

"That was Maieli?"

Ignoring his rhetorical question and without removing her glare, she grilled him further. "So how did you find me anyway? Stanton?"

"No, Jax. I tried calling you, but your phone was always turned off or your voicemail box was full, so I called him. He told me what happened. Especially, how you convinced Stanton to help you leave the hospital against his better judgement."

"So that's what he wanted to tell me?"

"Tell you what?"

"Never mind. I'll deal with Jax later."

"Honey, he was only concerned for your safety. Believe me; he has no idea that I'm on an assignment or that I'm in Italy. And he never told me who you were actually looking for."

"Don't 'honey' me—and I don't buy it." Max stomped her crutches on the ground.

"Do you always take everything way beyond the heart? I'm here because Jax said you were in trouble. I love you and I wanted to make sure you're okay. Now, does Maieli know who you are?"

"No!" Exasperation set in, but she took a deep breath, and with a modicum of calm, explained, "I was trying to get him to feel comfortable with me first."

Noble raised an eyebrow.

"Not that way you jealous fool. In fact, while you were glaring at us through the window, I came up with an idea."

"I'm sure you did—spill."

"Would you like to sit down?" Max offered, acknowledging her willingness to confide in him finally.

Noble took a seat in the chair next to the bed and sat in silence, waiting for her to lay it all out.

"I suspect Antonio, along with three other scientists, was scheduled to testify before Spark's committee. I have no idea what it was about, other than something to do with climate change. But whatever it was, it was powerful enough to get four people killed. If I can get Antonio to testify on videotape, then I can get it to the proper authorities. But now the president's involved—that's perfect! We'll have the leverage we need to protect his identity. I'll tell him tomorrow night at dinner."

"Where are you dining? I'll be joining you."

"No way! I can handle this Noble. Stay here and out of sight. In fact, did anyone see you arrive?"

"Don't change the subject. You know the minute you tell him you're investigating the Senator's murder, he's gonna want to flee. What do you plan on doing? Hit him over the head with your crutches?" *Oops*, he thought, sensing she was about to erupt.

"What part of 'I can handle this' didn't you understand?"

"Max, I'm the only one who can give him the assurances that the president will protect him and that it's in his best interest to cooperate."

"Then I'll bring him to you. And we'll convince him togeth—"

"Okay!" Noble cut her off in an act of surrender. "We'll work together—on your terms." He had no choice but to throw in the proverbial towel, although he openly confessed that Max could be an asset. "Admit it. You could use a little help," he said jokingly. He reached over to hold her hands, trying once more to show affection.

Max pushed back again, denying him the opportunity. Then she blasted him with a series of rapid-fire questions, refusing to be interrupted for a second time. "Incidentally, when did the president ask you to find Antonio? Was it before Senator Spark was discovered dead in the park? Is that why you tried to stop me from grilling the police chief?"

He checked his watch, ignoring all her questions. "Stay right here! I have a call to make." Noble made a quick getaway and left the room, taking the key with him.

"Don't let anyone see you!" she warned, as he slipped out through the door.

Max was furious at him for not answering her questions and leaving her dangling. But as she remained stranded on the side of the bed, her anger dissipated slightly. She realized how bizarre the case was turning out to be. She also realized that Noble could be an asset. Especially as the president's intermediary, one who could guarantee Maieli's protection. *This could turn out to be a good thing,* she surmised with more composure.

Noble eyed a spot on the terrace where there was no one seated, although he heard a few guests who were chatting down by the pool. Fortunately, Maieli was nowhere in sight. He pulled out his xPhad, the ingenious smartphone that, when unfolded, converted to a tablet. More important, it provided a secure line. It was 11:15 in the morning inside the beltway. He made the phone call.

"Did you find him?"

"Yes, Mr. President."

"Wonderful. I don't want to know where you are. But keep him safe until I figure out the next step. I'll get back to you shortly."

"Sir—there's a problem."

"What now?" the president asked with trepidation.

"Max is here."

"Jesus Christ! She really gets around. What the hell is she doing there—wherever you are?"

"She was also looking for Maieli, whom she has befriended." Noble elaborated how Max was hired by Senator Spark's wife to find his killer, which led her to the missing scientist.

"Shit. Neither of you know what you're getting yourselves into."

Noble thought it best not to ask the president the obvious question, but went ahead and described Max's plan to get Maieli to testify.

"Then all three of you will become targets. You'll be the only three to know."

At that point Noble needed the answer. "To know what, sir?"

"I don't know exactly. That's the problem." The president answered with full candor. He informed Noble that Senator Spark had come to his office when two of the four scientists had died suspiciously. "Sherman feared they were not accidental and that there would be more deaths to follow. He seemed depressed at the thought he might be personally responsible." The president hesitated and then admitted, "When it was reported that Sherman had committed suicide, I felt it was plausible given our recent meeting. What he told me at the time could be gobbledygook science or it could bring down a mega-trillion-dollar world-wide industry—I need to be sure."

Noble was shaken by the president's words, but he kept his emotions at bay. "Sir, how do you want me to handle the situation?"

"Get Maieli to testify. Tell him he has my word that his identity will never be revealed and he will be kept safe."

"Sir, how do you want me to handle Max?"

"She's no longer SIA. But knowing Max, she'll never lose the scent. Just keep her on a tight leash."

"You know you can trust her, sir."

The president knew Noble was correct. He also suspected Sherman's information was accurate and something nefarious was happening. Something that cost him his life. He had to trust her because she already knew too much. "Just get him to testify."

The line went dead.

Noble returned to Max's room and found her lying on the bed. He couldn't tell whether she was asleep until she rolled over and murmured, "Noble." All traces of anger had left her lips. He was relieved as he walked over to the bed and lay down beside her. Gently holding her, he whispered, "Looks like it's you and me kid, working together again."

Clack, clack, clack, the door knocker resonated from the other side of the door. "Signorina Ford—Signorina Ford," echoed a voice.

"Oh no! I forgot about dinner. Shh," she whispered and then called out, "One moment please! Noble, toss me my robe and go hide in the bathroom." Respectfully dressed above the waist, with the blanket covering the rest—and no evidence of a romantic interlude, Max hollered, "Come in please!"

"Good evening," Valentina said. Noting Max lying in bed, she apologized, "I'm terribly sorry if I disturbed you."

"Not at all. I was just taking a nap. I guess the combination of wine and sun, and of course, your luscious lunch knocked me out. I can't blame everything on jet lag." Max made every attempt not to sound as though she had been caught with a man in bed.

Valentina smiled inwardly, recalling the platter of food and the wine bottle that had been totally consumed by Max and her guest. "Would you like your dinner tray on the bed or on the table?"

"On the table please."

"Anything else I can get you this evening?"

"No, thank you, Valentina. You should go home and be with your family. It's been a long day for you."

"Yes, Signorina. I mean Max." Valentina excused herself and left Max alone with her dinner and the man hiding in the bathroom. *Evidently he had forgotten to tell her that he had already checked in.* Valentina chuckled as she closed the door.

———⟡———

Noble heard the door close and came out of the bathroom.

"Whew, that was close!" Max smiled.

Noble beamed a devilish grin.

"What is it?"

"It was so unnecessary. I checked in earlier as your fiancé. That's how I knew you were having lunch with your gentleman friend on the terrace."

"You rat!" she shouted, aiming her pillow directly at his head. "Good catch, but what are you going to have for dinner?"

Noble looked over at the dinner tray and Max's eyes followed. She saw the two wine glasses and a full bottle of wine.

All of a sudden, Max's face flushed. "Valentina knew all along! I must have sounded like an idiot—thanks a lot!"

Noble laughed uproariously as he went over and poured two glasses of wine and presented one glass to her. He made the first toast. "I love you, Max."

"I love you too—sometimes."

Noble wolfed down the pasta and polished off his veal chop, along with what remained on Max's plate. She had only picked at her food, still sated from her lunch. But she enjoyed the company, the wine, and watching Noble. She admitted to herself that it was great to have him there and glad they would be working side by side again.

The rest of the evening was spent talking about how she would approach Antonio and Noble would follow up the conversation by laying out the conditions. In part, it seemed like old times, but then those times were also fraught with danger.

"I'm exhausted!" Max was the first to cave.

"Let's get a good night's sleep. We have an interesting day ahead of us."

"Agreed."

Chapter 30

―――◦―――◦―――◦―――

FULL DISCLOSURE

"Daniel—Daniel—No—Come back!"

"Max! Honey, wake up! You're having a bad dream." Noble reached over and pulled her into his arms.

"What's the matter?" She had no clue as to why he had awakened her.

"You were calling out in your sleep. Before that you were thrashing me in the head."

With still no idea what he was talking about, she grappled for any excuse. "My last few days have been rather traumatic. I guess I'm suffering the ill effects."

Surprised by her strange behavior, Noble hesitated before asking, "Who's Daniel?"

"What?" Max bolted upright.

"You were shouting his name."

"It's nothing. Let's go back to sleep." Max rolled over with her back facing him.

"Max."

"Noble, let it go." Her voice was muffled as she talked into the pillow.

When he reached over to pull her close to him, he could feel her body trembling.

She pulled away again. "I said let it go!"

Instinctively, he feared whatever it was could not be pushed aside. He tried again to pull her into his arms. That time she did not resist. Slowly, she began to relax.

"Darling, we both understand that there will be times when we won't be able to talk about a case. But I don't think what's going on with you has anything to do with Spark's death or finding Antonio. And when it comes to our personal life, we promised to be open and honest with each other."

"Please, Noble—it's late," she replied wanly, but she remained tucked in his arms as her mind began to wander. *He's so wrong. It has everything to do with this case. But this is not the time to unlock the memory box.* She was driving herself into an unwonted territory. She tried to put her mind in neutral, but the thoughts kept flowing. *Can he handle it? Can I live through it again? Maybe it's just the tenacious jet lag screwing around with my head. Enough!* Without warning, Max shot up from her pillow and sat upright. "Any wine left in the bottle?"

Given the late hour, Noble thought it an odd question, but then again, she was acting oddly. He inched his way out of bed and walked over to check. "Some."

"Pour us each a glass, please. We're both gonna need it."

He obliged, albeit with a tad of self-admitted trepidation.

Max had already leaned herself up against her pillow and sat in a comfortable position. Then, out of the blue, she had another flashback. She was sitting on a couch in front of a shrink as part of the prerequisite to be certified as an agent. And when she was asked to bare her soul, she managed to keep her past sealed. Now, with her right knee pulled into her chest, and her encased leg lying helplessly prone, she was about to default on a solemn promise. She let out a lengthy exhalation and muttered, "Here we go."

Noble thought he heard her say something but missed her comment as he handed her one of the two partially filled wine glasses. But it did not really matter because at that point he was beyond curious and had only one question he wanted answered. He sat down in the chair next to the bed and asked, "Okay, Max, what's going on with you?"

"You're wrong about this case."

"Why! What's so special about this case? You've had worse."

"This case opened a floodgate of memories, memories I swore I'd never revisit."

"Honey, you're not making any sense. Tell me what's going on."

"I am telling you. I'm telling you something that I've been forbidden to speak about. Something you can never mention— to anyone—including me—ever again."

"Well, repressing whatever it is hasn't seemed to have worked. Maybe it's time to open up to someone you can trust. Like me, for example."

"At least you have top security clearance."

"Thanks a lot, Max."

"And—you're the only one I love enough to trust with this information."

Noble reached over and squeezed her hand. Then he pulled back and allowed her to continue in her own way, uninterrupted.

At first she hesitated. But after a few sips of wine, she started off with a disturbing question. "Do you remember the name Admiral Orris Irving?"

Noble concentrated. The name sounded terribly familiar. "Aha, of course! As I recall, he was a decorated war hero. Tragically, he killed his only daughter and three sons, and then he killed himself. I believe his actions were blamed on post-traumatic stress disorder attributed to his time in Vietnam. It was a horrible event. Wasn't it grotesquely referred to as the Thanksgiving Day Carnage?"

"No. It was the Christmas Eve Carnage."

"That happened a long time ago. Why the interest?"

"Actually it was in 1983. At that time, the admiral was in Naval Intelligence assigned to the National Maritime Intelligence

Center in Suitland, Maryland. Before that he was stationed at the base in Naples, Italy, during which time his wife developed breast cancer. He wanted to return stateside and requested a transfer to the Jacksonville Naval base. It was granted."

Noble took note of the expression on her face. It was disturbingly void of emotion, but he let her continue.

"The admiral had already prearranged for his wife to undergo treatment at the Mayo Clinic in Jacksonville, hence the request. Unfortunately, the cancer had progressed to stage four, and she died a few months later. Shortly after, he transferred to the National Maritime Intelligence Center and moved his family into a home in Falls Church, Virginia. That's where the admiral died." She paused before moving on with her story. "It was on Christmas Eve. He was in his living room with his oldest son Daniel."

Noble caught the reference but remained silent.

"His other two sons, Charles and Robert, were visiting friends nearby. His daughter Claudia was upstairs reading until suddenly she overheard an argument—and then a gunshot. When she ran downstairs, her brother Daniel was gone and her father was dead. He had been shot in the head once. Claudia saw her father sprawled out on the sofa with his right arm hanging toward the floor. A gun lay at his fingertips."

Noble listened to Max describe the horrible events in gruesome detail as she maintained eye contact with the wine glass in her hand. Her body language was strangely unaffected. And although her behavior concerned him, he said nothing.

"Claudia panicked. The only thing she could think of to do was to call her other two brothers and tell them to come home. But before her brothers arrived, two men appeared at the front door."

Noble could not hold back any longer. "Max, I'm really confused as to why you're telling me all this."

"Please." Max held up her hand to ward off any questions as she took another sip of wine. Then, in the same vein, she continued. "One man was short and stocky, but the other man was tall with a ruddy complexion. They told Claudia that they were from Naval Intelligence, but she refused to say anything until her brothers arrived. They agreed. As they waited, she remained seated in the corner, staring at her father's body. No one spoke a word. For Claudia, the time seemed eternal until her brothers returned home. At first there were wails and then shouting and then shock set in. Finally, when the men were able to calm them down, they moved everyone into the dining room and that's when their lives changed forever."

As difficult as it was, Noble had remained seated quietly as he listened to Max. But the dispassion in her voice suddenly frightened him. The urge became too strong. "Honey, how do you know all this?"

For the first time Max looked at him directly. "The admiral was my father." The quiver in her voice was apparent.

Noble's jaw dropped in shock, and more confusion set in. "Max, the admiral had only one daughter." Immediately it struck him. "Oh my God, you're Claudia!"

"Don't ever mention that name again! She's dead! She died that night!" Max took a deep breath, reeling in her composure, until she was ready to continue.

Noble respectfully gave her whatever time she needed.

"I told the tall guy, *Redface*, that I heard my father and Daniel arguing, but there was also another voice I didn't recognize. Then, after I heard the gunshot, I heard the front door slam. Then, I heard the door slam shut again. I insisted there was no way my father would kill himself. They seemed to ignore what I said as though they had already sized up what had happened. Charles asked them why they came to the house. Robert kept asking about Daniel. They refused to answer any of our questions. All Redface would tell us is that our father's murder was the upshot of a case he was working on and that now our lives were in mortal danger. Redface went on to tell us this wild plan of how they would help us to disappear to protect our lives."

"You mean new identities?"

"Yes. Redface said we would be given new names, replete with a past history, and money to start a fresh life in an undisclosed location. He spent hours trying to convince us. Ultimately my brothers folded and agreed to the terms. They strongly believed it was their only real choice. As Navy brats we had no roots planted. Furthermore, both our mother and father were dead, and we were unaware of any living relatives. For my brothers the decision was easy. They were older and already on their own. However, I was problematic, being eleven years old. But in the end, Redface convinced my brothers that it was in my best interest to be placed in a boarding school until I came of age. The deal also included a college trust fund. I virtually had been stripped of any choice and had no way of fighting the inevitable for the moment. But I'm my father's daughter. There would be another time and place and I was willing to wait. First, I pledged to find the means and the tools necessary to learn what happened. It became my obsession. Eventually, I would set the record straight."

"Honey, you were amazingly doughty for your age."

"I wasn't brave. I was just determined to get to the truth in my own way." Max let out a deep breath as she felt a peculiar sense of relief. "So there you have it—twenty-four hours after my father was executed—I became Maxine Ford."

Noble was speechless.

Max appeared nonplussed as she leaned back and sipped her wine. She waited for Noble's inevitable series of questions. Oddly, he remained mute.

However, Max was eager to get the inquisition over and unwilling to wait any longer. "Ask whatever questions you have now. After tonight we will never speak about this again."

Noble detected that she had more to say before putting it officially behind her. So at her behest he treaded lightly.

"What you're saying is the story about the family massacre was a complete fabrication?"

"Yes."

For the first time since detailing her tragic story, Noble noticed tears welling up in her eyes. He felt her pain and was torn between consoling her or backing off. Unable to resist, he reached over and caressed her hand. "It's okay to cry. You need to let it out."

"Been there, done that," she reproached. Max pulled her hand away and began to elaborate, remarkably with full composure. "They took us away to a safe house. It wasn't until much later that we read the false report in the newspaper, claiming all of us had been killed at the hands of our father. Not surprisingly, we were furious, but there was nothing we could do. According to the report, ambulances and police cars arrived late at night. The neighbors witnessed body bags being removed from the scene. There were five in total."

Noble noted the number of body bags. "You never mentioned what happened to Daniel?"

"I never heard from him again. None of us have."

"Did you ever think he had something to do with your father's death?"

"My brothers were convinced he was involved. I didn't believe it was possible. Someone else had to have been responsible. I was determined to find out who."

Noble suddenly got this strange sense that the dots were about to connect. "Don't tell me that's why you joined the CIA?"

Noble saw the hint of smile reflecting from her face serving up his answer.

"After I applied to the academy, an unexpected visitor arrived. It was Redface. I hadn't seen him for years, and although he was thicker around the waist and the hairline had receded, his face was still as ruddy. The one thing I'll never forget was his fear-provoking expression. Standing uncomfortably close, he whispered, 'Using the CIA as a way to find the answers is a very bad idea.' Then he turned and walked away. But it was clearly a warning and made me only more determined. For years he would periodically reappear on the scene. He must have thought his presence alone was enough to deter me from learning what happened to my father and exposing the truth. But even though I met stone walls everywhere I turned, I simply couldn't cope with the notion that we never existed, and that my father's reputation was disgraced."

"Did you ever get to the truth?"

Max paused before admitting, "No. And after decades of pursuit, I capitulated and ended my search. Mysteriously, when I stopped looking, Redface stopped showing up."

"You think he was putting up the stone walls?"

"I'm sure of it. I even tried to source out information on him, but he's as much of an enigma as my father."

"What about your other brothers? Do you still keep in contact?"

"We did in the beginning. But they wanted me to give up looking for Daniel and for the truth—I couldn't let it go. So we argued about it for years until we stopped talking altogether. Silence has prevailed ever since. Ironically, my brothers were correct. It was a waste of my life, with no hope in sight. But at least my job at the CIA allowed me to keep tabs on Charles and Robert. It gave me satisfaction knowing that they had created positive lives for themselves and were able to put the entire tragedy behind them. Until now, I thought I had as well—but apparently there are still unhealed wounds."

"When you saw Spark's body lying on the bench in the park, you recalled your father's death scene? That's why this case is so important to you?"

"I empathize with Isabelle, having had to suffer a similar experience. That's why she has the right to know the truth. That's why she has to know that her husband didn't commit suicide. At least she'll have closure."

"My love, it explains a lot, and not only about this case, but it clarifies why you are so difficult to read at times."

"Don't plan on renewing your library card."

"I'm happy to see your sense of humor is back, but I'm still worried about you. You seem so detached."

"I am detached from the horror that befell me. That's not me anymore."

"Are you sure you're really up for tomorrow?"

"Noble, I'm fine. I'm really glad that you know everything— so now we never have to speak about it again." Max shook her head and announced, "I've already put it behind me."

Noble was not so sure, but certainly understood there would be no further discussions on the matter. Resigned to the fact, he relented. "Okay. Are you ready to get some sleep?"

Without answering, Max set down her wine glass on the night stand, eased herself back into a reclining position, and closed her eyes.

But Noble lingered in the chair a while longer. As he watched her doze off, he wondered whether she had, in fact, let go of her past. Then other thoughts began racing through his mind. *Within the past hour, I discovered an unbelievable story about the woman I thought I understood so well.* His heart ached for what she had endured, yet it also swelled with admiration for the unbeatable odds she had overcome. He had fallen in love with an amazingly strong woman who punched above her weight. And while he understood why she had to move on, it was now an indelible part of his life that would not be easy to forget. *How can you know something so significant about the person you love and not discuss it? It's a question I'll have to wrestle with.* At once, in a moment of razor-sharp clarity, the answer came to him—*you don't.* After a few more moments of reflection, both the physical and emotional drain of the evening began to take hold. Noble assumed Max must have felt the same. Quietly he crawled back into bed and cuddled up next to her and drifted off to sleep.

Chapter 31

---○---

THE MORNING AFTER

M ax managed to reach dreamland in Noble's arms, snoozing restfully throughout the remainder of the night. Finally, she awakened and rolled over. Managing to open one eye, she saw Noble fully dressed sitting in the chair reading his xPhad.

"Hey, sleepyhead, welcome to the world."

"What time is it?" She was still crawling out of her somnolent world as she stretched and yawned.

"Eleven thirty."

"Why did you let me sleep so late?" she scolded. At that moment the phone rang. Max shot up into an upright position. "No talking," she cautioned as she reached for the handset.

"*Ciao bella,*" Antonio purred in an alluring tone.

"What a pleasant surprise!" Max listened to him wax on about how lovely their lunch was, and how he did not think it was possible to wait an entire day before spending more time with her. She cupped her hand over her phone and whispered, "It's Antonio."

Noble began to roll his hand, gesturing for her to move the conversation along. At the same time, he thought about how amazingly resilient she was, appearing as though the previous night had never happened.

Seconds later, Max silently mouthed the word *lunch* and Noble nodded in agreement.

"Antonio, that would be wonderful. Can you give me an hour?"

Noble flagged his hand and mimed the word *where*.

"Antonio, are we going to the same charming restaurant you mentioned yesterday?" She listened to his response. "Ah, yes, *Lo Sfizio di Bianchi*. Great; see you shortly." She hung up the phone.

"What's happening?"

"Apparently he wants to have lunch with me! He's going to call a taxi to take us to the restaurant. I'm to meet him in the living room at twelve-thirty."

"Then I'll show up at one-thirty. Make sure that you get a table with some privacy."

"Uh-uh, Noble! We agreed that you stay here. If you were to approach him now, he'd run for the Tuscan hills. Trust me to convince Antonio, and then you can make your pitch. I'll deliver him to you in an hour."

"Max."

"What is it now?"

"You're in Italy," he remarked with an impish smile.

"Okay, two hours, smartass. Now I have to shower and dress. And seeing as you're a registered guest in this luxurious establishment, would you please go and get me a double espresso? But don't let Antonio see you come and go from this room."

"You win!" Noble knew Max possessed an unerring arsenal of persuasive talents and would sway Antonio. In full surrender, he planted a kiss on her forehead and left to fetch her coffee.

Max made her way to the bathroom and into the shower. When she stepped out to dry off, Noble called out, "I left your cup on the counter next to the sink."

"Thank you!"

She sipped on her requisite caffeine fix between parts of her grooming ritual as she hurriedly dried her hair, dressed, and swiped on some lip gloss. Stepping back, she examined her appearance. Happily, the bruise on her forehead had begun to dissipate. *This should satisfy Antonio,* she mused.

When she walked into the room, Noble remarked, "Nice dress! Have I seen it before?"

"No, Stanton bought it."

"Stanton!"

"My trip to Sarasota was supposed to be an overnighter. Plans obviously changed. Besides, I ripped my jeans when I fell and I needed a few clothes. No biggie."

"Good thing he remembered your size—and your taste. Did he buy what's under the dress as well?"

"Let it go. I'm seriously not in the mood."

"Lighten up Max. It's going to be a long day."

Noble walked over to give her a farewell hug and was stunned by her returning a more forceful embrace, holding him close to her for several moments. He sensed it was a wordless acknowledgement that their relationship had reached the new apex. "Go get him tiger," he murmured softly in her ear.

Without a word, Max pulled back and left the room, quickly closing the door behind her.

As he heard the door close, Noble reflected on a time when he was considered a conundrum. *But Max takes the cake,* he thought. Although, he felt blessed that on the rare occasion when Max's hard shell revealed a slight crack she would let him see. *I couldn't love her any more than I do at this moment. Dear God, just let us get through this alive.*

Chapter 32

————◦◦——◦——◦◦———

THE PROPOSAL

O pting to leave the crutches behind, Max limped as elegantly as possible in her boot cast toward Antonio, who stood waiting.

"*Come sei bella.* How beautiful you are," Antonio gushed as he offered Max his arm. "Signorina, your taxi is waiting."

Within minutes, the taxi drove down the paved road and into the center of the square, the heart of Gaiole. Thankfully, the driver took the liberty of driving them directly to the restaurant, a route legally permitted for only town officials. Under the circumstances he was willing to take the risk. Soon they approached Lo Sfizio di Bianchi, one of the local restaurants recommended by the hotel.

"*Interno o fuori?*" the woman asked as they walked up to the entrance.

"Would you prefer to sit inside or outside?" Antonio asked.

"Let's sit over there." Max pointed to a secluded table in the far corner of the outside terrace with two sides surrounded by hedges.

"*Va bene,*" the woman responded and walked them to the table. Soon two glasses of the customary *prosecco* appeared.

"*Salute,*" Antonio said, being the first to make the toast.

"Our conversation at lunch yesterday was fascinating, and you seemed extremely knowledgeable in the area of science." Max's first attempt to solicit more information from Antonio failed.

"Bella, there are more interesting topics to discuss than climate change. For example, this beautiful little village." Antonio proceeded to rave about Gaiole, its ancient castles, fortified abbeys, and established wineries, among other local lore until their meals arrived.

Max succumbed and quite enjoyed their pleasant conversation that covered the gamut. But it was getting late and she could stall no longer. However, at that moment the server interrupted and asked if they wanted *dolci*. They both refused the sweet ending and opted instead for a *grappa*. So, once the server poured their *digestivo* and left them alone—a different conversation began.

"Antonio, I haven't been completely open with you."

"Yes, Max, I'm listening." Antonio replied, sipping his grappa, not seeming overly concerned.

"I'm a private investigator and I'm here to follow up on a lead."

Antonio recoiled, but he still seemed intent on hearing her out. "And why are you telling me this?"

Max reached over and touched Antonio's hand, sensing he may try to bolt. Evidently her gesture put a spark in his eye. She hoped it would not turn into a flame. She took it slow. "I'm investigating the death of Senator Sherman Spark. And the deaths of three scientists by the names of Claus Veunet, Luca Doerfinger, and Jonas von Boehmer, who were scheduled to testify before a committee Spark co-chaired that focused on climate-change initiatives."

He forcefully jerked his hand back. His face filled with instant anger. And even though he appeared to be ready to exit at any moment, he remained seated.

Max stayed on alert as she proceeded. "We don't believe it was a coincidence that all three men were killed before they had the opportunity to testify. Or that Senator Spark's death was unrelated."

Antonio's face lost its expression. Evidently he was not going to make it easy for her, especially on the off chance she did not know his true identity.

"Antonio Maieli, you are the fourth scientist." Max saw him flinch. She waited for the backlash.

"You knew all along? You lied to me!" He stopped. His eyes projected the predictable fire.

"I just reordered the truth. But putting that aside, we need your help. We need to know the reasons surrounding your friends' deaths. We need to know about the testimonies."

"You can't be serious. I'd be signing my death warrant." He was adamant.

"Antonio, there is someone I want you to meet before you make any decisions. Please hear him out. He's someone who can offer you iron-clad protection."

"No one can protect me."

"That protection comes by way of the President of the United States."

Antonio stared into Max's eyes, trying to calculate her sincerity. "Who's this person you want me to meet?" He refused to give a hint of whether he would capitulate.

"His name is Noble Bishop. He's the director of the States Intelligence Agency. And he's here on direct orders from the President."

"Here—where?" Antonio asked, still showing no sign of emotion.

"In my hotel room, waiting to speak with you."

Suddenly, Antonio's facade cracked. "Is he your emotional problem?" he chided, acting like a jilted lover.

At times, Max thought, but simply offered a slight smile. She continued in a more serious tone, one he had not yet heard. "Antonio, you can hate me, but you'll soon learn that Noble and I are your best chance for your safety and freedom. Hear us out before you decide. Now let's return to the hotel and discuss your future."

Antonio hesitated, contemplating his options. None presented themselves for the moment. He motioned for the check. Promptly, the server returned and handed him a slip of paper. Without speaking a word, he tossed the required euros on the table and then stood up to help Max out of her chair.

So far, so good, she thought, exhaling her pent-up tension.

The taxi was waiting as promised and quickly sped them up the hill to Capannelle.

Chapter 33

THE DEALMAKER

Noble heard their voices as they entered the living room. He shot up from the chair and stood next to the bed.

Max and Antonio entered the room together.

"Signore Maieli, I presume," Noble said as he walked over to shake Antonio's sweaty palm. His nervous grip was obvious. Noble tried to relieve the strain without further fanfare. "I've been asked by the President of the United States to find you and keep you safe. I'm pleased to see I'm not too late."

"Not as pleased as I am—that it's not too late, I mean," Antonio wisecracked, trying to stave off the tension.

"Would you care to see my credentials?" Noble had hoped to further relieve any lingering concerns Antonio may have had.

"I'm well aware of your reputation, sir." Antonio's passive response masked the fact that he was momentarily juggling reality. Then it hit him. Seeing the director and Max in the same room, he finally put it together. He turned toward Max. "You were his deputy director? *Mama mia*, I read about your resignation but I never deciphered the connection—shame on me."

Max said nothing.

Noble ignored Antonio's revelation in lieu of moving the discussion along. "Please take a seat." He signaled Antonio to sit in the chair against the wall. Noble sat in the chair next to the bed.

Max had already taken her place on the side of the bed and was prepared for the first question, one that had plagued her. "Antonio, I'm curious as to why you didn't change your first name as you did with your last?"

"What's the point? Antonio is like Alessandro or Massimo. There are millions of us running around," he droned sardonically. "Besides, I'd be less likely to make a mistake."

"Except when someone calls you by your last name."

Antonio remembered flinching when Max addressed him by his surname. "Touché. I guess I'm not so clever." He grinned, seeming more relaxed.

Noble sensed it was time to step in and close the deal. "Max has already informed you that we need to know the details of the testimonies your friends were to give before the Committee on Climate Change Initiatives. We need to understand what was so damning to cause their deaths. You will also need to describe your involvement to provide authenticity. Your testimony will be videotaped."

"I already told Max I'd be signing my death warrant. But videotaped—no way!"

"Antonio, if you value your life, I suggest you take the offer." It was time for Noble to sweeten the pot. "If you do this, you will be provided with a new identity, money, and safe passage to wherever you wish to go—all courtesy of the US government."

Max quickly added, "Other than Noble and I, only the president will be aware of your identity. Bear in mind: Antonio Maieli will cease to exist." *Just as I did*, she thought.

Max and Noble maintained their vigil and waited for Antonio's reaction—but surprisingly, none came. They both found him extremely difficult to read.

"Antonio!" Max said harshly and then toned it down a notch. "This is the one and only chance you'll have for a new beginning. Otherwise, you'll be spending the rest of your life looking over your shoulder. Take this opportunity! I guarantee you the president will make good on his promise."

Antonio's face was bereft of emotion until he reluctantly nodded his head. He had tacitly agreed to take the deal. "I'm listening."

They took it slow, chatting up a series of germane questions in an attempt to ensure Antonio's personal data was valid before jeopardizing the president's position. Then, after a few hours, and mildly satisfied, Max decided to dig deeper.

"We know that Jonas took a leave of absence to work on a special project with a group of scientists. Did that include Claus, Luca, and you?"

Antonio instantly clammed up and became a bit mumpish.

That went well, she thought and tried again. "Antonio, we know that all of you attended the same university in Switzerland, and somehow you all got back together?"

"Yes!" he blurted out, becoming exasperated by the questioning, but then quickly calmed down reasoning it would be even worse during the videotaping. "We all attended École. But our scientific interests took us in different directions. Only Claus focused on climatology at the time. It wasn't until years later that we somehow found ourselves embroiled in a controversy."

"What controversy?" Noble asked.

This time Antonio appeared more willing to reveal portions of what he knew. "It started after the *Climategate* scandal when the CRU reported that the climate data initially showed that the temperatures were cooling, not warming. Phil Jones, the director of the CRU at the time, instructed Claus' team to add real temperatures to each of the groupings since 1981 and then hide the decline that had occurred since 1961."

"That doesn't sound like standard protocol?"

"Absolutely not! All scientific exploration is based on a hypothesis and utilizing a method where it can be tested. In CRU's case maybe it wasn't rocket science, but it certainly wasn't climate science either. What's so bizarre is that even after the scandal broke, some of the top world scientists supported the original false hypothesis that had been invalidated and continued to use it as their guiding premise. No one thought to disprove CRU's phony report because it had already been sanctioned by the United Nations Intergovernmental Panel on Climate Control and accepted as gospel." Antonio was fired up.

Max and Noble were pleased.

"Then Claus received an email."

"From Phil Jones?" Max asked.

"No, after the scandal Jones had been moved aside into a newly created role as Director of Research, reportedly not a demotion, just a reduction in administrative duties to concentrate on research. The only public criticism noted in the media was that the CRU had not 'embraced the spirit of openness,' whatever that means. But Jones certainly embraced it later. I understand he publicly conceded that global warming may not be a man-made phenomenon after all." Antonio was obviously not pleased with the outcome. He continued in the same fiery manner. "That prediction alone sent the IPCC scurrying to Stockholm in September of that year for a pre-summit session. They published their fifth assessment report the following month. The report continued to substantiate their earlier findings that humans were the cause of global warming, although the succeeding reports they issued were rather evasive and lacking statistics. The IPCC stated that after adjusting the computer climate models to measure more accurately the increase in CO_2, additional years of testing would be required before issuing conclusive evidence of global warming. And according to Claus, the numbers they used were fabricated."

Max reeled him in. "Antonio, let's get back to the email. What was in it?"

"It was a directive that all deniers of global warming be excluded from the IPCC process, that any examination of the IPCC reports be restricted, and strict control over the peer-review process be maintained to prevent any deniers from being published in scientific journals. The email circulated throughout the scientific community, including thousands of scientists who volunteer their expertise to the IPCC. It was meant not only to add peer pressure but also as a warning to the recipients. Claus was furious at the implications and that's when he met privately with Luca and Jonas to seek their advice."

"Why didn't Claus seek your advice?"

"I was working for NASA in a totally unrelated field, so they didn't involve me at that time."

Max recalled the scribbling on the back of the photo with Antonio's initials. She quickly retrieved the photo from her smartphone and flashed it at Antonio. "What can you tell us about this?"

$$\text{Temp}(\text{year}) - \text{Temp}(1850) < 1.8\{\text{Log}[\text{CO2}(\text{year})/\text{CO2}(1850)]/\text{Log}[2]\} \text{ deg C}$$

"It's one of many formulae used to challenge the computer-driven climate models. That equation happens to compute only the GMST, the Global Mean Surface Temperatures." Antonio appeared to be nonplussed as the explanation rolled off his tongue. "It describes the actual data trends of the last 165 years of global temperature change that bounds the net warming effects of CO2, other greenhouse gases, and aerosols in our atmosphere that can be used to forecast maximum possible anthropogenic-global-warming temperature rise for the future."

"Why was it scribbled on the back of a photo next to your initials found in Senator Spark's family photo album?"

Antonio turned ashen. "Evidently," he said after a brief pause, "it was his way of connecting me to the others and their activities. Look—I said I wasn't involved at the time. The full explanation will have to come later. Sorry; you'll just have to wait."

Max looked at Noble. She sensed that he had picked up on the defensive retort. She also assumed he was as curious as she was as to how Antonio eventually became mixed up in the affair. But for the moment she had a more pressing question. "If Phil Jones didn't send the email, who did?"

Somehow that question put out Antonio's fire. He withdrew into a nonresponsive mode.

"Okay, let's talk about the actual testimony. What did Senator Spark want the committee to hear?" Max probed, trying a different tack.

For the next hour, Antonio reluctantly responded with brief answers, until he pronounced, "*Sono stanco!* I'm tired! That's all you get out of me until tomorrow. *Finito!*"

Nothing he revealed was earth-shattering enough to cost the lives of so many, but the little they heard shocked them. It provided enough assurance that there was treachery afoot and that he would be forthcoming during the videotaping. Regrettably, they would have to comply with Antonio's demands and wait.

From the window they could see that the sun was about to set on the horizon. It provided the perfect opportunity for a time-out. Simultaneously, Max's insatiable appetite had reappeared. "Let's take a short break and get something to eat," she suggested.

Fortunately, Noble was able to sweet-talk Valentina into preparing dinner for the three of them. So while they sat straddling plates of pasta on their laps, reaching periodically for their glasses of wine, they switched the conversation to lighter topics. Then Noble tried again.

"There's a crucial part of the story you're not telling us!" He intentionally sounded unyielding.

"What is it with you two? You'll have to wait for the videotaping. The crux of what you want to know—you'll only hear from me once." Antonio was equally determined, but at the same time he seemed ill at ease.

Even the dinner wine didn't loosen his lips. At that point, it was doubtful that they would get any more information from him. The hour was late. And Antonio was obviously holding his cards close to the vest. Noble and Max realized they would have to hold off until tomorrow for the moment of truth.

"Meet us back here in the morning, promptly at eight o'clock," Noble specified. "We'll begin recording then."

Antonio agreed, having already resigned to his fate. He got up from his chair, said *"Domani,"* and walked out of the room.

"You haven't lost your stuff, kid. Good job."

"Thanks!" She held up her fist.

Noble returned the fist bump on his way to the door. He stood there and listened to Antonio's footsteps as he walked up the stone staircase to his room. A few seconds later Noble turned the doorknob.

"Where are you going?" Max was surprised by his sudden move.

"I'm going to sleep on the sofa in the lounge outside of Antonio's room. We can't lose him now."

"You think he still might run?"

"One never knows, but I'm not taking any chances. Will you be okay?" he asked, thinking about her fitful night of sleep.

"Aside from this damn ankle, you don't have to worry about me anymore. Sweetheart, what's done is done. It's ancient history. And thanks to you, I can truly put it behind me."

"That's exactly what I needed to hear." He gave her a passionate goodnight kiss and then forced himself to leave, carrying along a disappointed heart.

For several seconds he stood motionless on the other side of the door, wanting desperately to turn around and make love to her. This was the first time they had worked together as both partners and lovers. And as much as it hurt, he recognized the assignment had to take precedence. *Welcome to the spy business,* he thought.

Chapter 34

---○———○———○---

ESCAPE FROM CAPANNELLE

The noise was muffled but detectable. The stealth design and black sheen were menacing. It caught the attention of all those working in the vineyard. Abruptly, the laborers stopped in their tracks and looked upward.

Max saw Noble's expression. Slowly their eyes drifted toward the ceiling as they listened to the familiar sound. "You think they found us?" She uttered the words in a muted tone, hoping not to distract Antonio as he prepared mentally for the videotaping.

Minutes passed. Nothing seemed to deter the helicopter as it stubbornly continued to hover above the vineyard, maintaining its position. The constant humming sound was becoming unsettling. Especially for the three entranced guests inside the hotel.

"I swear I've been extra careful. I've paid cash for everything," Antonio insisted, shattering the silence inside the room.

Both Antonio and Noble shifted their attention to Max.

"Don't look at me! Stanton paid for my airfare, and I paid cash to the driver."

Noble switched his attention toward the nightstand. "Max, what about your phone?"

"It's secure. Stanton loaded encryption software on both mine and Jax's." Immediately, her expression changed to one of dread. Her eyes moved over to the dressing table.

"What's wrong? Max—what happened?" Noble had seen that expression on rare occasion. Somehow she had screwed up.

"I bought a few toiletries for this unplanned excursion and makeup to cover this frigging bruise."

"Where?"

"Duty-free—on the plane."

"With your credit card? What were you thinking?"

"I was thinking about how crappy I felt." Max's expression remained deadpan, but she could not believe her own stupidity. Whether it was the near-death experiences, the concussion, or fleeing hastily, she simply never focused on the fact that her credit card was being traced thirty-thousand feet up in the wild blue yonder. *I have to stop behaving like a P.I. and reflect back to the days when I was a damn good spy,* she chastised herself.

Noble sensed she was confronting her costly mistake and laid off from further recrimination. "Forget it Max. Let's focus on getting out of here."

Antonio entertained that very thought. "The winemaker might be able to help."

"Go find him, but make sure the way out of here avoids the main road," Noble cautioned.

Antonio left straightaway, almost before Noble had finished issuing the order.

"I'll gather my stuff." The sound of defeat in her voice was obvious.

Noble gave her a quick hug and assured her they would all be okay. Then, he moved into action. "Pull your things together as fast as you can. I have a fast call to make."

"To whom?"

"Enzo."

Luckily, Enzo answered. "*Ciao, amico mio.* What a pleasant surprise."

"I need your help!"

Enzo could tell from Noble's strained voice that he was in real trouble. "*Calmati.*"

"It's no time to be calm. I really need your help!" he repeated. Then he gave Enzo a hasty snapshot of what was happening, divulging only what was necessary.

"Okay, get yourselves to San Marino as fast as you can. I'll be able to protect you there." Enzo thought for a second longer and then instructed, "Check into the Hotel Titano. The room will be in my name and they won't require a passport or any identification."

"There'll be three of us."

Just then Antonio rushed back into Max's room.

"Enzo, see you soon." Noble hung up. "What did you find out?"

Still out of breath, Antonio sputtered, "Simone showed me a tunnel. It starts in the wine cellar under the main gardens and leads to another vineyard about a kilometer away. Here!" Antonio handed Noble a key. "It belongs to an old Laforza they leave at the vineyard until after the harvest. It's parked on the side of the road, close to where the tunnel ends."

"May I ask, what's a Laforza?" They were in enough peril. Noble wanted to make sure that were not adding to their woes.

"It's an Italian SUV made by Rayton-Fissore. Trust me; it will be fine."

"Great; go grab your things. We're getting out of here—now!"

"Hey guys," Max lamented, "there's no way I can make it, in a LaForza or otherwise. Noble, you'll have to get Antonio to safety alone."

"We're not leaving you here," Noble insisted.

Antonio agreed.

While Antonio left to fetch his belongings, Max asked one more time to be left behind.

"No, we're all going together!" Noble was emphatic. "And on the way to San Marino let's take the opportunity to see if we can get any more information out of Antonio. Maybe even an inkling as to his testimony. We need to be one-hundred-percent sure he's for real. Our lives and the president's reputation are on the line."

Max relented even though she suspected it was Noble's ploy to make her feel essential.

It took them close to an hour to reach the vineyard with Noble and Antonio taking turns carrying either Max's luggage and crutches or Max. Finally, they reached the end. As Simone promised, an old Laforza was parked alongside the road. They still heard the ominous sound of the helicopter whirling off in the distance and knew they had no time to spare. Hurriedly, they threw their belongings into the rear of the vehicle and helped Max into the back seat. She managed to sprawl out and get reasonably comfortable. Noble and Antonio sat up front. Antonio drove.

Chapter 35

A GHOST FROM THE PAST

"Ford Investigations."

"Hey, if it isn't Jackson Monroe."

"Who am I speaking to?"

"You don't remember your old spy buddy Sam?"

"Casper?" Jax was taken aback.

"Shush, that was a long time ago. But right now you and your lady spy are playing with hell's fire—or should I say ire—or should I just say 'L.'"

Jax shuddered at hearing the one letter that would frighten the bejesus out of anyone. He had heard all the stories about Henry Edmond Little. Henry was in the same Special Forces Unit as he and Sam. Except Henry left the forces as the consequence of a court martial. It was often rumored that while he was serving time in the brig, he would make veiled threats that "there'll be *Hell* to pay" after his release. Henry kept his word and became an unrivaled hired assassin known only as 'L.' There was nothing little about him and his trademark—all methods he devised for his hits—started with the letter 'L.' It became his deadly calling card.

"You have my attention."

"When Max met me in Sarasota, she told me that Claus Veunet died climbing Lou Passo with a virtual stranger. Luca Doerfinger died when his brakes went out on a rented Lexus an hour after he picked up the car. Jonas von Boehmer, an extremely fit German, also met his fate. How did he die, exactly?" Sam asked.

"He was supposed to have been given an adrenaline injection to stop a cardiac arrest. But the autopsy revealed traces of sodium thiopental and potassium chloride. Von Boehmer's cocktail was probably laced with sodium thiopental causing him to become dizzy and then unconscious. And I suspect, instead of adrenaline, he was given the potassium chloride that would have induced cardiac arrest." Jax was trying to figure where Sam was leading.

"Remember the doctor treating Max was attacked with a syringe?"

"Yeah, I still get the shudders thinking about it."

"The doc's a friend of mine and he told that the toxicology report showed over a hundred milligrams of pancuronium bromide. All three of those drugs in combination are used for a *lethal* injection given to prisoners being executed."

"I'll be damned. They all start with an L. How the hell did I miss that?" Jax was floored.

"Oh, let's not forget Sherman Spark died with a Luger pointed at this head." Sam paused. Then it was his turn to confess. "I didn't make the connection myself old boy until I ran the plates on the car that hit Max. It was a Lincoln Continental rented by someone using a fake I.D."

"Oh my God, the syringe that landed in the doc's neck was meant for Max. Sam, she's up to her usual tricks. She's in a winery in Italy on a hunch."

"The name of the winery is Capannelle."

"What! How do you know?"

"I'm afraid that was my fault. I gave her the clue that led her there. And there's one more thing. When I went to visit Max in the hospital room, I noticed that someone had sent her a bouquet of edelweiss. I caught a glimpse of the scribbled note on the card that was left on the night stand. It was clearly a warning."

"Odd," Jax interjected. "Max received a bouquet of the same flower at the office right after taking the case."

"Jax, the Latin name for edelweiss is *Leontopodium alpinum*. It appears they may have come from the fine and fatal hand of L."

"But why would L first warn Max to back off and then try to kill her?"

"I've met our lady spy. She's quite the looker. Best guess, our deadly assassin had a weak spot and only wanted to finish her off in his own sweet time. Whatever the reason, get to Max and warn her." Casper hung up.

Jax immediately tried to call Max, but her phone was unavailable. Then he contacted the winery directly, but they told him that she had checked out a few hours earlier. *She'll be okay,* he thought. *Noble must have caught up with her by now.* But that gave him little comfort. His heart beat more vigorously as the initials for Henry Edmond Little, along with his calling card, spun in his head. "There'll be HELL to pay, you sadistic bastard!" Jax shouted out to an empty room. He was outraged and at the same time frightened for Max. Suddenly, one more scoundrel came to mind. He dialed the number.

⊷⸻•⋘⋙•⸻⊶

"Senator Erog, please. This is Jackson Monroe, an associate of Max Ford."

"One moment," the secretary replied.

"Yes, Mr. Monroe, what can I do for you?" the senator asked impatiently.

"I recently came across documents that you may find of interest. I understand they have to do with the testimonies Claus Veunet, Luca Doerfinger, and Jonas von Boehmer were to give before your committee."

There was complete silence on the other end of the line.

"Senator, are you there?"

"What makes you think they are of any interest to me?"

"All I know Senator, is that four men have died, all of whom knew the contents of their common testimonies."

"We're all shocked at these horrible accidents. Out of respect, my hearings have been delayed by these unfortunate tragedies."

"Then Senator, can I assume you're no longer interested in these documents?"

Ahem was the strained sound from the end of the line as Erog tried nervously to clear his throat. "I'll call you right back." The phone went dead.

"Son of a bitch, my suspicions were right. He's up to his pudgy neck in this fiasco." Jax spouted out loud again and then reverted to a smile. "But the lily-livered senator fell for my bluff. Max was right. He'd make a lousy poker player."

Jax had hoped that if he served himself out as bait, the senator would contact L and L would want to take out his old buddy. He waited patiently for the phone to ring, but the call never came. Instead his phone vibrated as a text message was being received—it was an address. "Perfect! Now we go *mano a mano!*"

But he also needed Sam.

Jax redialed the number Sam had called him from before. There was no answer. Frantically, he searched his desk looking for the piece of paper with the phone number he had scribbled down, the one Max had shown him earlier, the one with Sam's other number. He dialed it.

"We're done talking," Sam grumbled.

"Wait! I have a plan. Meet me tomorrow in Washington at two p.m. I'll text you the address." Jax hung up.

Chapter 36

—⊶◦—◯—◦⊷—

ON THE ROAD
TO SAN MARINO

S an Marino was a three-hour drive from Gaiole. Noble used the navigation on his secure phone to guide them. Once underway, Antonio took the opportunity to ask two gnawing questions.

"Who's Enzo? And why are we going to San Marino?"

"Enzo Borgini is a dear friend and the executive director of police headquarters at Interpol." Noble could see Antonio wince, but continued. "He's headquartered in Lyon, France, but oftentimes he's in San Marino where Interpol plays a vital role in promoting cooperation between its tiny republic and other member countries. Fortunately for us, he's in San Marino at the moment."

"Fortunately for me—he's Italian," Antonio jested.

"Hey, slow down! Who do you think you are, Fabrizio Giovanardi?" Max bellowed as she almost rolled off the back seat.

Antonio chuckled as he looked at the rear-view mirror. "So you know our famous race car driver?" Easing slightly up on the gas pedal, he continued to wend his way up and down the meandering roads on SS73.

"I'm just a head full of trivia."

"There's something else bugging me," Antonio said. "How could the credit card transaction on the plane lead to Capannelle?"

"I'm sure Max would also be happy to explain that anomaly." Noble felt her punch the back of his seat with her fist. He laughed inwardly.

Max huffed. Then she droned as though she were reading a textbook. "The transaction was traced to a specific flight. From the security cameras at the airport it was easy to find a woman fitting my description, being wheeled through Fiumicino, and outside to a car waiting. The license plate on the car was easily visible on the outdoor security camera. All it took was to track down the driver and ask where he delivered his fare." While Max laid out her *Spy Tracking 101* theory, she realized how simple it sounded. Her self-incrimination began to resurface.

Abruptly she switched the conversation.

"Antonio, you told me that when you and Simone discussed global warming, you disagreed as to the cause. So what is your take on climate change if it's not global warming?"

"Nice try, but I'll only discuss the testimony on videotape." Antonio caught her sunken expression in the mirror.

"She's just making small talk, Antonio," Noble interjected. "But I'd be interested in your opinion as well."

Antonio thought, *What's the harm?* and moved in with his pitch. "The UN Intergovernmental Panel on Climate Change, the IPCC, is posturing that manmade CO2, when released into the atmosphere produces warmer temperatures. But in reality, overall manmade emissions have little effect."

"I'm all ears!" Max caught Antonio eyeing her again in the mirror. She made sure she appeared interested.

"There's a total disconnect between CO_2 in the earth's surface temperatures. What's being touted by the IPCC does mesh with the numbers. I place my money on the analytical stats."

"So reducing CO2 will have little long-term effect on temperatures?"

"Yes. But there's overlooked evidence that CO2 has a salutary effect. It's making Earth greener, which will be beneficial to crops and forests."

"Greener?" Max asked rather dubiously.

"Yes—greener. There's science that bears me out. Recently, a team of scientists using satellites has determined that in the last thirty-five years Earth is becoming greener. I'm sure you remember from your high school science class the term photosynthesis?"

"Sure. The process by which plants and other organisms convert carbon dioxide and water, along with nutrients from the ground, into sugars producing energy."

"You get an A-plus. But don't forget that energy is the main source of fuel from which plant life thrives and some of that CO2 comes from fossil-fuel production. Also, as Earth becomes greener the biomass absorbs more of the CO2 and the entire ecosystem as a whole flourishes."

"So anyone citing CO2 as the basic source of global warming is crazy?"

"To be polite—I would say ill informed! There are so many factors that dictate climate change, starting with the normal cycles of the sun and moon and the unpredictability of clouds and rainfall. In the final analysis it makes more sense to adapt our lives to the reality of natural climate change instead of somehow thinking we can alter its outcome."

Noble adjusted his position to face Antonio. "Are you suggesting that maybe one day we won't be growing corn in Nebraska, but Greenland will have a new major export product?"

"Spot on, Director. In fact, Greenland will be green again, but not due to the CO2 emissions in the air as the alarmists would have you believe. In this case, the melting ice is due to a strong geothermal irregularity from an ancient source of heat deep below the surface."

"You give absolutely no credence to global warming?" Max jumped back in.

"Manmade global warming—NO!"

"So we just sit back and do nothing to protect our environment?" Noble challenged.

"Don't get me wrong. I'm a good citizen of the earth and believe in reducing my own carbon footprint. I conserve energy in all possible ways. I use the proper lightbulbs, drive fewer miles, waste less food, as I would encourage anyone to do. However, this push for renewable energy must be evolutionary, not revolutionary. In either case, it's not going to change the weather."

"Then what do you suggest?" Noble pressed.

"Instead of spending trillions of dollars on green energy to prevent global warming, something we have no control over, we should consider rotating crops and looking for technological alternatives to manage the weather we are dealt. As I stated before, common sense dictates that if we can't change something we need to adapt. We're simply investing in the wrong science, but it fits the global warming alarmists' misleading narrative."

"Hey, slow down!" Max was being tossed about each time Antonio rounded a curve.

"Sorry." He eased up on the gas pedal, realizing the topic of conversation was juicing up his adrenaline.

With both the car and Antonio operating on less octane, Noble asked, "Has Harold Doiron affected your rationale?" He saw Antonio react, but evidently he still had his attention.

"I see you've done your homework, Director."

Max caught Antonio glimpsing at her again in the mirror. *He realizes we knew a lot more about him than just his name. He has to be wondering what else we know.*

Antonio refocused and responded to Noble's question. "I assume your homework also included Doiron's group." Antonio smirked, but then acknowledged, "When Hal first introduced me to The Right Climate Stuff research team, I became captivated by their findings. Some of its members like Tom Wysmuller and Jim Peacock, along with Hal, greatly contributed to solidifying my layman's views. First and foremost, the science predicting that anthropogenic global warming will produce catastrophic climate change is not settled. There's simply no resounding evidence to support the theory. On the contrary, a small amount of global warming with more CO_2 in the atmosphere will definitely be beneficial to crop production, which goes back to the vast amount of CO_2 greening research."

"Did you ever meet Jonas' boss Dennis Avery?"

"No; why?"

"Just curious. Avery has made similar assertions."

That explains a lot. Antonio kept his revelations to himself. "Doiron's research team also predicted that the maximum additional rise in temperature by the year 2100 will not exceed one-point-zero degrees Celsius, making the two-degree by the year 2050 threshold established by the Paris Agreement redundant. With their prediction also comes the realization that by the year 2150 all economically recoverable fossil fuels on the planet will have been consumed, which would then make the CO_2 argument superfluous."

"The attempts to abandon fossil fuels have already been economically devastating." Noble recalled the turmoil when the prior administrations tried to stamp out the coal-mining regions in the US.

"Wait! The US government hasn't finished. They'll spend billions of dollars more trying to end the use of fossil fuel completely—and centuries from now—their efforts will have no meaningful impact on the climate. Other than to perhaps stunt the growth of our forests and agriculture. Yet, the UN and world governments continue to ignore, for political reasons, the reality-based science in favor of their global-warming theory." Antonio's frustration was clear.

"Obviously the activists are running the asylum." Max's failed attempt at levity only perpetuated the conversation and Antonio's heavy foot on the pedal.

"Even with their failure to predict the warming effect over the past two decades, they still beat the drums. Although there is reason amidst the insanity. There was another man whom I came in contact with at NASA. Interestingly, I disagreed with his views on CO_2 being responsible for global warming, but his view on how to manage climate change are quite enlightening. Are you familiar with a man named Piers Sellers? He's a British-American meteorologist and a veteran astronaut with three space-shuttle missions under his belt."

"His name sounds vaguely familiar," Noble admitted.

"Not to me," Max responded. "Tell us more."

"Well, sadly, he was diagnosed with stage-four pancreatic cancer. But what I found encouraging was his perspective. He talks about his 'God's-eye view of Earth and his recognition of its fragility. He said that changes in climate are inevitable, sometimes producing disastrous effects, other times positive. But he has faith that 'new technologies have a way of bettering our lives in ways we cannot anticipate,' and that 'there is no convincing, demonstrated reason to believe that our evolving future will be worse than our present, assuming careful management of the challenges and risks.'"

"But wouldn't reducing CO_2 emissions be managing the challenges and risks?" Max asked.

"If it were a viable risk, yes. As I said, I disagree with Sellers' view on CO_2 because it's widely accepted that the earth has different temperatures. Average temperatures are susceptible to manipulation and not a reliable scientific measurement. However, Sellers is correct when he states that new technologies will come along and improve our lives."

Noble was puzzled. "Making clean energy cheaper would be a game-changer. In fact, I understand that carbon-capture technology is available, although currently expensive."

"Expensive or otherwise, the technology has no valid scientific merit. Of course, that is my opinion," Antonio admitted. "But the one frustrating aspect goes back to there being no structure in place for dealing with climate-change disparities on a regional basis. All the models are predicated on a global basis."

Time passed quickly and the intellectual banter appeared to produce the positive effect. Antonio had become more relaxed and forthcoming. But Max and Noble sensed the question of trust still hung in the balance.

For the next hour they sat in relative silence as Antonio continued to maneuver the roads Italian-style. Noble took the opportunity to focus on devising a plan. Max dozed on and off.

Antonio, unexpectedly swerved to the right and pulled into a parking area on the side of the road. Both Max and Noble were startled by the sudden move. Then the car came to an abrupt halt.

"Hey, what's going on?" Max asked in a half-awakened tone. She edged herself into a seated position and noticed a hill town off in the distance. "Where are we?"

"That's Anghiari," Antonio replied. "Let's get out and stretch our legs or crutches." Antonio turned around and flashed Max a smile.

"Ha-ha."

Antonio, in need of moving his own legs, hopped out of the car and walked over to an historic sign that stood along the wall at the edge of a cliff.

Noble immediately went to help Max. It also provided him a moment to hold her in his arms. He knew she still blamed herself for their predicament and wanted to assess how she was doing. "Holding up okay?"

"I'm ready to kick up my heels—at least one of them." She smiled and then reached up to give him a reassuring kiss.

They stayed back a few more minutes to enjoy time alone. Then they went to catch up with Antonio.

All the while, Antonio pretended he had missed their interlude. When they finally arrived at his side, he proudly explained that Anghiari was known as the site of the famous battle that took place between Florence and Milan in 1440.

The three of them stood in silence and admired the view until Noble became antsy. "It's amazing, but we need to get going."

"First, we must take a coffee," Antonio insisted. "Otherwise, Noble can drive."

"Splendid idea, the coffee that is," Max teased, feeling better as she breathed in the fresh crisp air.

The small café was about fifty feet from where they had parked, which was obviously Antonio's motive for stopping there in the first place. After Max insisted that she could make the trek, they walked over together. Finally, feeling fully fueled, they got back in the car and continued to tackle the hills.

Earlier, during the tranquil part of their drive, Noble had conjured up a series of particular questions. Now he chose the occasion to catalog the answers. "Antonio, do you speak any languages other than Italian and English?"

"I'm proficient in French as well from my time at École Polytechnique."

"Where's your family from originally?"

"Catania. It's the second largest city in Sicily, after Palermo." Antonio wondered what was to be gained by all the personal questions, but he played along.

"You've already told me why you didn't change your first name when you checked into Capannelle, but why take the name Di Stefano?"

"It was my grandfather's family name."

Noble persisted with the inquiries for another half hour until Antonio broke off the inquisition.

"Why all the questioning?" he asked, slightly annoyed at the intrusion.

Noble didn't respond at once but then said, "I'm creating your new life."

Antonio was speechless. He began to have serious second thoughts about his decision. His mind began to race looking for an alternative solution. But he came up empty—it was his only salvation. He finally decided he had to trust them.

Max also remained silent but not for any esoteric reason. She was becoming edgy as she continued to watch the scenery whisk by the car window. Her damaged leg was cramping and her mind was focusing on a nice, soft bed waiting for her up ahead. "Are we there yet?" she called out, feeling slightly neglected.

Providentially, Antonio spotted the sign for the Republic of San Marino. "We're getting close."

"Finally!" Max groaned.

Without any prompting, Noble switched the topic and took to the virtual podium. He began to relay what geography he had learned from his conversations with Enzo. "Technically, the tiny republic is located on Mount Titano wedged between two Italian regions, Emilia Romagna to the northeast and Montefeltro in the Marche to the southwest, but she still remains independent."

"Impressive, Professor!" Max's sense of humor seemed to have returned as they got closer to their destination.

"Once we reach the top, we'll be just over 2400 feet above sea level."

"Sounds like the perfect hideaway for the time being." At least Max desperately hoped so.

Antonio veered sharply at the fork in the motorway and began the ascent up the twisting country road. Noble and Max braced themselves as the car corkscrewed at a fast pace up the mountain. Fortunately, it would be only minutes before they would walk inside the walls of the oldest independent city-state in the world, dating back to 1243. They also knew there was a possibility they were placing their lives in further jeopardy.

"Prepare yourselves for a beautiful, charming medieval treasure, as I've been told." Noble kept trying to relieve the tension he sensed they felt.

"I was under the impression you've been here before?" Antonio asked curiously.

"Enzo has been coaxing me to visit for years, but I'm afraid my travelogue comes only by way of conversation."

After rounding the last curve, they had finally arrived at the top of Mount Titano. Following Enzo's instructions, they located the parking lot next to the Jolly Café outside the walled city and ditched the car.

"I'm afraid we'll have to walk from here, but the hotel shouldn't be too far." Noble led the way, helping Max with her crutches as they battled the cobblestone street. Once they passed through the ancient walls, they inched their way up a gentle incline and arrived at the hotel.

Antonio trailed behind carrying the luggage.

Chapter 37

—————◦◦————◦O◦————◦◦—————

THE HIDEAWAY

"Welcome to the Hotel Titano," enthused the desk clerk. Thanks to Enzo's influence, the check-in procedure went smoothly with little to no questioning, leaving them all breathing a huge sigh of relief.

"You'll find the Cesta Suite at the end of the corridor that way." The clerk pointed and then signaled the bellman to help them with their luggage. Then he handed Noble the key. "Please follow this gentleman. He'll take you to your room. I wish you a pleasant stay."

The three of them straggled down the hallway and then once safely tucked away in the two-room suite, Noble called Enzo.

"We're here."

"I trust you didn't have any difficulty with the usual Italian folderol and you're all checked in?"

"No, it all went according to plan."

"Good. Now, tell me what I can do?" Enzo had been in the business long enough never to start off with the question "What's going on?"

"I need a US and Swiss passport with dual citizenship, a Swiss driver's license and birth certificate, the usual array of documents. They are for Antonio Di Stefano. He is six feet, two inches tall with dark brown hair and brown eyes. He was born on April sixth, nineteen seventy-five in Bellinzona, Switzerland."

"Stop a second! Let me get this all down."

"Enzo."

"Okay, okay, go."

"He speaks fluent Italian, French, and English. Father's name was Alessandro Di Stefano, first generation Italian, born in New York. Mother's name was Lena Ottinger, born in Bellinzona where they resided. Both parents died in a car crash in 1990 driving home one evening from Locarno, a neighboring town."

"You've planned this down to a tittle, my friend. But I'll still need a photo."

Noble looked over at Antonio who had been listening in on the conversation as he nervously flipped through the pages of a magazine. "I'll send you one in a few minutes."

"I'm sure there's more," Enzo presumed.

"I also need one million euros deposited in a Swiss private bank account, along with some pocket cash." Noble looked over at Antonio. "I think ten thousand will do."

"What!"

"Enzo relax. You'll be fully reimbursed. You have the president's word."

"And?"

"A way to get Antonio out of here unseen. I'll need a fishing trawler standing by in Ancona to take him to wherever he wants to go. Also bring along two secure smartphones with you as well."

"Is that all?" Enzo asked, half-afraid of the answer.

Noble glanced at his watch. It was late and everyone was tired. He would delay the interview until the morning. "I'll need everything by noon tomorrow. Also I'll have a parcel that I need delivered to the president under the highest security."

"*Mama mia*, what have you gotten yourself into?" Enzo could no longer hold off. He had to ask the pesky question.

"Later Enzo."

"I thought I'd give it a shot." Enzo chuckled. "*A domani*. And don't forget to send me that photo."

"Will do. See you tomorrow." Noble hung up the phone and then turned to Antonio. "How long have you been sporting the circle beard?"

"For over twenty years. Why?"

"Go shave it off now. Quickly!" Noble commanded.

"Oh, no—first my name, now my good looks!" Antonio stomped into bathroom. A few minutes later, he returned looking ten years younger.

Noble then pulled out his reading glasses and handed them to him.

"Put them on."

"I have twenty-twenty vision and now you want me to look like Woody Allen," Antonio challenged, but again he obeyed.

"Perfect!" The horn-rimmed glasses with a medium width frame gave Antonio a professorial look and sufficiently disguised his face.

"Except I can't see a bloody thing."

"You will. Stand against the wall." Noble snapped a few shots of Antonio with his xPhad and then forwarded the best photo to Enzo. He attached the following message: *Bring along a similar pair of glasses with no refraction lenses.*

Max remained in a reclined position on the sofa, while listening intently to Noble's conversations with both Enzo and Antonio. She assumed Antonio's constant joking was an attempt to stifle his anxiety. Now, he spared his audience and began to take it out on carpet threads.

Chapter 38

THE LAST SUPPER

"It's late, and we could all use a good night's sleep before the interview," Noble suggested. "We'll start first thing in the morning—now, who's hungry?"

Two hands shot up in the air.

"I noticed a pizzeria across the plaza. And considering I'm the only one that's not being hunted down, I'll go fetch dinner," Noble volunteered.

"Pepperoni for me," Max requested.

"Ha-ha," Noble chuckled.

"What's so funny?"

"Pepperoni doesn't exist here, but *peperoni* with one 'p' means red peppers, not salami. And I know how much you like peppers."

"Yuck. I'll take anything with meat."

"Antonio, any special requests?" Noble assumed he had missed the repartee. "And please stop pacing! You're wearing out the carpet."

"Easy for you. In fewer than twenty-four hours I cease to exist."

"Yes, but Antonio Di Stefano has a long future ahead of him."

Antonio exhaled forcefully. "*Prosciutto.* I think Max will like it as well." He smiled. He had not missed a word.

Noble left with their orders and Max went to freshen up in an attempt to revive herself after the long ride. Antonio continued to pace.

Twenty minutes later, Noble returned with two pizza cartons and two plastic bags. "Dinner's served."

"Nice touch. How did you manage that?" Max asked.

"I used my charm." He winked.

Evidently he had been able to scrounge up some plates and utensils from the desk clerk, who was happy to provide the accoutrements from the breakfast room. The moment he set them down Antonio's Italian roots sprouted. He swooped in to retrieve the wine bottles from one of the bags and was already tackling one of the corks.

Finally, circled around the coffee table, sat the president's attaché, the crippled detective, and the man about to disappear to parts unknown—all sharing pizza and wine as though it were just another Saturday night. For a while they traded friendly jabs and nonsense chitchat, and managed to steer clear of discussing their actual circumstances—until all the pizza had been devoured. But with wine still remaining in their glasses and the second bottle half-full, Noble decided to break the verboten ice.

"Antonio, how did you ever get yourself so entangled in this mess?"

"You guys don't give up easily, do you?" This time around the wine seemed to have a calming effect. "Look, both of you know I'm not a climate scientist. And yes, I have been plunked right in the middle of this fiasco. Why? —You'll have to wait until tomorrow to find out." Antonio's *gotcha* smile was obvious.

"Okay then, tell us what you are willing to divulge." Noble tried a different tack.

"If you insist. Since the 1880s the earth's temperature has increased one-point-seven degrees Fahrenheit. Granted, we've experienced extreme weather conditions in the past two decades, including record high and record low seasonal temperatures. It's estimated that sea levels will continue to rise a foot a century. But here's the crack in CO2's foundation. At the September 2016 London Climate Change Conference, the renowned Swedish Oceanographer, Nils-Axel Mörner and one of Hal Doiron's NASA colleagues, Meteorologist Tom Wysmuller, conclusively showed that there was no relationship between CO2 acceleration and sea level rise—none at all! A stunning figurative *sabot* of hard empirical data thrown into the mix, grinding to a halt the propaganda gears of the catastrophic sea-level rise proponents."

"So in scientific speak, correlation is not, of necessity, causation?" Noble asked.

"Precisely! You're actually quoting Margaret Thatcher's policy advisor, Lord Christopher Monckton of Brenchley, who praised the great Nils-Axel Mörner's integrity with a staccato of accolades at the London Conference. As I said before, while there may be a flaccid intermittent relationship between increased levels of CO2 and rising atmospheric temperatures, there is certainly none with sea levels. And according to the Global Warming Policy Foundation—"

Max cut in. "That's where Luca Doerfinger worked, correct?"

"Yes, and as I was saying, quoting a compendium of scientists on a global scale, 'there has been no increase in frequency or intensity of storms, floods or drought,' points driven home by Wysmuller at the London conference with his unassailable graphics showing just that! There are those with altruistic motives who foolishly believe they can control the weather. But science shows that while humans can affect the atmosphere, overall we're just bit players and are unable to compete with Mother Nature. Our best choice is to forecast future weather patterns accurately and prepare for the outcome as I stated before—now is that what you two wanted to hear?"

Max took the challenge and jumped in. "Okay, wise guy, we know you don't buy the theory that man is the source of all the problems, but you do believe in climate change and that it's a naturally occurring cycle. And we know that you're a good citizen of the earth. So how should the world proceed?"

"You double-team quite nicely and you understand that the terms are not synonymous. But have you noted that with all the talk about global warming, CO2 emissions, greenhouse gases, however the phenomenon is described, the sun's primary role seems to be underrated as to its impact in climate variability?"

"In what way?" Max readjusted herself on the sofa, curious as to his point.

"There's a man named John Casey, whose bio is a bit sketchy, but he was a consultant for NASA at one time. He's been discredited by some over the years, most likely for his claim that the perpetuation of the global-warming epidemic was costing taxpayers twenty-two-billion dollars a year. He blatantly called it a scam. But his basic assertion that the earth surface and oceans are not getting warmer, but colder—and that humans are not responsible in either case, asserting that the temperatures changes have everything to do with the natural cycle of the sun—has merit."

"So the earth is actually getting colder?" Max's head was spinning. "This is crazy. All this talk about our planet sizzling and now we are heading into an ice age?"

Antonio suddenly became anxious. But they were eager to hear his response and let him continue.

Ahem, Antonio cleared his throat. "That's—not what I'm saying. But Casey claims to have irrefutable evidence, based on highly reliable climate models that study the sun. He purports that Earth is now transitioning from an ongoing cycle of global warming to what he calls 'a solar-induced, cold climate epoch.' If you're really interested, you'll find his book *Dark Winter* a fascinating read. It details his theory. Enough of Casey!"

218

Noble looked over at Max. He sensed she also thought Antonio wanted to get off the topic. It seemed strange, but they left it unchallenged.

"Besides, I already told you that I hold true to Piers Sellers' belief that human ingenuity will devise technologies that will continue to improve our lives."

"So we just go on about our business as usual?" Max was enjoying the devil's advocate role, perhaps a bit too much. But Antonio continued to play along.

"Let's set the occurrence of climate change aside for the moment. Because the real *inconvenient truth* is that there is no consensus within the scientific community that the real cause of global warming is man-made as the public has been led to believe." Antonio's earlier reluctance rapidly disappeared. He was geared up to extend their intellectual discussion.

Max and Noble were delighted. The pizza and wine had proven to contribute greatly to their relaxed mood.

"The great uncertainty expressed in various IPCC reports, considered the holy grail of climate science, has helped only to foster the skepticism. The Paris Agreement is another example. Effectively, it's non-binding. And certainly, it's a foolish attempt to get countries to put aside their own political and economic agendas for the greater good of Mother Earth. Interestingly, the two-degree figure bantered about is arbitrary. Climate models can predict only a range."

"Certainly, it would be impossible to coax every country to jump on the global warming bandwagon—because they don't share common interests."

"Therein lies the lunacy. For example, China the number one CO_2 emitter and India, number three after the US, continue to build new coal-fired power stations, increasing emissions in pursuit of their economic growth. Australia repealed their pro-environment carbon emission laws and later laid off their leading climate scientist, shifting their focus toward more commercial projects of greater national interest. And for Russia, it's a balancing act. Any reduction in global warming would greatly impede agriculture and mining in her colder regions. On the whole, decarbonization, the radical move to eliminate CO2 from the atmosphere, is proving to be incredibly costly and unrealistic for many countries. In fact, it would be impossible without significantly reducing the standards of living, which goes to Avery's argument."

"But it didn't stop the Paris Agreement from going forward," Noble added.

"To seal the deal only fifty-five nations needed to sign on. Not even a majority. The number itself is convoluted, being the equivalent of fifty-five percent of the world's total greenhouse gas emissions. What's important is that one-hundred-forty-one nations are allowed to renege and as the political winds change it is likely to happen. Take the Philippines, for example; after the May 2016 election when Rodrigo Duterte became President, he disavowed his country's commitment to the Paris Agreement after learning that it would limit Philippine growth. He stated 'That's stupid. I will not honor that.' And followed up with, 'That was not my signature. It's not mine. We'll make a new one...'"

"So in the end, it will be like dipping your toe in the ocean. After you pull it out, you discover you've had no impact." Max was astonished by the whole concept.

"Despite the logic, it wasn't enough to slow down the bandwagon, even with a few missing wheels. Effectively, the Paris Agreement was a giant step toward global-governance, exerting more political control over the world's human and natural resources. The outcome would likely stymie entrepreneurship and technological advances that Piers Sellers referenced."

Agenda 21 flashed into Max's mind, but she held back making the reference. "What's the end game?" she thought was the better question.

"Frankly, I contend it doesn't have to do with climate per se. In fact, Christina Figueres, the Executive Secretary of the UN Framework Convention on Climate Change, may have unabashedly revealed the true mission cloaked behind the Paris Agreement. If I remember correctly, she stated 'This is the first time in the history of mankind that we are setting ourselves the task of intentionally, within a defined period of time, to change the economic development model that has been reigning for at least 150 years since the Industrial Revolution.' I assume she was referring to capitalism."

"Have they no shame?" Noble asked.

"No, and they've found the perfect weapon. It's clear from their actions that they intend to silence *climate deniers,* a derogatory term for anyone challenging the alarming predictions of the extent of manmade global warming."

"Whoa! That sounds like a return to the Inquisition. It didn't fare too well for Galileo."

"Do you have fondness for Galileo?" Antonio asked, remembering Max had brought him up in past conversation.

"What's not to like about a man who speaks his mind?" She grinned.

"Well, Galileo would be rolling in his tomb in Santa Croce if he knew what was happening. In fact, if it weren't so scary, it would be almost laughable. A Rasmussen survey a few years ago reported that twenty-seven percent of Democrats in the US are in favor of prosecuting climate skeptics. Two attorney generals, one from California and one from New York, investigated whether ExxonMobil lied to their shareholders and the public about the degree of global warming that exists."

"Didn't I read somewhere about a professor at George Mason University leading the charge?" Max inquired. *Ironically, the same university where Fred Singer, Dennis Avery's co-author taught,* suddenly flashed in her mind.

"His name is Jagadish Shukla. Shukla, who had received more than sixty million dollars in grant money from the federally funded National Science Foundation, led the charge. He, along with twenty other professors wrote a letter addressed to the former President Obama and the then-Attorney General Loretta Lynch. They called it the RICO20 because, Shukla, with the help of Senator Whitehouse from Rhode Island planned to use the RICO law."

"The same law used to go after organized crime?" Noble was confused.

"Yes, I guess they thought using a civil suit to threaten financial ruin would silence them. Clever, huh? Anyway, Shukla was later discredited for his misuse of the funds. But Senator Whitehouse continues to go after the fossil-fuel companies for misleading the public about carbon pollution."

Noble pointed out, "In the case of the tobacco companies it was a valiant effort."

"Yes, because there was scientific proof as to the hazards of tobacco smoke," Antonio highlighted.

Max let out an uncontrollable yawn. "Sorry, guy. But it sounds like the drums are still beating from congresspersons to academics to other officials, including the man who started it all, the former Vice President Al Gore, *the carbon millionaire*. Ten years after his documentary *An Inconvenient Truth*, his predictions have apparently failed to materialize."

Antonio shrugged his shoulders in disbelief. "Exactly my point. For nearly two decades there has been no significant increase in global warming. The record high polar bear population is still romping around on the ice-filled surface of the Arctic Ocean, and Antarctica is not melting as fast as predicted. In fact, the ice mass is growing progressively in some areas. Avid explorers are still scaling the year-round snow-covered surface of Mount Kilimanjaro, hurricane activity has decreased and the number of disasters from storm activity, including forest fires, is static."

"Yet, the push for the government to pursue civil actions against so-called deniers continues." It was Max's turn to express disdain.

"Except, the former Attorney General told the Senate that her department would refer all requests to prosecute climate dissent to the Federal Bureau of Investigation. Doesn't sound very civil to me."

"This is truly shocking!" Max had apparently regained her stride.

"What's shocking is the proposed prosecutorial overzealousness all based on no scientific consensus!" Antonio stressed.

"But then again, it's the same government that said it was non-debatable," Noble added.

"When it rises to this level—it's serious!" Antonio's voice reflected the gravity by further explaining, "Whatever anyone believes, science must be scrutinized. What the opposition is trying to do is dumb down science by making it non-debatable. And right now there's a lot of oppression coming down on those who take the current faulty assumptions to task."

"But if it's proven that humans aren't responsible for global warming, then God could be the next target?"

Antonio missed Max's humor but picked up on the God reference. "It would seem that climate change has become a topic you don't discuss in polite company, right up there with religion, politics, and which lavatory you use."

Noble noticed the time, and as much as he was enjoying the conversation, it was getting late. He made one last point. "I certainly can see how it could create a *Ferguson effect* among scientists. Especially if they become unwilling to challenge the climate models; to go against the house of cards considered *the norm*."

"Science can only achieve credibility with total transparency," Antonio insisted. "However, the layers of secrecy blanket the transparency to the point its smokescreen is nonexistent."

"Speaking of blanket, yours is over there, along with this sofa bed. It's time to get some sleep." Noble stood up and helped Max off the couch.

"I'd be happy to trade places with you," Antonio offered.

"I'm sure you would," Noble responded.

"Goodnight Antonio," Max said, as she and Noble headed for the bedroom.

Chapter 39

———oo—○—oo———

THE INTERVIEW

"Stop fidgeting," Noble requested, "and bring me six bottles from the mini bar—beer, wine, whatever you can find."

Antonio was not in the least bit thirsty himself and thought imbibing six was overkill, especially for that time in the morning, but obliged.

In the meantime, Noble plugged a device into the HDMI socket in the back of the large flat screen TV. He then opened his xPhad to the tablet mode and replaced the SD memory card that was in the slot with another one. Finally, after tapping a few of the icons, the tablet began to stream the video app to the TV. He stood the tablet upright on the coffee table and positioned the webcam directly at the chair in the corner of the room.

"Hand me the bottles."

Antonio watched as Noble used the bottles to prop up the tablet and hold it in place, still allowing for access to the control panel.

"What's happening?" Max asked as she entered the living room.

"The technician is setting up the studio for my screen test," Antonio teased.

"Lots of laughs—guess what? You're starring in the guest role. Now, would you please take a seat in the chair over there?" Noble nodded in the direction of the chair and then went to take his own seat next to Max. She had already adjusted herself into a comfortable position on the sofa.

The picture on the large flat-screen TV was a view of Antonio, with his face blurred out.

"Hey, how did you do that?" Max asked, impressed with Noble's technical skills.

"I used a face-off function to distort Antonio's identity. It's designed to automatically track the position and rotation of his face."

"Thanks! What's next? I go poof and disappear?"

Noble ignored Antonio's quip. Then, with everyone in place, he said, "Take a deep breath," and then reached over to hit the *Record* button on the tablet. "It's show time!"

Max led the questioning and asked: "State your name, occupation, and relationship to Claus Veunet, Luca Doerfinger and Jonas von Boehmer."

Noble would intervene only when necessary for clarification.

Antonio, staring directly at the tablet, complied. He answered the basic questions methodically and then gave a full accounting of his time at NASA and his association with the other scientists. Then he began to describe the contents of the email and the circumstances that brought him in contact with the others.

Max and Noble let Antonio speak freely without interruption, listening carefully to his tale, but also kept a watchful eye on his body language as they viewed him on the TV.

Antonio paused and took a sip of water from the glass placed on the table by Noble. He waited a few minutes longer to collect his thoughts before resuming.

"Let's move on." Max suspected they still had a lot of ground to cover.

"During the Climategate scandal, other critics of global warming popped up."

"What does this have to do with Veunet and his testimony?" Noble interjected, sensing he was getting sidetracked.

"Claus knew that Jonas' colleague Dennis Avery had compelling scientific evidence that the sun played a key role in climate change along with cloud formations and shifts in the ocean, concluding that reducing fossil fuel use would have no discernible effect on rising temperatures. Claus assumed these factors had not been accounted for in the computer-driven climate models. Ironically, at the same time, Luca was following reports from the Global Warming Policy Foundation about disputes among independent climate scientists." Antonio continued to throw out names and scientific dogma with ease, but his tempo was a bit unsettling for his audience.

"Antonio, please slow down. The SD memory card has plenty of storage, so we'll give you all the time you need." Noble wanted to hear it all.

At a calmer pace Antonio went into further detail and then explained, "The conflicting views added only more fuel to the global-warming skeptic's bonfire. But it provided information that Claus needed to support his hypothesis."

Antonio took another nervous sip of water before continuing. Clearly he was tiring, but Max reminded him of the importance that they get the entire story on tape without delay.

"You still haven't explained what this has to do with Veunet's testimony? Noble repeated. And what is his hypothesis?"

"With the mounting evidence against manmade global warming, Claus wanted to disprove the CPU climate models with empirical certainty. He believed with the additional information Jonas had collected from Avery and the scientific findings Luca had uncovered, he would finally be able to end the controversy. But he needed Luca and Jonas to work with him to prove his theory. That is when they started working together. He needed to be absolute before making a public statement and releasing the email."

"Was this an attempt to expose the IPCC in the cover-up?" Max's expression was more than dubious.

"Not completely, becau—" Antonio stopped in mid-sentence. Clearly, he was about to broach another subject, but then quickly reverted to topic. "Luca and Jonas agreed to work with Claus to run independent climate models to see if they could formulate different results. They believed that the models were conflating correlation and causation."

"How did you end up working with them? You said earlier that your work at NASA was unrelated to climate science." Max was overly curious considering he seemed to be the linchpin to the entire conspiracy.

"Because of my association with Doiron, Claus knew that I had a direct link to The Right Climate Stuff research team. He asked me to funnel scientific data from the team to him. But Claus didn't want me directly involved at that time. He said it could get dangerous, and they needed someone on the outside. He said I would be their failsafe."

"Failsafe—now I'm more than confused?

"Remember the equation Spark wrote on the back of the photo?"

Max and Noble nodded, wondering where this would lead.

"Claus and Luca decided that instead of trying to mimic the computer-driven climate models they would use empirical data from The Right Climate Stuff research team to calculate the various metrics such as Equilibrium Climate Sensitivity, Transient Climate Response, Total Radiative Forcing, and Representative Concentration Pathway, including the Global Mean Surface Temperatures, the same equation you discovered on Spark's photo." Antonio glared at Max, gauging how much more information to reveal.

"And?" she asked impatiently.

"The equation for the Global Mean Surface Temperatures was crucial. It forecast that no more than one-point-zero degree Celsius of global warming above current levels will occur in this century from burning fossil fuels, proving that the current alarmism regarding CO2 emissions is scientifically unjustified. Claus called me. He was ecstatic. He said that they finally had the undeniable proof that man-made CO2 emissions were not a major factor in global warming—but the impact was even greater than they had imagined!"

"What did they discover?" Max was clearly tiring at pulling teeth.

"Claus wouldn't tell me. He wanted to arrange a meeting with both Avery and Doiron to show them the results personally before he made the findings public. All he said was for me to hang tight and emphasized it was for my own safety. He promised it would be over soon."

"Did you ever find out what happened at the meeting?" Noble asked.

"It never took place." Antonio moved his head from side to side and then bemoaned, "Claus died the day before. Evidently he was scheduled to meet prior to testifying before the Committee on Climate Change Initiatives. I had no idea about Claus' death or the testimony until Luca called me. Needless to say, I was thunderstruck."

Noble got a sudden sense they had just scratched the surface. "What happened next?"

"Shortly after, Luca started receiving threats and after his subsequent death, Jonas had to step up to the plate and prepare to testify before the congressional committee to report their findings. It was then that Jonas involved me directly. According to him, Claus had agreed to testify on the condition that no one else in the group would be exposed to the committee. But Spark was desperate to discredit what he viewed as the global-warming swindle. Evidently he threatened to unleash the fact that Claus had stolen the scientific records from the CRU, which is why he agreed to testify in the first place. I can only assume Spark had something on Luca and Jonas as well."

"Did Jonas tell you the results of their findings?"

Antonio was clearly rattled by Max's question.

She laid the pressure on. "Antonio, did Jonas tell you what they discovered?"

"Yes!" After his outburst, he took a moment to regain his composure. Then, he methodically unleashed the startling results, test-by-test.

Noble and Max sat back and listened as they watched Antonio on the large screen. They were aghast by what they heard. The implications would have indescribable consequences.

Max feared the answer, but they needed to know. "Did anyone else know about the testimony, other than the four of you and Senator Spark?"

"Spark told Claus that Senator Erog knew only that he had evidence to disprove the computer-driven climate models. Evidently Claus freaked out, but Spark assured him that he did not give Erog any specific information, just enough for him to agree to allow the testimony. Jonas told me he suspected Spark had some dirt on Erog and used it as a persuasive weapon."

"Why didn't Spark go directly to the president?"

"I can only presume he didn't want the president to have to decide between covering up a scam or cause a multi-trillion-dollar worldwide economic collapse."

Both Noble and Max flinched at the same time. They sensed they were getting to the crux of the case.

"Personally, I thought it was rather naïve for Senator Spark to think the consciences of the other senators would be in his court," Antonio posed.

"Noted. But putting that aside, let's back up a minute. You still haven't answered the question as to who sent the email." Noble was starting to wonder whether the ending would have the hoped-for startling conclusion.

"I'll get to that in a mome—"

"You're losing me!" Max was equally frustrated.

"Antonio, who sent the email to Claus?" Noble's request had clearly converted to a demand.

"The email that circulated through the scientific community came from the IPCC's Secretariat. It was also cc'd to the Secretary General of the UN."

Max and Noble were stunned by the blatant attempt to control the debate. But from Antonio's body language they sensed they were getting close to the core of the issue—and it was something big. They remained silent.

"It was the email that put Claus in such a lather and caused him to seek advice from Luca and Jonas—but then there was another email."

Both Max and Noble picked up on the unusual expression on Antonio's face and made a mental note, but they were eager to let him continue.

"Claus was having coffee at his favorite corner cafe during his usual morning stop. While he was there he was approached by a man who handed him a plain envelope. The guy abruptly turned and walked away before Claus could identify him. But in the envelope was a copy of another email with orders to cut and paste the contents and then destroy the original email. It contained the same language that Claus received in the email from the Secretariat."

"Okay, who sent that email?" Noble was losing his patience, beginning to wonder whether Antonio was playing them.

Antonio took a deep breath and then blurted out, "The Director of the Consortium."

"The Consortium!" Max and Noble responded in unison. They were overwhelmed for a second time.

Noble immediately hit the *Stop* button.

The room went silent.

Chapter 40

———◦◦———◦——◦◦———

CUT TO THE CHASE

They were not sure how much Antonio knew about the Consortium. There was no reason he should be acquainted, but they chose to tread carefully. For many the Consortium was considered a mythical legend. But for those in the upper echelon, its membership was rumored to mimic the roster of the Bilderberg Group as well as their mission: to debate the future of the world and ensure the survival of over seven billion humans. But whether the Consortium was comprised of the same prominent business moguls and heads of state, there was no question they wielded enormous power in the slurry of the political swamp. They professed democracy, but in reality it was clear they considered public participation a rather cumbersome concept that would only stymie their superior goals.

When a popular political candidate suddenly dropped from a race, or a Supreme Court Judge voted counter to his or her beliefs, or a prominent senator unexpectedly stepped down, the Consortium's calling card was omnipresent. Their behind-the-scenes power was controlling the metrics of the entire world. But its members remained cloaked in anonymity by imposing the *Chatham House Rule* as evidenced by their circulated documents without attribution, an extreme measure to remain clandestine. The Consortium was also rumored to be the ghost-whisperer for groups like the Bilderberg, or the Illuminati, even extending to some factions of the United Nations.

Max sat motionless, grappling with the idea that the Consortium was pushing the narrative, until she could hold back no longer and broke the silence. "There has never been any tangible proof as to its membership or its elusive Director. It's akin to the iconic question: Who is John Galt?"

Noble was not completely satisfied. He needed further confirmation. "Antonio, are you positive that it came from the Director?"

He hesitated for a few seconds and then confirmed, "There's no doubt."

"Then—let's continue." Noble reached over and hit the *Record* button. "Antonio, what do you know about the Consortium?"

"I know the Consortium has great influence to push the concepts of global warming and the sustainability of Mother Earth. They go to great lengths to perpetuate the myth, to protect their unmistakable agenda to seek power fueled by greed, which underlies all of their activities. The Consortium is comprised of charlatans who created the Potemkin Village called global warming. In the process they created a highly profitable cottage industry. But because of the Consortium, the global-warming fairytale will remain off the debate stage, even though it's predicated on pseudoscience. They're willing to kill deniers. What better proof than when they killed my friends, who became deniers in the name of true science. I hold the Director personally responsible!" Antonio had finished his fiery delivery and slouched back into his chair.

"If this is true, then it is the greatest hoax ever perpetrated on the world," Max averred, almost disbelieving her own words.

"That's what all of us in the thick of it believed," Antonio muttered.

Max and Noble were astounded by his seeming level of knowledge. His depth of anger was also clear. He had not only lost friends, but he was forced to begin a lifestyle cloaked in secrecy. They understood his level of distress—but it did not negate the fact they still needed proof.

"Antonio, let me cut to the chase—it's not enough! We need something other than your word." Noble's tone made it clear that his testimony thus far, was not sufficient.

Antonio seemed overly hesitant. In his mind he started to question his level of freedom.

Noble and Max feared he did not have the silver bullet to confirm the conspiracy.

Noble tried one more time and stressed, "Antonio, you are indicting some very large fish and one extremely dangerous shark. What proof do you have?"

After a deep breath and another gulp of water, he told them what they needed to hear. "When Jonas sensed danger was around the corner, he gave me a going-away gift. He told me that if anything happened to him, I would be the only one to have the proof—to have the scientific findings and the supporting documents." Antonio flashed his wrist. "They prove the Consortium was controlling the IPCC. It will make the *Panama Papers* look like a leaflet."

Max noticed for the first time a newly formed scar on Antonio's arm. She was curious as to its significance.

"Do you have a sharp knife?" Antonio asked.

"You're not serious!" Max recoiled.

Noble didn't hesitate. He hurried into the bathroom and retrieved his Swiss army knife from his toiletry kit. When he bolted back into the living room he asked, "Need help?"

Antonio shook his head and then bit down on his lip. Trying not to grimace he deftly sliced open the scar.

Max did all the grimacing for him as she watched him perform self-surgery on the flat screen TV.

Under the flap of bloody skin, Antonio dug out a micro SD, a secure digital memory card about the size of a fingernail.

"This also contains photos of the emails along with tracking information and the location of the Director's extremely private and impenetrable network. The truth can't be distorted. I think you'll agree this is better than any hearsay."

Max and Noble had listened intently throughout the entire interview, oftentimes questioning his testimony. But then when Antonio handed Noble a stick of dynamite in the form of a memory card, his words could no longer be ignored.

Antonio was overcome with exhaustion. Not surprisingly, having to resurrect the timing of events leading to the deaths of his classmates was difficult physically and emotionally. But it was finally over. He sat back and pressed his thumb and forefinger to the bridge of his nose and tried to rub away the fatigue.

Noble hit the *Stop* button. "Astounding!" Immediately, he retrieved his xPhad from the table and placed the micro SD in the additional slot. Quickly, he copied the data from the micro SD to the SD card containing the interview. Once he confirmed all the data had been transferred, he encrypted the data and then removed both SD cards. He placed the SD card with the interview and incriminating evidence in a small envelope and placed it in his pocket. Then, he walked over to the microwave oven at the make-shift kitchen and placed the micro SD card inside. He set the timer for ten seconds.

"Hey, what are you doing?" Antonio asked, coming out of his haze.

At the sound of the *ding*, Noble opened the door to the microwave and pulled out the black molten glob. "Now only the President of the United States will know what truly transpired."

A hush filled the room.

Suddenly there was a rap on the door. They instinctively froze.

Noble looked at his watch. He had not realized it was already noon. "It's Enzo," he said, trying to put Antonio at ease.

Chapter 41

TYING LOOSE ENDS

"*S ono io,* it's me," sounded the faint voice from the other side of the door.

Noble shot up in a flash and opened the door to let Enzo into the room.

Max remained on the sofa.

"Well I'll be damned!" Enzo brandished a huge smile at the sight of Max and Noble in the same room. He wagged his index finger in between them as he maintained his grin.

"Yes, Enzo, we're together." Max responded indifferently, still shaken by Antonio's testimony.

"*Splen—di—do!*" As soon as the word left his mouth he sensed something was wrong. He scanned their faces and thought perhaps they could use some good news. "News flash. I just received a text from the main office. Your country has proof that the deadly assassin known as L was found dead outside a bar in Washington near the Navy Yard. The circumstances are unknown, other than one more really bad guy is gone. Great news, eh?"

Max, all at once perked up. "Was it at The Bachelor's Mill?"

Simultaneously, an inquisitive look appeared on the faces of both Enzo and Noble.

Noble took the challenge. "How did you know that?"

Max stared back at the two of them. "I'm a detective." Then, out of nowhere, she got this wrenching feeling that either Jax or Sam, or perhaps even both, had something to do with the hit. A thought she kept to herself.

Antonio remained seated in the chair as he waited for the chitchat to halt. He was still emotionally drained from the last few hours' events and did not mind delaying the inevitable. But then finally Noble made the formal introduction to Enzo, and he was forced to stand up.

"And Noble," Enzo chided, "you forgot to mention also a dear friend who has come to the rescue."

Antonio's face instantly relaxed. *"Mi piacere."* He shook Enzo's hand.

"Let's all take a seat," Enzo suggested, trying to alleviate the obvious tension in the room. He grabbed a seat in the chair next to Antonio and then focused all his attention in Antonio's direction. "These should fit you nicely." He handed him a gray T-shirt with "San Marino" emblazoned on the front and a baseball cap decorated with the initials "SM." He also handed him a pair of horn-rimmed eyeglasses and a smartphone. "All of these items will help you get out of here safely."

Antonio was confused, but said, "Grazie," and gladly accepted them.

Enzo reached over and handed Noble the other smartphone along with a key and said, "Now, here's the plan." He redirected his comments to Antonio.

Max and Noble listened closely. They knew their turn would come later.

"In thirty minutes you're to go to the lobby. A man wearing an identical T-shirt and cap will get out of the passenger's side of a green Jaguar parked out front. He will come into the hotel carrying a large parcel and will exit through a back entrance. Wait five minutes. Then walk out of the lobby and get into the Jaguar. The driver is Giovanni Righi, one of San Marino's finest citizens. No one will stop or question him. He will take you to Ancona, where a fishing vessel will be waiting. The ship's captain is instructed to take you wherever you want to go. *Va bene?*"

"*Ho capito.* I understand." After days of contemplation, Antonio had finally concluded the safest place on Earth was in a small village on the coast of Sicily, the home of his grandfather's birth. Something the others did not want to know.

Enzo then handed Antonio a large envelope.

He opened the envelope and pulled out all the contents. He inspected the passports and the photos closely, along with other documents. There was also another envelope inside that contained ten thousand euros in five hundred and two hundred denominations. "What's this?" Antonio asked, holding up a sheet of paper with a series of numbers that was tucked in with the euros.

"That's the phone number and account number for the Swiss private bank account that holds another one million euros at your disposal." Enzo could see that he was satisfied. "Spend it wisely, Antonio Di Stefano. Now, get ready. It's almost time."

Antonio, almost trancelike, stood up and changed into the T-shirt and placed his other clothing, along with the euros, into his backpack. He put on the eyeglasses and slowly placed the cap on his head. It was the final gesture in his transformation— Antonio Maieli no longer existed.

Enzo stood up to shake his hand one last time. "*Il resto sta a voi.* The rest is up to you. Godspeed."

Antonio, with a strangely sad expression, thanked everyone. He offered Noble the two-sided air kiss and saved a long, strong hug for Max. Then, without speaking another word, he turned and left the suite.

"What's this?" Enzo asked, as he inspected the envelope Noble handed him.

"It's a trillion-dollar bomb," Noble replied with caution in his voice. "Only the president can decide whether it should be detonated. Until that time, our lives are in your hands my friend."

"Grazie!" Enzo said grudgingly, not especially pleased with his new burden.

"Arrange for this to be delivered by special Interpol envoy. The package must reach Agent Stan Stanton by tomorrow. He will personally ensure it reaches the president. Then in the next few days, we'll need a helicopter to fly us to the Aviano Air Force Base. I'll let you know when."

Enzo knew the airport was north of Venice about four hours driving time, but a helicopter could make it in about thirty minutes. "I assume you want me to have you cleared for a military jet transport."

"Please. I want the US government to have minimal involvement. In the meantime, we'll sit tight."

"Okay, your wish is my command. Just stay safe. And please, you two, don't wait so long to pay me a visit—but next time make it simpler." Enzo hugged his dear friend, kissed Max goodbye, and departed.

⁕

Noble would not be able to relax until receiving his final orders. "I have a call to make."

"POTUS?"

"Yes."

"I'll give Jax a call." She was eager to hear what he had to say about L.

Noble handed Max the smartphone that Enzo delivered.

"I told you my smartphone is secure."

"At this point, let's not take any chances. And be careful how much you tell Jax—and nothing about Antonio's testimony."

Max flashed him an *I don't need a reminding* look.

He was well aware that she understood the risks and that they were not home free. But an unusual edginess was plaguing him. Without further delay, he stepped into the bedroom and closed the door behind him so as not to be distracted.

Max remained seated on the sofa.

Noble exhaled and placed the call. Soon after he heard the president's voice on the other end of the line.

"Noble, was it them?"

"Yes, Mr. President. It's the Consortium as we suspected."

"You have the proof?"

"Yes, sir. Once you view the evidence, you'll be convinced. The package is on its way."

"What about Antonio Maieli?"

"He no longer exists. It's all been taken care of, and I've kept the US involvement out of it."

"Enzo Borgini?"

"Yes sir, but it will cost the US taxpayers roughly one million, one hundred and forty thousand dollars based on the current exchange rate today."

"A fair price to pay. Stay put until I figure out how to handle this whole mess. Good work, Noble. And I mustn't forget, please extend my thanks to Max as well." The president ended the call.

"Case solved!"

"Max, how nice of you to check in—but where the hell have you been?" Jax's tone was more out of concern than anger.

Max took it as such. "Sorry, I should have contacted you sooner, but it's been a little unpredictable to say the least."

"So where are you, exactly?"

"Jax, I should be limping home in a few days, then I'll bring you up to date. Now, what's happening on the home front?"

"Have you seen the headlines? The notorious world assassin known as L has been found dead."

"I heard—what a coincidence that he was found dead outside The Bachelor's Mill. The very same place Isabelle located Spark's cellphone." She waited for his response.

"Actually, it may not be such a coincidence. The chief came back with the autopsy results for von Boehmer. Apparently, his drink was spiked with sodium thiopental, causing him to pass out. In the ambulance he was given an injection of potassium chloride."

"Wait a minute, the doc in Sarasota was injected forcibly with pancuronium bromide." *An injection that was meant for me,* she thought.

"You go girl! The same combo of drugs they use to execute those unfortunate souls on death row. Coincidently, both the bartender at the restaurant and the EMT on duty in the ambulance were newbies. They were fill-ins for the two who called in sick. The chief was also able to locate the Lexus Doerfinger rented from Hertz. It looks like the brakes were tampered with. Now he's trying to track down the mechanic."

"And Spark was shot with a Luger," Max interjected.

"You're firing on all cylinders today. All three crimes started with an L and took place in Washington."

"That begs the question. Was L, Ernst, the same person who went climbing with Claus Veunet?"

"According to Ray, who finally got through to the French authorities, someone had drilled around the bolts that had been permanently placed up along the rock face at Lou Passo. They were tampered with enough to break free when harnessing weight.

Get this! The day before, another climber had reported that a set of bolts on the St. Leger rock face had also broken loose."

"St. Leger is where Claus and Ernst first climbed. And according to Veunet's wife, it was Ernst who had insisted on climbing Lou Passo the next day. It had to have been L."

Jax thought for the moment that it was best not to tell Max about the edelweiss and freak her out. She had enough on her plate. Besides L was no longer a threat.

"There had to be a mole," she alleged. "Each man died before he was supposed to testify. Someone's been leaking info like a sieve."

"Exactamundo! Weeks before von Boehmer was killed, L made a multitude of calls that included a mechanic and two ex-cons that fit the descriptions of the bartender and the EMT at the Old Europe Restaurant. There were several other calls made to the same number. With a little help from my seraph hacker, I traced that number to a private line. Ta-da...guess where?"

"Senator Erog's office."

"You got it! Your suspicions were right about that guy. He had to be the conduit between whoever ordered the hits and L."

"Excuse me," Max said, without hesitation. "How do you know who the assassin was calling?" She was sure Jax had something to do with L's assassination, but she wanted to hear it directly from him.

"Max, trust me. What's important is that while we may not be able to prove the direct link, we do have proof that Erog has been misappropriating stimulus money to green-energy companies— along with his little familial conflicts of interest lining his family's pockets. I'm sure there's a crime in there somewhere. Erog's going down. Although it would be interesting to find out who else Erog was calling from his private line."

Max presumed the answer was the Director of the Consortium. But sharing that little piece of information would have to wait until she was home safe and sound. "Good work,

Jax," she praised. A nanosecond later the vision of L lying in the back alley at The Bachelor's Mill appeared on her mind's eye screen. Standing over the body was a tall, thin, bald, shadowy figure of a man. She shook her head as though the thought would disappear without further contemplation. It did not work. She hastily said, "Gotta go."

"Max, don't hang up!"

"What is it? I really have to go."

"Should I inform Isabelle Spark that her husband's killer has been identified?"

"No, I want to tell her personally. And would you ask the chief to hold off as well?"

"Will do, but you never did tell me where you are. Did you find Antonio? Did Noble catch up with you?"

"Yes, Antonio's safe. And Noble's here. Which is something you and I will discuss later," she stated with mild admonishment, and then she changed her tune. "Relax; I'll be there in a few days. I'll fill you in on everything when I return."

"I guess I have no choice but to wait, partner. But prepare to be busy. We have a few more cases lined up when you return."

"Get started without me. Just don't forget to invoke my name." Max heard Jax's devilish laugh as he ended the call.

Noble walked back into the living room at the same time Max hit the red phone icon. "We need to stay here for a while longer until we get the okay from POTUS to come home. By the way, he sends his thanks."

"Great! But I have to get back to work. Jax pulled in some new cases. And I have to inform Isabelle Spark."

"Right now we have to stay safe. We're not out of the woods yet."

"What if Antonio is wrong—what if the science is wrong?" Max was suddenly uneasy. Especially knowing that both the evidence and the herculean decision was about to be placed in the hands of the president.

"And if he is right?" Noble's rhetorical question was unqualified. "Let's go."

"What's going on? You said the president wants us to stay here until he can ensure our safety."

"We'll discuss it later." Noble grabbed their luggage and helped Max to the elevator just outside their door. Shadowing the key pad as best he could, he hit a button.

"Hey, funny guy—we're going up, not down." She frowned until she spotted his cocky expression.

The door opened. That time Noble carried their luggage off the elevator and Max followed behind. They entered another suite. The name on the door was Montefeltro.

"What's going on?" she asked with a suspicious grin.

"Compliments of Enzo." Noble flung open the draperies and revealed a large terrace. Perched outside the French doors was an enormous hot tub.

Max broke out in hysterical laughter as she pointed down to her cast.

"Don't worry; we'll figure something out." He winked.

Chapter 42

————◦◦———◦———◦◦————

DOOMSDAY DECISION

The president sat alone in the Oval Office, donning a pair of headphones. Playing on the screen in front of him was the video recording of Antonio Maieli. His eyes were fixated and his ears were sharp, but he was not prepared for what he heard at the 1:08:14-second mark. He was stunned. "And he has the proof!" he uttered aloud, as though the proverbial bomb had dropped. He hit the *Stop* button and rewound to the 38:00-minute mark and again listened carefully to Maieli's words.

"There is irrefutable science that proves Earth is heading into a 100-year cold spell. During that time the sun will be emitting less energy. Despite this evidence, the scientific community has been ordered to support the global-warming narrative with the sole focus to reduce anthropogenic CO_2 emissions by two Celsius degrees. Any effort to remove CO_2 from the atmosphere will certainly cause temperatures to drop. However, there is no scientific evidence that once greenhouse gases reach a sustainable level that they can be contained. If rapid decarbonization were to occur in combination with a naturally reoccurring solar-induced, cold climate epoch, in conjunction with the Atlantic Multidecadal Oscillation producing cooler temperatures—there is the grave possibility the world could plummet into not just a little ice age as the expected cycle indicates, but the Big Ice Age. The world will be unprepared. The lack of food resources, riots in the streets, and untold deaths will become the norm. Yet, the current directive is unlikely to be overturned. It comes from the Director of the Consortium."

The president hit the *Stop* button again. "Damn them!" He pounded his fist on his desk in outrage. Abruptly, he stood up and walked into the anteroom and opened the presidential vault. He carefully removed the *President's Book of Secrets* and held it in his hands. Surprisingly, the book had a calming effect. He thought about the sacred ritual—the private conversation that took place in the Oval Office between the former president and newly-sworn-in president. It was at that time that the book containing the most serious notations from all past presidents was handed over. During the historic conversation, it became the responsibility of the outgoing president to put into perspective how vital it is to study the notes so the new administration is not doomed to repeat the same mistakes.

The president returned to his desk in a more relaxed state, but continued to fondle the book a bit longer as it induced the memory of the first time he read the sacred tome. The recognition that he was dealing with the handwritten words from the first president was as overwhelming then as was it now. He remembered reading Washington's vision for his new country, Lincoln's aspirations, Roosevelt's predictions, Kennedy's conflicts, Nixon's fears, and Reagan's hopes—each former president providing a trove of useful insights.

As he held the book close to his heart, he took another moment to reflect. Then after exhaling deeply, he humbly opened the book and turned to the page where he recalled seeing a number and a code. He noted that there was no mention of how the information was obtained, only that the entry was written into the book several administrations ago. For what purpose was unknown until now. It was the only direct link to the Director, the controlling head of the Consortium.

As the president continued to gather his thoughts, he glimpsed at the computer screen. The video had ended, displaying a copy of the email, along with its tracking information. The ISP address was familiar. A block of similar addresses had been set aside for private servers to be used only by those with the highest security clearance in the offices of government. The GPS coordinates attached, identified its location. The speculation about the identity of the mysterious Director had finally ended.

Heavily weighing his options, he knew he would not be able to connect the Consortium directly with the activities of the assassin named L, an assassin who was now dead. *Although his assumptions could be used as leverage if the Director needed convincing,* he thought, a thought he held in abeyance. Then he began to consider the economic impact. Using his tremendous gift for numbers and his mind that was a virtual calculator, the costs began toting up in his head. He thought about the annual budget for climate-change expenditures that had grown to $25 billion and climbing, the total cost of subsidizing the faltering green-energy companies that had hit over $8 trillion. He remembered that New York City alone spent $2.2 billion on coastal protection and urban drainage to adapt to climate change, only one of many major cities to do so. And there was the $100 billion a year the United Nations expected to spend as an offshoot of the Paris Agreement. He considered the effects climate-change legislation had on the increase in green-energy jobs and green-energy investments, spurring an increase in taxes that would offset only a fraction of the cost. He knew he had only scratched the surface, but the consequence of the green economy was not only a US event—it was a global phenomenon.

The president rubbed his forehead as though his brain physically hurt. *The fallout from exposing the deception would be disastrous. Disgrace and distrust would befall world leaders who enforced their green policies. It could lead to another Brexit on an enormous scale. The sound of companies folding, jobs being lost, and markets crashing would be a curdling screech heard around the world.* He agonized at his thoughts, but the choice was clear. He dialed the number.

From the obvious number of clicks, the call was being rerouted through various transmission points. Finally, he heard an electronic voice resonate on the end of the line.

"Enter the ten-digit code," ordered the robotic sound.

The president followed the instructions and then heard a few more clicks until a real, but obviously disguised voice announced, "Identify yourself."

"This is the President of the United States." He waited for a response; none came. "Director, I have in my possession evidence that includes an email from you to the Secretariat of the IPCC stating your intentions. It is clear that the Consortium has intentionally perpetrated a fraud of gargantuan proportions— with the potential to collapse the world-wide economy—if it were exposed." The president paused slightly and let out an inaudible breath. Then he continued. "The information will be withheld on one condition. The Consortium must dial back the rhetoric and slowly denounce the claims of anthropogenic global warming. If I see any drastic movement in the markets to the contrary, I will expose not only the fraud—but your identity."

The Director was silent. Then he challenged, "You're bluffing."

"As I mentioned, I have a copy of the email you sent to the IPCC with your directives." The president paused. It was time to call the bluff. "I also have evidence that the Consortium hired the deadly assassin called L to kill three scientists and Senator Sherman Spark, and that Senator Winston Erog is your messenger."

Again, silence.

"Done!" The line went dead.

It was settled.

The president placed the phone back in its cradle. His posture remained stiff as he sat in his chair. He studied the Oval Office as he contemplated the myriad of pronouncements that had come to fruition in that room. He hoped his judgement had not betrayed his oath of office. But he was certain—L was dead, Erog was going to jail, and the Consortium was forced to stand down. He glanced at the *President's Book of Secrets* lying open on his desk. He now would be forced to enter the first notation of his presidency. Next to the telephone number and code he wrote in two more sets of numbers: *Latitude 36.108564 Longitude -86.819957*, identifying the location of the Consortium's private server. Then he placed the SD memory card in between the pages and closed the book.

Confident he had made the right decision, he returned the sacred tome to its rightful place inside the vault. He said a prayer and then texted Noble: *The sky is clear.*

Noble texted Enzo: *Tomorrow.*

OTHER POINTS OF VIEW

"Few challenges facing America and the world are more urgent than combating climate change. The science is beyond dispute and the facts are clear."

—President-Elect Barack Hussein Obama,
November 19, 2008

"Climate change is a terrible problem, and it absolutely needs to be solved. It deserves to be a huge priority."

—Bill Gates, Founder Microsoft, Philanthropist,
November 11, 2010

"We are running the most dangerous experiment in history right now, which is to see how much carbon dioxide the atmosphere can handle before there is an environmental catastrophe."

—Elon Musk, CEO Tesla Motors, Inventor,
April 22, 2013

"I am not a scientist, but I don't need to be. Because the world's scientific community has spoken, and they have given us our prognosis, if we do not act together, we will surely perish."

—Leonardo DiCaprio, Actor,
September 23, 2014

"Today, there's no greater threat to our planet than climate change."

—President Barack Hussein Obama,
April 18, 2015

"Climate change is a global problem with grave implications: environmental, social, economic, political, and for the distribution of goods. It represents one of the principal challenges facing humanity in our day."

—Pope Francis,
June 18, 2015

"...The scientific community has been extremely clear—no debate—climate change is real, climate change is manmade, and climate change is already causing severe damage in terms of drought, floods, forest fires, rising sea levels, and extreme weather disturbances..."

—Senator Bernie Sanders,
September 4, 2015

"It's hard to believe that people running for president refuse to believe the settled science of climate change."

—Hillary Rodham Clinton,
July 1, 2016

ACKNOWLEDGEMENTS

The Editor: After the completion of each novel I'm faced with a dilemma: how to recognize someone who has had the greatest impact in the creation of the novel. After using the Dedication and the Acknowledgment in past novels, neither appeared sufficient. Joe Fernandez, my loving husband, avid supporter, and incredible content editor, deserves the highest recognition. After 38 years together, he made it possible for me to embark on this amazing journey as an author; to produce entertaining, intellectual, and informative novels. His literary contributions alone are invaluable. Additionally, his diligent, in-depth editing enhances my narrative. His scrutiny of segue, nuances, facts, and the content that assures plausibility is priceless. My mantra has become, "If Joe doesn't get it, neither will the reader." Because of him, my writing style has improved immensely; because of him I've written five novels of which I am proud. Perhaps, the only place to fully appreciate the sacrifices he has made is in that special place in my heart that he occupies.

The Publisher: Both Joe and I offer our deep appreciation to my publisher, David Dunham, for his continued confidence in me as a novelist. And for giving of his own time to see my projects to fruition. But I know David could not do it without his amazing colleagues at Dunham Books, Managing Editor Crystal Flores and Associate Publisher Joel Dunham. Thanks to all of you.

The Alpha/Beta Readers: Our profound thanks go to my special inner circle of talented readers whose objective insights and valuable feedback from various perspectives continue to help enrich my stories. It's amazing after the number of rereads and edits Joe and I run the manuscript through, this group still finds the nagging oversights and offer helpful hints: to Kenney

DeCamp, Richard Halpern, Ann Howells, Donna Post, and Alfredo Vedro.

The Fact-Checkers: A special thanks goes to those who have granted me permission to use them as real-life characters in my fictional story and for conducting a fact-check review: to Harold Doiron, Tom Wysmuller, Jim Peacock, Laurence Gould, and all members of The Right Climate Stuff research team. These former NASA Apollo Team heroes and other accomplished researchers who joined their research team deserve special recognition for continuing to take *giant leaps for mankind*. To Dennis Avery, former senior fellow of the Hudson Institute and co-author of the *New York Times* bestseller, *Unstoppable Global Warming: Every 1,500 Years*, who worked tirelessly alongside S. Fred Singer, to ensure the integrity of science be maintained through their dogged research and pursuit of the truth. To Police Chief Bernadette DiPino, James ("Sully") Sullivan, and Dr. Paul Yungst; Sarasota, Florida's finest citizens whose roles helped to enrich the plot.

The Italians: To all my Italian friends who have also allowed me to use them as real-life characters in my fictional story: Dottore Franco Della Piane, Simone Monciatti, Manuele Verdelli, Giuliana Ferrucci, and Valentina Catinari, who have always welcomed us with open arms during our stays at Capannelle. To Giovanni Righi, who not only opened the doors to his fabulous restaurant Ristorante Righi generously, but to the wonders of the Republic of San Marino during each of our frequent visits. To all the staff at the Hotel Titano who have always exceeded our expectations. And to Carmine and Massimo Maieli, for allowing me to use their family name, and for their amazing artistic talents to transform our US home into a Tuscan Villa; *mille grazie*.

Family and Friends: Lastly, I am indebted to all my family and friends from around the world, too numerous to mention, for all the love and support they have given me throughout this endeavor.

ABOUT THE AUTHOR

If you relish suspense thrillers with a tinge of conspiracy, you'll enjoy Sally Fernandez' novels. Readers have said she pens riveting plots of intrigue and political awakening, seamlessly blending fact with fiction…or fiction with fact…you be the judge.

Fernandez, a novelist of provocative political thrillers, wasn't always twisting facts with fiction. Heavily endowed with skills acquired in banking, she embarked on her writing career. Fernandez' focus on computer technology, business consulting, and project management, enhanced by business and technical writing, proved to be a boon. Her books of fiction reflect the knowledge garnered from her business experiences, while living in New York City, San Francisco, and Hong Kong.

Fernandez' foray into writing fiction officially began in 2007 when the presidential election cycle was in full swing. The overwhelming political spin by the media compelled her to question the frightening possibilities the political scene could generate. As a confirmed political junkie, she took to the keyboard armed with unwinding events and discovered a new and exciting career.

Redemption: Aftermath of The Simon Trilogy is her fourth and final novel in a series following *Brotherhood Beyond the Yard*, *Noble's Quest*, and *The Ultimate Revenge*. Each book provides an exhilarating platform for *Redemption*, with a gripping narrative that challenges the reader to put the book down. The ever-elusive Simon's daring escapes add unheard-of dimensions to the classic cat and mouse game. Her development of the other characters is destined to create a lasting bond between them and the reader. Despair not; Fernandez has a new series featuring Maxine Ford as the female protagonist. *Climatized* is the first Max Ford Thriller.

A world traveler, Ms. Fernandez and her husband, also editor-in-residence, split time between their homes in the United States and Florence, Italy.

BROTHERHOOD
BEYOND THE YARD

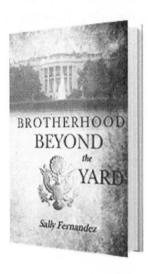

In 1990, an extraordinarily talented young man was discovered on the streets of Florence, Italy. His gifts are readily apparent, his ability to lead unmatched, and the possibilities for his future endless. Several years later, a group of scholars at Harvard known as La Fratellanza devise a brilliant thesis in the form of an intellectual game. When the game morphs into a real-life experience with the election of President Abner Baari, no one could have foreseen the consequences—or ramifications.

Director Hamilton Scott of the States Intelligence Agency is dispatched to Florence to coordinate a sting operation with Interpol to trap a terrorist, but as he digs deeper, he finds himself in a complicated mystery that has the fate of the United States, even that of the president himself, on his shoulders. As Hamilton drives the investigation forward with clear-headed integrity, *Brotherhood Beyond the Yard* provides an array of disturbing possibilities while delivering a rush of thrills.

Sally Fernandez's crackerjack international thriller expertly weaves seemingly disparate events into a cohesive whole leading to a shocking, shattering climax; a classic blend of character study and well-plotted action sequences keeps the pages turning faster and faster. There are no sacred cows here as Fernandez drives straight to the highest seats of Washington and questions anyone—and everything. A hair-raising page-turner from start to finish, *Brotherhood Beyond the Yard* examines political ideology, the international banking crisis, the role of Internet technology, and international terrorism with ferocious insight.

www.sallyfernandez.com

NOBLE'S QUEST

Fresh on the heels of her acclaimed first novel, *Brotherhood Beyond the Yard*, Sally Fernandez has penned a sequel that will add more sparkling thrills to the trilogy she is authoring. Major earth-shaking events in Europe and the USA converge to fuel Interpol and the States Intelligence Agency to join forces.

Although seemingly detached, the threats prompt Noble Bishop, Director of the SIA, and Enzo Borgini, Executive Director of Police Services for Interpol, to conduct joint investigations. Leading-edge technology is used to unravel the labyrinth of connections. The events are not coincidental. The enormous risks facing the USA and the world eventually draw the newly elected president into the picture.

Land grabs, political manipulation, and a terrorist camp—along with sea changes in the American psyche—are skillfully woven to form a tapestry of intrigue. Readers of *Brotherhood Beyond the Yard* will renew their acquaintanceship with some of the characters in the sequel. This time their roles are more expansive and transparent, adding to the lingering intrigue. The widely sought mastermind of the global terrorist threat adds a breathtaking twist that lends even more intrigue to the narrative.

Written in the author's patent style, readers will be beguiled by the artistic marriage of established facts with a storyline that lifts creativity to new heights. Readers are challenged to separate fact from fiction, in the true Fernandez style.

www.sallyfernandez.com

THE ULTIMATE REVENGE

The Ultimate Revenge is the explosive conclusion to The Simon Trilogy that has held political thriller readers tightly in its grasp. The author's earlier books, *Brotherhood Beyond the Yard* and *Noble's Quest*, provide an exhilarating platform for the launch of this final chapter of a gripping narrative that challenges the reader to put the book down.

The ever-elusive Simon's daring escape from a high-security prison allows him to add unheard-of dimensions to the classic cat-and-mouse game he has played with Noble, the SIA Director. The manhunt for Simon engages two geniuses and a collection of talented operatives, all immersed in a chase with more twists and turns than a rodeo bull. In the process chicanery and double-dealing at the highest levels is unfolded, continuing some of the manipulations of the earlier books. Max, Noble's trusted partner, comes into her own, as she uncovers startling evidence and suggestive connections that reveal the nation's power grids are at risk.

Of greater significance, are the hidden agendas of some of the world's most powerful recognized leaders to pursue their goals toward a supra-national one-world government under the guise of global warming. Simon, the deposed President Baari, and the Jihadists find themselves sharing the same boat, each driven by separate motives but all resulting in a potential disastrous national emergency of huge proportions. The future of the United States is precipitously at stake. The capture of Simon becomes the highest priority as he continues to elude his captors with his usual bag of tricks. Meanwhile, Noble staves off a massive national emergency with his technical prowess. Simon, finally cornered, provides an explosive ending to a fast-paced trilogy that is not for the faint of heart.

Fernandez has proved once again that she has mastered the art of blending fact with fiction, leaving the readers to make their own judgments. Whatever the outcome, it raises the inviting question, "What if?"

www.sallyfernandez.com

REDEMPTION: AFTERMATH OF THE SIMON TRILOGY

It was April 2017. The nation was gripped by the shocking news that Simon Hall, the notorious terrorist, had leaped to his death off the Peace Bridge in Buffalo, New York. Moreover, the fact that the body had yet to be recovered raised doubts among many. Had Simon cleverly eluded his captors once again?

But for the newly elected president, there were greater threats looming. President Randall Post had inherited a rapidly sinking economy that brought chaos of gargantuan proportions. And with the push for global governance threatening America's sovereignty, the country was in dire need of solutions.

Meanwhile, the American populace was clamoring for a full governmental offensive on the clear need to create more jobs. The economic sinkhole had been accelerated by the paucity of employment throughout the country, which was largely ignored by the former administration in favor of their agenda. Internationally, a loss of esteem, coupled with a rising support of global governance among powerful forces, gave birth to a prediction of a permanent decline in America's stature. Unrest among the masses had surfaced in frequent demonstrations against the government, many of which included violence. There was a blatant crisis of confidence facing the nation.

The increasing turmoil threatening the future of the US was addressed head on by the newly-elected president. He filled the leadership void boldly and without hesitation—but he needed of the support of the American people. The downtrodden mood that permeated the society forced his primary objective to design a strategy to address the crucial need for more jobs. Borrowing a page from the Manhattan Project, the president's chosen course was to assemble some of the country's best minds to offer solutions. The clandestine group known as La Fratellanza was enlisted to fulfill the role. Their superior intellectual skills and experience as Washington insiders, made them eminently qualified to meet the President's needs. Noble Bishop, director of the States Intelligence Agency was tasked to bring them together and to provide the leadership and guidance. The timetable had been set. To deliver on the immediacy of his stated goals, the President expected an overall strategy in only sixty-five days—a challenge of overwhelming dimensions

With the country's sinking economy and sovereignty in peril, can President Post rescue America?

www.sallyfernandez.com